The Super Spies and the Cat Lady Killer

by
Lisa Orchard

The Super Spies and the Cat Lady Killer
by Lisa Orchard
Published by Astraea Press
www.astraeapress.com

THE SUPER SPIES AND THE CAT LADY KILLER
Copyright © 2012 LISA ORCHARD
ISBN 13: 978-1479177158
ISBN: 1479177156
Cover Art Designed by Elaina Lee
Edited by Laura Heritage

This book is dedicated to my wonderful husband Steve, and two boys Kyle and Ethan. To my family and friends who encouraged me and read my first drafts of this book and offered suggestions.

Chapter One

"Do you know who that was?"

Sarah Cole whirled around and spied a tall, skinny girl standing a few feet behind her. "Are you talking to me?" Shading her eyes, Sarah cocked her head to get a better look at the girl.

The skinny girl nodded, her mop of wild curls dancing with her movements. "Yeah, do you know who she is?"

Sarah gazed down the street at the wizened old woman shuffling away. She wore a faded housedress, which appeared to have been slept in for at least a couple of nights. It looked like the wrinkles had wrinkles.

The woman's hair was a listless gray, trapped in a feeble bun at the nape of her neck. Some of it had escaped and trailed behind her as she walked, the limp strands swaying with the old woman's faltering steps. Minutes ago, Sarah had helped her with her cart—it had gotten stuck on the doorjamb as she left the corner drug store.

Pulling her honey colored hair out of her eyes, Sarah spun and studied the skinny girl, not quite sure what to make of her. "No, I don't."

Sarah continued her scrutiny and noticed the skinny girl stood at least five inches taller than she did. Her curly hair burst from her scalp in a frantic frenzy. She looks like an exploded cotton swab. Pursing her lips, Sarah suppressed a bubble of laughter.

"She's the Cat Lady," the bony girl said, an expression of guarded curiosity mixed with fear on her face.

"Who's the Cat Lady?"

The skinny girl pointed at the old woman shuffling away. "She's a crazy lady. A witch."

"A witch?" Sarah scoffed. "I don't believe in witches."

"It's true," the skinny girl whispered emphatically. She stared at Sarah, her dark eyes reflecting the conviction behind her words.

"I don't believe you."

"No one has seen her in years. She never leaves her home." The skinny girl glanced toward the Cat Lady again, and then walked closer to Sarah.

Realizing the skinny girl was scared, Sarah glanced down the street a second time. She watched the hunched, old woman make her painful shuffle down the sidewalk. The Cat Lady didn't look dangerous to Sarah. She appeared to be a weary old lady making her way home.

"There's no such thing as witches," Sarah said.

"She's a witch, an evil witch," the scrawny girl insisted. She nodded her head again, sending her dark curls into another wild dance.

Sarah glanced down the street a third time and watched the old woman limp away. She didn't look like she had the strength to pull her cart, let alone perform black magic. "How do you know? Does she practice voodoo or something?" Sarah smirked at the skinny girl, realizing she had a flair for the theatrical. "And if she never leaves her home...why is she out on the street now?"

The girl opened her mouth to speak, and then shut it again as if she realized Sarah had a point. "Well...the delivery boy must have quit." She pulled on a wayward curl and frowned. "Because there's no way she leaves her home. I haven't seen her in years."

"Uh huh," Sarah said, raising her eyebrows and pursing her lips.

The skinny girl must have seen the doubt in Sarah's expression, because she crossed her arms over her bony chest and moved another step closer. "Just let me tell you the whole story; I'm sure you'll change your mind. My name's Jacqueline Jenkins." She drew out the syllables emphasizing her name like a movie star or the Queen of England, JAAAQUELEENE JEEENKIINS. Jutting out her hip, she faced Sarah as if she were posing for a magazine. "What's yours?"

"Sarah Cole." Speaking through tight lips, Sarah was able to stifle another bubble of laughter.

"You can call me Jackie, though. That's what my friends call me." She studied Sarah for a moment. "You're new in town, aren't you?"

"Yeah. We're staying with my aunt and uncle while my parents are on vacation."

"We?"

"Me and my sister, Lacey." Sarah scrutinized her surroundings. "Is this the whole town of Harrisburg?"

"Yep, this is it," Jackie said. She opened her arms wide as if she were presenting the town to her.

Sarah stifled another giggle. *She looks like Vanna White on the Wheel of Fortune.*

"Where are you from?"

Sarah cleared her throat and sighed. She wasn't looking forward to being stuck in this podunk town for the summer.

Looking down the street, she realized there were only two traffic lights in the tiny burg.

"We're from Walker, you know, the big city." Sarah held up her hands and formed quotes with her fingers when she said the words 'big city'. "Do you guys have a bookstore?"

"Nope, but we do have a library." Jackie pointed to a weathered, old building standing on the corner. "But no one goes there this time of year."

"Why not?" Sarah's spirits sank even lower as she realized she wouldn't be able to buy her True Crime novels.

"Because, it's summer, silly."

Sarah rolled her eyes. "Oh, I thought you were going to say it was haunted by the Cat Lady."

Jackie cracked a wide grin. "Nope, she never comes out of her house."

"Except for today." Sarah shot Jackie a skeptical look.

"Once I tell you the whole story, you'll be a believer." Jackie hooked her arm through Sarah's. "Good thing you ran into me, otherwise you would have gone the whole summer without this knowledge. Come on, let's follow her home."

Sarah chewed on her thumbnail. "I don't know—"

Jackie pulled on her arm. "Come on...she's a legend in this town. Don't you want to see her house? People have gone in...and never come out." Jackie's eyes darkened with the mystery and her voice dropped for emphasis.

Sarah continued chewing on her nail; she thought about her options and realized she didn't have many. She could go home and hang out with her younger sister, *yuck*, or check out the *supposedly* crazy Cat Lady's house.

Sarah's inquisitive nature got the better of her and she pulled her thumb out of her mouth. "Okay, let's go."

Jackie beamed and pulled Sarah down the sidewalk. "So, what grade are you in?"

"Ninth."

"Hey, me too." Jackie put her arm around Sarah.

The girls trailed the crazy lady, staying a good block behind her. As they walked Jackie filled her in on the Cat Lady legend. According to Jackie, at least three people had mysteriously disappeared from the town of Harrisburg, all of them victims of the Cat Lady curse. Sarah couldn't help but be drawn in by the stories. There was the former grocery delivery boy, Gus, who delivered her groceries and never returned to the store. The next victim was the good doctor, who used to do house calls until he disappeared inside her house, and then last but not least, old lady Farnsworth who was discovered dead after a dispute with the Cat Lady.

Listening to her new friend drone on, Sarah watched the infamous woman wind her way home. She couldn't help but notice how frail she appeared as she shuffled down the street. The poor woman didn't look strong enough to make anyone disappear, let alone cause the death of a grouchy old lady.

The air was thick with humidity. Sweat formed on Sarah's brow as she rounded the corner toward the Cat Lady's place. Sighing, she wiped it away. *How much farther do we have to go?* Glancing at the huge oak trees lining the sidewalk, Sarah realized this was an old part of town just because the trees were so big. Sunlight dappled the walkway, leaving dark shadows as it forced its light between the leaves. No one roamed the streets; Sarah thought this was odd and her heart picked up its pace. *Jackie's stories are getting to me.*

"Okay," Jackie whispered, clutching Sarah's arm. "We're almost there." Jackie stopped and cast a skittish glance around her. "Let's cross the street."

Strolling across the street, Jackie tried to appear casual by swinging her arms and whistling, but Sarah knew she was faking it.

Sarah stopped her when they reached the opposite sidewalk. "Okay, what are we going to do?"

"We're going to watch her."

"Watch her?"

Jackie pulled on one of her curls. "Yeah, see if she does anything...you know...witchy."

Sarah furrowed her brow. "Won't she see us?"

"Trust me." Jackie winked.

Sarah followed her new friend to an old church, reaching it just after the Cat Lady disappeared inside her home. They scurried behind an old oak tree growing on the church's lawn. With a thudding heart, Sarah hugged the tree. *These stories are definitely getting to me.* Feeling the rough bark of the tree calmed her. She was hidden and this made her feel safe. *After all, what could happen in broad daylight?*

Peeking out from behind the tree, Sarah stared at the house. It sat in the middle of the block on Jefferson Street in a state of disrepair. Ancient gutters sagged at one end, and it needed a fresh coat of paint. The front porch ran the full length of the structure, settling on the south side. It reminded Sarah of a drooping smile, the kind of smile she might get from someone whose mouth had been shot full of novocaine. Dirty windows, which resembled sinister eyes, peered at the girls with their unblinking stare. A chill ran down Sarah's spine. *It's like the house knows we're here.* She noticed the grass hadn't been mowed in weeks and the house appeared abandoned. Cats dawdled on the stoop, the only signs of life around the place.

"Go up on the porch," Jackie urged.

Sarah raised her eyebrow and smirked. "You go up on the porch."

Jackie shook her head. "No way."

"Are you scared?" Sarah teased, grinning at her.

"Absolutely. I could go up on her porch and never be seen again." Jackie's solemn expression told Sarah she believed her own words.

The girls watched the house, waiting for a glimpse of the infamous witch. After what seemed like hours, there was still no sign of her.

Sighing, Sarah fidgeted. She was antsy, her legs cramping from staying in one position for so long. "Let's go," she said, doing a deep knee bend. "I've got to get home. My aunt and uncle will wonder where I am."

"Okay, we can come back tomorrow."

Just as the girls were about to leave, three rough looking boys swooped down the street on their bikes. Jackie grabbed Sarah's arm and pulled her back behind the oak.

"It's the Wykowski boys."

Sarah didn't move. She had no idea who the boys were, but from Jackie's reaction she figured they were trouble.

"These guys are total creeps," Jackie whispered as she peered out from behind the tree.

Sarah hoped they would ride past them and be on their way. Much to her dismay, they slowed and began circling in front of the Cat Lady's house. She groaned. *We're never getting out of here.* The three boys stopped circling and Sarah poked her head out to see what was happening. They were in the middle of the street whispering to each other.

Jackie pointed at a tall boy with dark, shaggy hair. "That's Tim. He's like the leader."

Suddenly, Tim yelled at the house. "Hey! Cat Lady! Do you eat cat food with all your cats?"

The boys hooted with wicked laughter and then grew quiet. Sarah could tell they were waiting for a reaction from the withered old woman. When one didn't come they took up their screams once again, yelling for the Cat Lady to come out on her porch.

After several minutes of ranting and getting no response the boys produced three huge, overripe tomatoes. They glanced up and down the street, and then hurled the tomatoes at the house. A couple of them hit with a loud splat, smearing red pulp all over the dingy siding. Sarah's heart skipped a beat. *This will definitely get the Cat Lady out of her house.*

The rowdy boys took off on their bikes, laughing at their prank. Tim, the shaggy haired boy, rode ahead of the other two and jumped the curb, as if by coming closer to the house he dared the Cat Lady to come out. Glancing back he laughed, and the two other boys joined in. He didn't pay attention to where he was going and Sarah watched as he smacked right into a stop sign. Yelping, he fell in a heap and his brothers stopped to help him. They weren't laughing now. Climbing back on their bikes, the boys took off down the road. Sarah noticed Tim glanced back at the house, his expression filled with a mixture of fear and bewilderment.

"See, I told you she was a witch," Jackie whispered.

"That kid ran into the stop sign all by himself," Sarah scoffed.

"No way. He's lived in this town all his life. He knew the stop sign was there. It was the curse of the Cat Lady."

"Whatever." Sarah rolled her eyes. "I have to get home."

The girls waited a few minutes, and then left the safety of the tree. They ambled down the street away from the infamous house and all the secrets it held. Sarah stopped and glanced over her shoulder. She had a tingling feeling someone or something was watching them.

"I'll walk you home," Jackie said, linking her arm through Sarah's and pulling her. "We can get together tomorrow and I'll show you the willow tree."

"Okay." Sarah allowed Jackie to pull her forward.

They moved down the street and Jackie told Sarah all about the town of Harrisburg and its quirky characters. Sarah listened intently, forgetting the tingling feeling. *Maybe being stuck here for the summer won't be so bad.*

Looking at the homes lining the streets, Sarah wondered what it would be like to grow up in such a tiny town. She lived in the city and enjoyed the hustle and bustle. Here everything moved at a slower pace.

Reaching her aunt and uncle's home, Sarah made plans to see Jackie the next day. After she said goodbye, Sarah climbed the stairs to the large front porch. She plopped down on the swing hanging from hooks above the stoop. Sarah always thought of their house as friendly, with its yellow siding and ample porch. This could be a great summer after all. Exhaling a contented sigh, she looked forward to the next morning.

****

Sarah woke bright and early the next day. Bounding out of bed, she dressed in denim shorts and a yellow T-shirt. As Sarah brushed her hair, she realized she was excited about seeing her new friend again. Giggling, she remembered how much she enjoyed Jackie's dramatic flair. It was like Jackie was the ying to her yang. They went together like peanut butter and jelly.

Suddenly, Sarah remembered a song she had learned at Y camp a few years ago. The song drifted into her mind... *Peeeanuuut, peanut butter....jelly. Peeeanuuut, peanut butter... jelly. First you take the peanuts and you smash them, smash them, smash them —*. She had sung it with her best friend Melanie and they would swing their hips to the beat, pretending to smash peanuts with their hands. Sarah laughed at the memory and realized she clicked with Jackie, not quite the same way as with Melanie, but in a way that was still fun. *Things are definitely looking up for the summer.*

While waiting for her aunt to finish cooking breakfast, Sarah walked out into the backyard. She could tell it was going to be a scorcher, because it was only eight o'clock and already the dew had dried on the grass. Smiling, she turned her face to the sun, enjoying the heat.

Sarah listened to the sounds of the morning, the twittering of birds, the buzzing of insects, and the occasional bark of a dog. She loved this morning melody and her body tingled with anticipation.

Jackie arrived right after breakfast. Lacey beat Sarah to the door, and when she met Jackie she insisted on being included. Sarah didn't put up much of a fight and the three girls sat on the stoop making plans for the day.

Jackie studied Lacey. "Hey, you guys could almost be twins."

Sarah laughed. "No way."

"Way," Jackie insisted. "You guys have the same blonde hair and green eyes."

"But, Lacey's taller than I am and her hair goes all the way to her waist," Sarah pointed out. "Mine stops at my shoulders."

"Yeah," Lacey agreed.

"Besides, our personalities are like night and day."

"So, where does it say twins have the same personality?"

Sarah rolled her eyes. "Whatever."

"We should go to the willow tree," Jackie said, pulling on one of her curls.

"What? Bored with the conversation already?" Sarah teased.

Jackie cracked a wide smile. "Yeah. Let's go to the willow tree."

"Where's the willow tree?" Sarah asked.

"It's down by the creek." Jackie stood and descended the stairs. "I know. We can play truth or dare. Have you ever played?"

"I have." Sarah stood to follow Jackie.

"How do you play?" Lacey asked.

Jackie explained the rules of the game as they walked to the creek. Sarah tuned her out and focused her attention on the world around her. Listening to the neighborhood as it came to life, she heard the roar of a lawnmower as a neighbor fired it up to mow. She heard the *spish, spish, spish,* of a sprinkler as it watered someone's parched lawn, and then the buzz of a bee as it flew by, searching for flowers. When she felt the sun's prickly heat on her skin, Sarah realized she loved summer.

The Cole girls followed Jackie to the end of a cul-de-sac. Beyond it, Sarah spied a sandy trail stretching through the weeds like a discarded shoelace, long and skinny. Walking single file behind Jackie, Sarah winced when the weeds clutched at her calves.

When the girls reached the creek, they continued to follow their new friend. She walked along the bank, chasing the current downstream. The scent of wild flowers wafted past Sarah and she took several deep breaths. Her chest loosened as her lungs filled with the heady perfume. Sarah cracked a smile as her body tingled. *This summer is definitely better than I expected.*

The smell of wildflowers mixed with the sound of the water making its way to the ocean sent shivers of delight down Sarah's spine. It surprised her to find the creek only a few blocks away from her aunt and uncle's house. In the city, there wasn't a body of water within walking distance of their home. *Even finding a mud puddle is a rare occurrence.*

Walking along the bank, the girls came to the large willow tree and quickly claimed it as their secret hiding place. Creeping beneath the pliable branches, Sarah sighed, happy to be out of the sun. Jackie sat down on the ground and started playing in the soil with a stick. Sarah and Lacey plopped down next to her.

"Okay, Lacey why don't you start," Jackie said.

"Okay...Jackie, truth or dare?"

"I guess…truth."

"Oh, you big chicken," Lacey whined, a disappointed pout on her face.

"I'm not chicken. I just think you'll give me a wimpy dare," Jackie said thrusting her nose in the air. "So, truth."

"Okay, would you ever French kiss a boy?"

"Oh, what a lame question," Sarah grumbled. "I can tell this is the first time you've played this game."

Lacey shrugged. "So what if it is? Just answer the question, Jackie."

"Boy, you can tell you're only fourteen," Sarah said with a superior air.

"Ooooh, you're a whole year older." Lacey rolled her eyes. "Okay, Jack, answer the question."

"All right," Jackie studied the toe of her shoe for a moment. "It depends."

"On what?"

"On whether or not he chewed tobacco." Jackie nodded. "Yeah, if he chewed tobacco, no way…but if he didn't then I'd think about it."

"What a lame question." Sarah gazed at Lacey and raised her right eyebrow, and smirked. This was her infamous 'are you brain dead?' look.

"Be nice, it *is* her first time," Jackie said, smacking Sarah on the arm.

"Whatever." Sarah rolled her eyes.

"Sarah, truth or dare?" Jackie asked, a mischievous smirk playing on her lips.

"Dare." Sarah pulled her hair behind her ears and she sat up tall.

"Okay," Jackie laughed. "You have to go up on the Cat Lady's porch and ring her doorbell."

"Who's the Cat Lady?" Lacey asked as she pulled on the grass growing beneath her and tossed it in the air.

"She's a witch." Jackie whispered the words as if the mere mention of the woman would conjure her up.

"Holy Cow!" Lacey chortled. "You're history now!"

"No way," Sarah scoffed.

"Way." Lacey threw a handful of grass at her sister.

"Well?" Jackie asked. "Are you going to do it, or wimp out?"

"I'll do it."

"Are you sure?" Jackie wheedled. "You know, she's a witch."

"Yeah," Lacey piped up, relishing the teasing. "I bet she casts evil spells."

"You remember what I told you about Mrs. Farnsworth, don't you?" Jackie continued.

"Knock it off." Sarah crossed her arms over her chest. "I know you're just trying to freak me out."

"What happened to Mrs. Farnsworth?" Lacey asked, taking the bait.

Jackie deepened her voice. "It was a long time ago."

"I'm not going to listen to this." Sarah stood and brushed the dirt off her shorts.

"What? Are you scared?" Jackie teased.

"No, I'm not scared," Sarah said as she glared at Jackie. "But this is the hardest dare in the history of this game."

"Yeah, it is," Jackie snickered. "Are you up to the challenge, girlfriend?"

"Yep, let's go." Sarah turned, and began walking out from under the green canopy. The willow branches stroked her face and arms as she moved through them.

Lacey and Jackie stood and followed her.

Sarah squinted and shaded her eyes against the sun as she waited for the other girls to catch up.

"So, what did happen to Mrs. Farnsworth?" Lacey persisted.

"She used to live next to the Cat Lady. They were always fighting over something," Jackie began.

"So what," Lacey shrugged. "A lot of neighbors argue."

"Let me finish," Jackie scolded. "Anyway, the biggest feud they had was over the Cat Lady's apple tree. Every year it dropped a ton of apples in Mrs. Farnsworth's yard. They made a huge mess."

"I bet Mrs. Farnsworth was totally ticked," Sarah said.

"Yeah, it bothered her so much, one day when the Cat Lady wasn't home, she hired someone to cut down her tree."

"Oh, I bet the Cat Lady was so-o mad." Lacey frowned and twirled her hair around her finger.

"She sure was." Jackie nodded. "The story goes, the Cat Lady was so angry she cast a spell on Mrs. Farnsworth. She got some mysterious illness and died a week later."

"I don't know if I believe that story." Sarah shot Jackie a skeptical look.

"It's true," she insisted. "She died with huge warts all over her face and body."

"Oooh, so-o gross." Lacey grimaced and subconsciously wiped her hands on her shirt.

"Yeah, it was. They were oozing yellow pus."

Lacey gagged. "Gross! She had some horrible disease, the kind you get from an evil spell."

"Did you actually see the warts?" Sarah's upper lip quivered with suppressed laughter.

"No."

"Then how do you know it's true?"

"I just do," Jackie asserted. "They were green and oozing yellow pus."

Sarah hooted with laughter. "Come on, Jack. You don't believe that, do you?"

Jackie glared at Sarah. "Yes, I do. Everything I've told you is true. Remember what I told you about Gus Baker?"

"Yeah, I remember, but I don't know if I believe that, either." Sarah gave her the raised eyebrow smirk she usually gave her sister.

"Stop looking at me like that!"

"Come on. You don't believe those stories, do you?"

"Do you have any evidence they're not true?"

"No, I don't," Sarah admitted. "But we don't have any evidence that they are true, either."

"You mean Mrs. Farnsworth's wart-covered body isn't enough for you?" Jackie demanded. "What about Gus Baker?"

Sarah sighed and shook her head.

"So tell me about Gus Baker," Lacey said.

"Not now," Sarah interrupted. "We're here."

The girls stopped and Sarah noticed the sun vanished behind a cloud. Suddenly, the atmosphere around the house changed. Without the sun, it appeared dark and foreboding. Sarah stood across the street and stared at the Cat Lady's place, looking for signs of ominous danger.

The house sat hunkered down as if it were poised to spring like a cat stalking a mouse. Sarah shuddered at the thought of going up on the porch and she chewed on her thumbnail.

Looking behind her, Sarah studied the church facing the Cat Lady's home. It was a strong structure built of huge stones. She could tell it was as old as the town itself and its presence made her feel safe. Motioning for Jackie and Lacey to follow her, she moved from the sidewalk to the huge oak tree growing on the church's lawn. The girls hid behind it, peeking out at the witch's home.

"Are you still going to do it?" Jackie teased.

"Yep."

"Do you think she's inside?" Lacey asked wide-eyed.

Sarah smirked at her. "Where else would she be? I hear she never leaves her house."

"Be nice." Jackie smacked Sarah's arm.

"What are you waiting for? Are you afraid of the witch?" Lacey asked as she stared at the house.

"She's not a witch. She's just a freak, that's all."

"Well, then what are you waiting for?" Jackie snickered.

"I just want to make sure the coast is clear."

"Hey, you guys, look at all the cats," Lacey whispered. She pointed at the clusters of felines lolling about on the porch and walking in the yard. "There has to be at least twenty of them."

"Yeah, that's why she's called the Cat Lady." Sarah rolled her eyes and then felt the sting from Jackie's slap.

"Do you think she put a spell on those cats?" Lacey asked with an innocent expression, twirling her hair with her finger.

"Could be," Sarah snickered. "Or maybe she just...you know...gives them food."

"Knock it off, Sarah." Lacey glared at her sister. "What's her real name, anyway? I'm sure she hasn't gone by Cat Lady her whole life."

"Mrs. Fedewa," Jackie said, as she stared at the infamous house.

"Okay, I'm going for it. I'll meet you back here."

"Cool beans," Jackie said.

"Cool beans? Is this town still in the nineties?" Sarah teased.

"Shut up." Jackie smacked her arm again.

"This is physical abuse." Sarah rubbed her arm, trying to appear injured.

Jackie laughed. "Be thankful, I like hanging out with you."

"All I have to do is ring her doorbell, right?" Sarah poked her head out from behind the tree. She noticed the tomato pulp still clinging to the siding and peered up and down the street for the notorious Wykowski boys.

"That's right," Jackie chuckled.

Sarah took a deep breath and sprinted across the street. She stopped at the porch stairs. A group of cats were sunning themselves on the steps. They meowed at her as if they were hungry. Jumping when one of them rubbed against her legs, she bent down and stroked its back, never taking her eyes off of the house.

Sarah petted the cat, while she worked up the courage to climb the stairs. She heard the loud purr of the contented feline and it eased her anxiety. All of a sudden, she felt a hand squeeze her arm. Her heart leapt in her chest and she let out a yelp.

Turning, she spied Jackie. "I almost peed my pants!"

Jackie giggled.

"What are you doing here?" Sarah muttered and gave Jackie the evil eye.

"I couldn't stay behind the tree and miss all the action."

Sarah glanced around and pointed to some overgrown bushes in front of the porch. "You can hide over there."

Out of the corner of her eye, Sarah spied her sister running toward them and stifled a groan.

"I didn't want to stand by myself," Lacey whimpered, slightly out of breath. She tugged nervously on the hem of her T-shirt as she eyed the house.

Sarah groaned and her shoulders slumped as if she carried a heavy burden. She sighed and pointed at the bushes again. "You hide over there with Jackie and be quiet."

Sarah waited until the other girls were out of sight, and then climbed the stairs. Stopping when she reached the porch, Sarah took some deep breaths before stepping onto the sagging stoop. Walking gingerly, she hoped the porch would support her. Her stomach clenched when it groaned. She took another step and then another, the porch complaining with every footfall. Halfway across the stoop, she heard the girls behind the bushes.

"She's almost to the door," Lacey said in a low voice.

Sarah bit her lip, stifling the disapproving remark dancing on the tip of her tongue. Instead, she turned and glared at the bushes, willing its occupants to shut up. She made eye contact with Jackie, who quickly ducked behind the shrubs, pulling Lacey with her.

What in the world is she doing?" Lacey asked.

"Shhh," Jackie responded.

Sarah shook her head and continued her journey. She felt Jackie and Lacey watching her as she crept toward the door. Reaching the entryway, she was surprised to find the storm door wide open. The only barrier between the Cat Lady and the rest of the world was a flimsy screen door hanging askew on its hinges.

Alarm bells rang in Sarah's head. *This has got to be out of character for someone who never leaves her home.* She turned back and whispered to the other girls. "Hey!"

Jackie poked her head out. "What?"

"The storm door's open."

"So?"

"So what do I do?"

"Duh, ring the doorbell."

Sarah shrugged and pushed the doorbell. It let out an irritating buzz and she had the feeling it had been broken long ago and never fixed. She dashed down the stairs. The cats scattered, alarmed by the sudden activity. Reaching the shrubs, Sarah hid with her sister and Jackie.

Gasping for breath, Sarah waited for a reaction from the old woman. Her heart pummeled her ribs and she pressed her hand to her chest to calm it.

After a few minutes, Sarah started to pace. "Well, nothing's happened." She peeked out from behind the shrub and saw the screen door hanging ajar. "I bet she's not even home. I'm going to try again."

Jackie shrugged. "Be careful, remember she's a witch."

Sarah shook her head, and then peered out from behind the shrubs. Once again, she climbed the stairs. She was braver this time and it didn't take her as long to make it to the door.

She looked inside, her heart lurching in her chest. She tiptoed to the picture window and peered through it. Gasping, she ran back to the entryway. Pulling it open, she lunged inside.

Sarah stared, unable to tear herself away. Shock ran through her body like an electrical current as she eyed the scene before her. The crumpled form of the Cat Lady lay on the living room floor, just inside the door. No life flickered in the old woman's staring eyes. Her mouth gaped open in a silent scream and her hands were up around her head as if she were warding off blows. Turning away from the Cat Lady's body, Sarah gagged as the coppery scent of blood assaulted her. There was blood splattered everywhere, on the wall, on the carpet and under the Cat Lady's body.

Suddenly, Sarah's throat constricted and she gasped for breath. Fearing she would faint, she stumbled back out the door and collided with Jackie and Lacey on the porch.

Jackie grabbed Sarah's arm and shook her. "What are you doing? Are you crazy? I never said to go inside!"

Sarah didn't speak. She just stared blankly at the porch.

Jackie shook her again. "Are you under the Cat Lady's spell?"

Lacey whimpered. "Hey, Sarah...Can you hear me? Sarah?"

"She's under the Cat Lady's spell," Jackie said waving her hand in front of Sarah's eyes.

"Oh my—" Sarah moaned and clutched Jackie's arm.

"What is it?" Jackie shook her again. "Speak...say something!"

"Th-th-the C-C-Cat Lady, sh-sh-she's—" Sarah stuttered.

"She's what?" Jackie demanded.

"Sh-she's dead.

Chapter Two

"What?" Jackie asked, her voice so shrill Sarah winced.

Taking a deep breath, Sarah stared at her new friend. She noticed Jackie had the wild-eyed look of a horse ready to bolt.

She took another deep breath and clenched her hands, hoping they would stop shaking. Grabbing the hem of her shorts, she dropped her head and gulped more air. Her heart thundered in her chest, and the sound of her blood rushing through the veins in her ears, reminded Sarah of the roar of a lion. As Sarah tried to get a grip on the scene she had just witnessed, she raised her head and stared at Jackie.

"You won't believe this," Sarah wailed. She stood and wiped her face with her sleeve, and then gestured with her hands. "Sh-she's d-d-dead!"

"Are you sure she isn't sleeping?" Lacey asked.

Sarah glared at her sister. She fought the overwhelming urge to slap her. "She's lying on the floor and there's blood everywhere."

"No way! I don't believe you," Jackie said.

"Go look."

"No way. This is one of your tricks." Lacey folded her arms across her chest.

"It is not," Sarah insisted and pointed at the door with a trembling hand.

"Are you sure?" Jackie asked. "This better not be a joke."

"See for yourself."

Jackie eyed her suspiciously. "You do look kind of freaked out." She studied Sarah.

"What?"

"Just making sure this isn't a joke."

"Go look." Sarah pointed at the door.

Jackie cautiously opened the screen door. The squeak of the hinges unnerved Sarah even more. It was an eerie sound that seemed out of place on this lazy summer day. Following Jackie into the dim interior, Sarah stopped and blinked several times. She waited for her eyes to adjust, hoping she would see a different scene the second time.

Sarah watched as both girls gasped at the site of the Cat Lady lying on the living room floor. Her body lay in a large pool of blood. She gawked at the wide, staring eyes again and shuddered.

Lacey shrieked, "Oh no! Oh no!" She started to shake and tears welled in her eyes.

Sarah put her arm around Lacey and squeezed her tight. "Shhh."

"It smells like pennies in here." Lacey gulped. "Where is that smell coming from? I think I'm going to be sick." She clung to Sarah and took huge gulps of air.

"Calm down, Lacey." Sarah squeezed her tight. She knew by the sound of Lacey's voice, her sister was on the verge of going over the edge.

"She was murdered!" Jackie said in a horrified voice.

"Someone killed the Cat Lady!" Lacey shrieked again.

Sarah squeezed her tighter and noticed her sister's eyes

were wide with panic, and her voice filled with hysteria. Lacey pushed her away and pivoted, throwing up on a pile of newspapers stacked behind her.

Sarah held her hair away from her face and rubbed her back. "Are you all right?"

Lacey nodded, clinging to Sarah for support. "What is that smell?"

"I think it's the blood." Sarah wrinkled her nose.

"I don't believe it. The Cat Lady's been murdered," Jackie said.

Sarah glanced at her and saw the dazed expression on Jackie's face. Her eyes were as big as saucers, and her face pale from shock. "We don't know that. Maybe she fell and cut herself."

Sarah stared at the body, transfixed by what she saw. She had never seen a dead body before or this much blood. The shock of it hit her like a tidal wave, and Sarah stumbled back and almost went down. Her throat tightened, squeezing the breath from her.

All of a sudden, the sound of sirens filled the air, breaking the spell the Cat Lady's body had on Sarah. She stared at Jackie and Lacey taking in their horrified expressions.

"The police!" they shrieked all at once.

"Let's get out of here," Sarah cried.

The girls turned toward the door just in time to see two police cars pull up to the curb.

"Crap!" Jackie yelled.

"We've got to hide!" Sarah shouted.

She spun back toward the living room, and collided with the other two girls as they scrambled to hide. Lacey lost her balance and fell to the floor, placing her right hand in the middle of the blood pool.

"Oh gross!" she gagged. "I've got blood on my hands!" She grimaced and stood, stepping in the blood.

"This way," Sarah yelled.

Leading the way, Sarah plowed down a trail between stacks of newspapers. Piles of newspapers were everywhere. It appeared that the Cat Lady kept every single paper she'd received for the last twenty years. There were so many stacks Sarah couldn't see any furniture. She led the girls through the trail left by the piles. Sarah felt like a rat in a maze. The girls continued their sprint and made their way into a narrow kitchen, which was just as cluttered as the living room.

Sarah found a door leading to the basement. She flew down the stairs with Jackie and Lacey right behind her. The eerie screech of the front door told Sarah the police were coming inside. Lacey closed the basement door behind her, before rushing down the stairs. Breathing heavily, Sarah climbed back up the stairs and huddled next to the door. Jackie and Lacey followed her.

Sarah wiped her sweaty palms on her shorts and took deep breaths to calm her breathing. As she wiped her hands, she glanced down into the basement and saw light coming through a window. She could see dust floating in the air, trapped in the sunlight. The basement smelled musty, but dry. Old boxes were piled against a wall and they were covered with a fine layer of dust. Next, Sarah noticed the dirt floor. There were no footprints in the dirt. Sarah realized no one had been in the basement in years.

"I can't believe I just saw a dead body," whimpered Lacey. "It was so gross and that smell." She continued to wipe her hands on her shirt.

"Shhh. I want to hear what the police say." Sarah placed her ear against the door. Her heart thundered in her chest. It was so loud she feared it would drown out any other sound.

"Can you hear anything?" Jackie whispered. She positioned herself next to Sarah and pressed her ear to the door. The two girls faced each other, their noses almost touching.

"No, I can hear voices, but I can't make the words out."

"I've got the weebeejeebees! All that blood." Lacey grimaced. "I hope I don't puke again."

Sarah glared at her sister. "Shhh."

"I'm going to catch some fatal disease." She scowled and continued wiping her hands on her shirt.

"Would you shut up!" Jackie whispered vehemently.

Lacey clamped her lips together and didn't make another sound.

"I wonder what happened to the Cat Lady?" Sarah asked.

"I have no idea," Jackie said.

"This is a real mystery. Just like this one true crime story —,"Sarah started.

"How come you guys can talk, but I can't?"

"Shut up!" Sarah and Jackie hissed in unison.

The voices grew louder and Sarah heard the conversation.

"They're in the kitchen," she whispered.

Jackie bit her lip and gave her curls a nervous tug.

"They're following some bloody footprints," Sarah reported.

Sarah heard the voices growing louder.

"They're coming this way!" She gasped.

"The footprints lead to this door," a police officer said.

Sarah made eye contact with Jackie as she realized Lacey's blunder had led the police right to them. Turning, she glared at her sister.

Seconds later, the basement door flew open and a bright light shone down on them. The policeman had his gun drawn and aimed at the girls. Sarah's heart lurched in her chest. She'd never had a gun pointed at her before.

"On the floor, now!" he boomed.

The girls scurried up the stairs and dropped to the ground, spreading their arms and legs.

At the sound of the officer's command, another officer loomed in the doorway and stared down at the girls.

"Klonsky, search them for weapons," the first officer said.

Lacey started to cry. "We didn't do it! We just found the body!"

"Yeah," Sarah piped up.

Her pulse raced as Klonsky probed her for weapons. His rough hands on her body made her skin crawl. Sarah winced and shivered. She made eye contact with Jackie, grimaced, and shook her head.

"No weapons, Walker," Klonsky said.

"Okay, let's get them cuffed and down to the station," Officer Walker said.

"Wait, we didn't do anything!" Sarah yelled. She glanced at Lacey and groaned. Her T-shirt was smeared with blood. Sarah's spirits sank. *We're in big trouble.*

"We're innocent!" Jackie screamed and flailed her arms.

"We'll talk about that downtown. Now get moving," Officer Walker said, pushing Sarah forward.

She moved a few steps to the right to get past the officer's belly. *A lover of donuts,* Sarah observed and stifled a nervous bubble of laughter.

"We're going to jail," Lacey sobbed.

"We didn't do anything," Sarah insisted.

"We'll talk downtown," Klonsky said, escorting the girls to the police car.

Walking to the cruiser, Sarah noticed a small crowd forming across the street. She studied the faces of the Cat Lady's neighbors and watched their expressions harden when they saw the girls in handcuffs. Suddenly, feeling like a criminal, she lowered her gaze.

Klonsky opened the car door. "Watch your heads."

The girls grunted in effort as they struggled to get inside the car.

"Hurry up!" Klonsky snapped.

Sarah snorted. "It's not easy getting into a car with your hands cuffed behind your back."

"You girls should've thought about that before you murdered the old lady."

"So she was murdered!" Jackie's eyes widened.

"We didn't murder anyone!" Sarah argued.

Her anger at being searched was no match for her rage at being unjustly accused. She sent Klonsky an angry glare before leaning her head against the seat and closing her eyes. Sitting close to her sister, she smelled the coppery scent of blood on her shirt. Turning her head, she tried not to gag. The tight space in the car was heating up and sweat formed on her brow.

"That's right, we're innocent," Jackie insisted.

"Save it for the station," Klonsky muttered as he slammed the door and walked back inside the house.

Sarah opened her eyes and raised her head. The sweat on her forehead rolled down the side of her face. "Ugh."

"What's the matter? Jackie asked.

"I can't wipe the sweat off of my face." Sarah wiped the side of her face on the back seat. "What's going on out there?"

"I don't know," Jackie said, trying to blow some of the curls out of her face.

After an eternity, or so it seemed to Sarah, Klonsky reappeared from inside the house and climbed into the car. He ignored the girls as he started the engine. As they pulled away from the curb, an ambulance came into view. Behind the ambulance were three more police cars. *This is definitely a crime scene.*

"This is going to be the longest car ride of my life," Sarah groaned.

"No doubt, girlfriend," Jackie grimaced.

Lacey started to sob. "We're going to jail!"

As the cruiser picked up speed, Sarah stared at the world from behind the tinted window. The full force of her predicament hit her like a sledgehammer. *What if this is the last time I see sunlight?* Her stomach fluttered. *It won't be,* Sarah argued. *You're innocent. You didn't do this.*

Lacey sobbed. "I can't believe we're going to jail."

"You just had to get blood all over you, didn't you?" Sarah snapped.

"Like I did it on purpose."

"Shut up, Sarah. It could've been any of us," Jackie said.

"Yeah." Lacey wiped her face on her sleeve.

"Maybe," Sarah conceded.

The cruiser slowed and turned into the parking lot of the police station. Klonsky parked the car and turned off the engine.

"What's going to happen to us, now?" Lacey sniffled.

"Hey, Officer, what's going to happen to us, now?" Sarah asked.

Without turning his head, Officer Klonsky said, "Since you girls are under seventeen, we have to call your parents before we can question you."

"We didn't kill the Cat Lady," Lacey whined.

Klonsky turned and glared at them. "That's what they all say."

Klonsky's dark eyes bored into the girls. They were bottomless pools of anger. Sarah gulped as she took in his size. His shoulders filled the front seat and his head, even with short hair, brushed the ceiling of the car.

"It's true." Sarah clenched her trembling hands.

"You ever heard of death row?" Klonsky glowered at Lacey.

"Yeah."

"The majority of those guys say they're innocent, too." He turned away from the girls and fiddled with the police radio.

Lacey began wailing. "We're going to be on death row!"

"Stop crying, we're innocent. We didn't do anything." Sarah glared at the back of Klonsky's head. "He's just trying to scare you."

"It's a good thing too. Have you seen what those inmates wear? Bright orange jumpsuits, they are the ugliest things I've ever seen. Orange is definitely not my color," Jackie grimaced.

Sarah made a face at Jackie and nudged Lacey, whispering, "We didn't do anything. Remember CSI? The evidence tells the story."

"What are you, a detective?" Jackie asked.

"Shut up."

"Don't worry. We'll get that CSI guy to help us," Jackie said.

Sarah gave Jackie one of her 'are you brain dead' looks. "That CSI guy you're talking about is a fictitious character on a TV show." She cocked her head and nudged Lacey. "No one is going to jail. We didn't do anything."

Lacey nodded and sniffed. "Okay."

"Inside," Klonsky said as he opened his door. When he rose out of the car, it seemed to sigh in relief. Opening the back door for the girls, he towered over them as they struggled to climb out. His sheer bulk blocked out the sun.

"I'll take the cuffs off when we get inside."

Sarah stared at the building housing the police department of Harrisburg. It was a two-story, red brick building with large, white-paned windows. The panes on the windows reminded Sarah of bars on a cell door. She shivered at the thought of going inside.

Once inside the station, a separate officer was assigned to each girl. The officer in charge of Sarah led her to a separate interrogation room, removed her cuffs, and left her alone.

Sarah slouched in a folding chair, waiting for her aunt and uncle to arrive. The air conditioning had turned the room into a deep freeze, and the chair felt cold against her legs. She shivered. Goosebumps appeared on her arms and she rubbed them while she stared at the gray walls.

The walls in the tiny room closed in on her, and she suddenly had trouble breathing. Looking at the big mirror placed in the middle of the wall, she studied her reflection. She noticed her pale face and her shock filled eyes. Her lips were slightly parted as she took shallow breaths. Focusing on her image, she took some deeper breaths, easing her panicky feelings.

"This is just great," she said to her reflection. "Just when summer vacation was starting to get fun."

Sarah shifted her weight, and her mind wandered. Why would anyone want to murder the Cat Lady? Crossing her legs, she drummed her fingers on the table as she thought about the old woman. *It doesn't make any sense. She didn't have any friends, except for the cats, and she never left home.*

Just then the door opened, and Sarah's uncle walked in. All thoughts of the Cat Lady flew from her mind. Sarah noticed Uncle Walt's wispy hair was standing on end. Whenever he got stressed he tugged at what was left of his hair. It always ended up sticking straight up. He resembled a balding Einstein.

Uncle Walt was a highly intelligent, congenial man who had a hard time remembering why he was sent to the grocery store. He would often call Aunt June after he had gotten there to ask what was needed. Sarah snickered at the thought and decided he appeared to be more of an absentminded Einstein.

Sighing to release some of the tension in her body, Sarah realized she was glad her parents weren't here. Dealing with her uncle would be much easier. "Hey, Uncle Walt."

"Hi, honey. What is going on here?" he asked, concern etched on his face.

"We found the Cat Lady's body." Sarah stood and suddenly grasped the table, her legs felt like jelly.

"Who's the Cat Lady?"

"Mrs. Fedewa."

Her uncle reached out to Sarah, and she ran into his comforting embrace. She stifled the sob trying to escape her throat.

"Are you all right?" her uncle murmured into her hair.

Sarah nodded.

"Okay, tell me everything. Start from the beginning."

They sat down in the folding chairs. He put his arm around Sarah in a protective gesture. She snuggled next to him, grateful for his warmth.

She took a deep breath. "Well, Lacey, Jackie, and I were playing Truth or Dare."

"And?"

"Jackie dared me to ring the Cat Lady's doorbell."

Her uncle chuckled. "I'm sure you didn't turn that dare down."

"You got that right." Sarah gave him a lopsided grin. " So, when I rang her doorbell, I looked in the window and saw someone lying on the floor."

"What did you do then?"

"I ran to the big picture window to see who it was. I figured she was the Cat Lady."

"Okay, so what did you do then?"

"I ran back to the door, went inside, and that's when I saw all the blood." Sarah shuddered at the memory.

"Why did you go in the house?" Uncle Walt frowned and spun in his seat to look at her.

"I don't know," she said, her voice cracking. "I didn't know she was dead. I thought maybe I could help her."

"You should never go into someone's home like that." Shaking his head, he placed his index finger on the table to make his point. He pressed so hard Sarah saw the white crescent above the pink on his fingernail.

"I bet you would've done the same thing."

"It doesn't matter what I would've done. I'm not a fifteen-year-old girl," he said with a stern look.

"I was trying to help." Sarah's stomach fluttered and she shifted uneasily in her chair.

"Do you realize the killer could've still been there?"

"I didn't know she'd been murdered!"

"Okay, okay, but use your head next time."

"I hope there won't be a next time."

Her uncle groaned and tugged at the hair on top of his head. "Honey, I just don't want anything to happen to you or your sister. How would I tell your parents if something did happen? It worries me when you take risks like this."

"I know, but I honestly didn't think we were in danger." Sarah shifted in her seat and gazed at her uncle. "I didn't see the blood until I was inside."

"Your heart's in the right place." He sighed, searching for the right words. "Sarah, you're a courageous girl. I admire that about you, but you need to be more careful."

"I bet if the Cat Lady had been alive, and we'd saved her life, you'd be telling me I did the right thing."

He gave Sarah a rueful smile. "You're probably right. The mistake you made here is that you didn't call the police right away."

Sarah frowned, and stared down at her hands. "Maybe you're right."

"Maybe?"

"All right, you're right."

"So, you discovered the body. That's why you girls are here. At least they don't think you murdered her."

"They do think that." Sarah squirmed in her chair.

"What? Why in the world would they think you girls murdered Mrs. Fedewa?"

"When I showed Jackie and Lacey the body, the police pulled up in the driveway."

"You mean you went back into the house a second time?" Uncle Walt leaned forward in his chair and stared at Sarah.

"Well, yeah. Those guys didn't believe me, so I had to prove to them I saw a dead body."

"And?" Uncle Walt was beginning to look ill.

"The sirens scared us. Lacey tripped and got blood all over her shirt."

He leaned back in his chair and groaned. Both of his hands began tugging at his hair. "Go on."

Sarah glanced at her uncle and suppressed a nervous grin. His hair was standing straight up. He looked like an aging punk rocker refusing to accept he was past his prime. The only things missing were the leather pants, tattoos, and the pierced ears and nose.

"Well, then we ran and hid in the basement."

"Why in the world would you girls hide in the basement?" Uncle Walt pulled his hands from his hair and flailed them wildly in the air.

"I don't know," Sarah threw her hands up. "We just panicked."

"All right." Standing, he patted Sarah's arm. "I want you to tell your story to the police. Just tell the truth, and everything will be all right." He walked toward the door.

"Uncle Walt?"

He stopped with his hand on the doorknob. "Yeah?"

"I'm so glad you're here. This is all kind of scary."

He pursed his lips. "I'm surprised to hear you say that, Sarah. Between my two nieces, you're the brave one."

Sarah gazed down at her hands. "Well, I've never been handcuffed before."

He turned toward her, clenching his fists. "The police handcuffed you?"

"Yeah."

"I don't believe it," he shook his head and frowned.

"Yeah, I couldn't believe it either. Especially after they searched us and didn't find any weapons."

"They searched you?"

"Yeah."

"That is no way to treat young girls."

"Tell me about it."

He shook his head. His face turned a frightening red color.

"Are you all right? You look like you're going to puke."

Her uncle took a few deep breaths and tried to smile at Sarah, but it looked more like a grimace. He pivoted and walked out the door, signaling for someone to come in. Officer Klonsky loomed in the doorway.

Sarah's heart skipped a beat when she compared her uncle to Klonsky. Uncle Walt seemed weak and shriveled.

"Sarah's ready to tell her story," Uncle Walt said.

"I'm ready to hear it." Klonsky sat down across from Sarah. Another officer followed Klonsky and sat next to him. "This is Officer Wilson; he's going to listen in."

Her uncle nodded. "Are these girls under arrest?"

"No. It's standard procedure for us to question anyone we find at a crime scene. Especially a homicide," Wilson said.

Sarah studied Klonsky as Officer Wilson answered her uncle's questions. She shuddered as she remembered how his large, calloused hands searched her for weapons. Looking at his face, her heart skipped a beat. He wore a permanent scowl and his dark, probing eyes stared at her uncle and then Sarah as if he could read their minds. Warning lights went off in Sarah's head, and goose bumps reappeared on her skin, only this time it wasn't because of the air conditioning. A shiver ran down her spine, and she quickly turned her attention back to her uncle and Officer Wilson.

"Then why were they searched and handcuffed?" Uncle Walt asked, keeping his temper in check, but Sarah could tell he was mad, because the little vein in his forehead was bulging.

"Again, standard procedure. At the time, we had to make sure they didn't have any weapons on them."

Her uncle sighed. "Okay, go ahead."

"Sarah, how do you know the deceased?" Klonsky leaned forward and stared into her eyes.

She gulped. "Just from what kids have said about her around the neighborhood."

"Tell me how you happened to be in her basement."

Sarah repeated her story for the officer. He jotted down a few notes as she spoke, but he never interrupted her.

"So, you girls just stumbled onto the body while you were pulling a prank?" Klonsky asked, with a sneer.

"Yeah."

"You don't expect us to believe that, do you?"

Officer Wilson stared at Klonsky, shock etched on his face.

"It's the truth." Sarah hid her trembling hands in her lap.

Sarah's uncle put his arm around her shoulders.

"Did you have any kind of relationship with the deceased prior to being in her basement?"

"No. Like I said, we only knew her from stories we heard around the neighborhood."

"Are you in the habit of harassing your neighbors?"

"What kind of question is that?" her uncle demanded. "These girls don't live here permanently, they're from out of town. They don't even know Mrs. Fedewa."

"Klonsky, just stick to the case," Officer Wilson said.

Klonsky ignored his partner and continued to stare at Sarah. "Answer the question."

Sarah gulped and shrank in her seat. She felt Klonsky's piercing gaze. Dropping her eyes, she studied the floor. Slouching further down in her chair, Sarah knew she appeared guilty, but she didn't care. Escape from those probing eyes was the only thing on her mind.

"Come on, you're acting like these girls are suspects," Wilson said.

"We found them at the crime scene," Klonsky retorted. He didn't take his eyes off Sarah.

Wilson spun in his seat and stared at Klonsky. "Yes, but they didn't have any weapons on them."

"One of the girls had blood on her."

"You can't seriously believe these girls murdered Mrs. Fedewa," Uncle Walt said.

Sarah noticed her uncle sat straight up in his seat, his body rigid with anger.

"Why not?"

"Klonsky, the girl didn't have enough blood on her to be considered a suspect." Wilson shook his head. "You know that, you've been on the force for ten years."

He seemed disgusted with Klonsky's belligerent attitude, and Sarah felt a glimmer of hope.

"That's right, ten years. You're just a rookie."

"Even a rookie knows there wasn't enough blood on her clothes. These girls are not suspects." Officer Wilson made eye contact with her uncle and shook his head again.

Sarah watched as Uncle Walt relaxed back in his chair, keeping his arm around her.

"What stories have you heard about the deceased?" Klonsky asked, as he once again captured Sarah in his unwavering stare. She could tell he wanted to ask more forceful questions, but his partner's presence kept him in check.

"You know, she was a witch. All the kids were scared of her."

Klonsky shifted in his seat. "So, you were never involved in an altercation with the deceased?"

"Altercation?" Sarah squirmed and chewed her thumbnail.

"A fight, or a disagreement."

Sarah shook her head. "No."

"Why did you run into the basement when you saw us coming?"

Sarah put her hand back in her lap. "We just got scared."

"Scared?"

"Yeah, we heard the sirens, and they freaked us out, so we hid."

"You hid because you murdered her!" Klonsky attacked.

"All right! That's enough!" her uncle stood, and placed his hands square on the table between Klonsky and Sarah. His face inches from Klonsky's.

"Yeah, Klonsky, you're out of line. Take a break. I'll finish up the questions here." Wilson placed his hands on Klonsky's chest and pushed him back.

Klonsky stood and glared at Sarah. "These girls murdered Mrs. Fedewa."

"I said out," Wilson stood and pushed him toward the door. After Klonsky left, he shut the door and sat back down. "Sorry about that. He's just a little riled up. Let's finish these questions, and we'll get you out of here."

"Okay," Sarah said. She tried to smile but her lips wouldn't work.

"How did Lacey get blood on her?"

"She tripped and fell, and put her hand in the blood, then wiped it on her shirt."

"That's the only place you girls have blood on you?" Wilson asked.

"Yeah, see?" Sarah stood and held out her hands, twirling slowly for the detective. "No blood."

Officer Wilson nodded.

"Officer Wilson?" Sarah asked as she sat back down.

"Yes."

She leaned forward. "I think the Cat Lady knew her killer."

"Why do you think that?"

"Because, she had all these newspapers in her living room, and they were in neat piles."

"Yeah, that's true. But I don't see what that has to do with the crime."

"Don't you think the place would be a mess if she were fighting for her life? I think she knew the killer and let him in." Sarah sat up straight and squared her shoulders.

Officer Wilson stared at her. "I'm impressed. You might be right. You'd make a good detective."

Sarah beamed at the compliment, her lips working this time. "Thank you."

"Well, you're very observant. That's a requirement to be a good detective."

Sarah felt her face flush. "I want to be a detective."

"Maybe you will." He winked at her. "All right, I'm going to check on the other girls." Wilson stood. He walked toward the door and then stopped with his hand on the doorknob. "By the way, are you Mr. Bennett, the science teacher?"

"Yes I am." Sarah's uncle stood and held out his hand for Officer Wilson to shake.

"My son had you for biology. He spoke very highly of you. He enjoyed your class."

"I'm glad to hear it. It's always encouraging when a student gets something out of my class."

"I'll go check on the other girls. I'll be back in a few minutes." Officer Wilson walked out the door.

"Aunt June with Lacey?" Sarah asked, fidgeting in her chair.

"Yeah." Her uncle nodded. He squeezed her hand. "This is one heck of a way to spend your summer vacation."

"Tell me about it." Sarah laughed, and some of the tension left her body. "Riding in a police car is not my idea of fun."

"This is almost over."

"Good."

Uncle Walt sighed and leaned back in his chair. He ran his hands through his hair in an attempt to tame it. "I'm glad I don't have to call your dad and tell him you and Lacey were arrested."

Sarah chuckled. "I am too." She knew her parents would be furious with her. "We don't have to tell them about this do we?"

Her uncle laughed, and Sarah saw his blue eyes twinkle with understanding.

"We'll see."

Sarah gave him a smile. She liked her Uncle Walt. He was easy going and didn't have a huge hang-up about rules.

They sat in silence waiting for Officer Wilson to come back.

Sarah took a deep breath and let it out slowly. "How much longer is this going to take?" Her stomach gurgled with hunger, and she felt pressure from her bladder. *I need to find a bathroom.*

"Not much longer."

"Uncle Walt?"

"Hmmm?"

"Have you ever seen a dead body before?"

"Yes, at the funeral home when Grandpa Joe died." He raised his eyebrow and studied her. "Why do you ask?"

Sarah shrugged. "I just wondered." She cupped her hands on the table and placed her chin in them.

"Yeah?"

"It was so gross. All that blood everywhere."

"Yes, I suppose it was. I'm sure Grandpa Joe didn't look anything like the Cat Lady did."

"I feel sorry for her, you know, the Cat Lady."

"Yeah, I do too." He paused, thinking. "Hey, when Lacey put her hand in the blood was it wet?"

Sarah thought for a second. "Yeah, otherwise she wouldn't have wiped it on her shirt. Why?"

"I'm just thinking about the time of death, that's all."

"What do you mean?" Sarah turned and gazed at her uncle.

"Well, I was just wondering how long Mrs. Fedewa had been lying there. Since it's hot and humid, it takes longer for the blood to dry. So she could've laid there for a couple of hours. So that would make her time of death early this morning."

"Hmmm...how do you know this?" Sarah asked, sitting up straight.

"I was studying to be a doctor when I met your aunt. I knew I was going to marry her on our first date." He paused and beamed at the memory. "After that, being a doctor just didn't seem important anymore, so I became a teacher instead."

"Wow, I didn't know that."

"Yeah, one of my classes was forensic science when I was pre-med. I've always been interested in that kind of thing."

"Oh."

"You girls probably found Mrs. Fedewa just hours after she was murdered."

Sarah stared at her uncle. "For real?"

Uncle Walt nodded. "Yeah."

"You know, all the kids thought she was a witch."

"No kidding?"

"Yeah, I mean, she was kind of weird."

"Weird is a far cry from being a witch, don't you think?"

Sarah rested her head on her clasped hands. "Yeah, I guess. I just can't figure out why anyone would want to murder her."

"I don't know either."

Sarah raised her head. "Do you think someone murdered her because they thought she was a witch?"

Her uncle patted Sarah's arm. "There's more to Mrs. Fedewa than the crazy rumors you've heard around town."

"Like what?"

"Well, she wasn't always weird. In fact, she was one of the richest ladies in town."

"For real?" Sarah raised her eyebrows and gaped at her uncle. "Man, you should have seen her house. It was piled high with newspapers all over the place. Are you sure she was rich?"

"Yep."

"You couldn't tell by the way she lived. Why in the world would anyone want to live like that?"

"A very good question." He pursed his lips and tapped the end of Sarah's nose.

"It's kind of freaky."

"I think this is a good opportunity for you."

"A good opportunity?"

"Yes, to do some investigating."

"Yeah, but where do I start?"

"I would start by finding out as much as I could about the Cat Lady," her uncle cracked a smile. "You might be surprised by what you find."

Sarah gave her uncle a wide grin. "Okay."

"But use your head. I don't want you kids taking unnecessary risks."

The door opened and Officer Wilson walked in, stopping any further conversation.

"Well, it looks like your stories check out," Wilson said.

"What does that mean?" Uncle Walt asked.

"All three girls told the same story. So we're satisfied they're telling the truth."

"Great, we can go, right?" Sarah tried to stand, but the skin on the back of her legs stuck to the chair.

"Not exactly."

"What do you mean?" her uncle asked.

"We have to get elimination prints from the girls."

"Elimination prints?"

"We need to get their fingerprints, so we can eliminate them from any other prints we find at the crime scene."

Sarah finally detached herself from the chair. She could see the heat residue her legs had left. It was rapidly disappearing because of the chilled room.

"Follow me please, and we can get this done quickly." Officer Wilson opened the door and stepped out into the hall. He stopped and waited for Sarah and her uncle to follow him.

After all three girls had been printed, everyone walked down the hall toward the lobby. Sarah felt almost giddy with relief until the group happened upon Klonsky and another officer talking. As they walked by, Sarah glanced up and caught the cop's eye. He gave her a menacing stare.

"There go the killers right there." Klonsky pointed at the three girls.

Klonsky's words sent a chill down her spine. *Didn't the other officer just say we were free to go? Doesn't that mean we're in the clear? Why is this guy on our case?* These questions paraded through Sarah's mind, and her stomach churned. The strongest feeling came over her, the feeling this wasn't over by a long shot. She strained to hear the rest of the conversation.

"You're out of your mind, Klonsky." the second officer shook his head.

"Yeah, everything's going like clockwork for those three, but I'm going to catch them."

Uncle Walt scowled at Klonsky. "Knock it off, or I'll issue a complaint with your superior."

Klonsky glared at them, but kept his mouth shut. Sarah glanced down, refusing to meet his gaze. She chewed on her thumbnail as the group continued past the officers and out the door.

Chapter Three

Once outside, Sarah squinted against the brilliant sunlight. Tears welled in her eyes as she pulled on her uncle's arm. "Uncle Walt?" Sarah blinked and wiped her eyes.

"Yeah?"

"What's his problem?"

"I'm not sure." He glanced back at the police station.

"It's like he thinks we killed the Cat Lady." Sarah stopped and stared at her uncle.

He placed his hand on her shoulder and gave her a reassuring squeeze. "It doesn't matter what he thinks, it only matters what he can prove. He has no evidence."

"I know, but..." Sarah gnawed on her thumbnail again.

Her uncle put his arm all the way around her and squeezed again. "Don't worry about him."

"But he's a cop. He could do all sorts of things to make it look like it was us." Sarah felt sick to her stomach.

"Don't worry. You're innocent."

"Yeah," Lacey piped up.

"Yeah, true." Sarah glanced over her shoulder, but she

didn't feel any better.

"Don't worry," Uncle Walt said. "Harrisburg is a small town, it's not like they can manufacture evidence against you. This isn't a TV show."

Sarah faked a smile for her uncle's benefit. "That's true. I feel better now."

Uncle Walt cracked a wide grin and puffed up his chest.

"Can we go to Hinkle's?" Sarah asked.

"Right now?" Uncle Walt pulled back and frowned.

"Yeah."

"After the day you've had?"

She nodded. "Yeah, I think a little ice cream would help."

"I guess it's all right." He looked to Aunt June for confirmation.

Sarah glanced at her aunt and gave her a tentative smile. Aunt June resembled her mother so closely they could have been twins. They had the same blonde hair and green eyes. Both women shared the same worry line between their eyebrows. It was creased now because of their recent tangle with the law.

She gave Sarah a smile and relaxed. The crease disappeared. "Just be home before dark."

"Okay."

"I'm going home. I need to disinfect," Lacey sniffed.

"Do you need some money?" her uncle asked.

"Yeah."

He pulled out his wallet and handed Sarah a five. "Have fun."

Sarah hurried over to Jackie. "Hey, how about Hinkle's?"

"Absolutely," Jackie gave her mom her best Vanna White smile. "Mom, we're going to Hinkle's."

"I don't know." Jackie's mom hesitated. "You've had a horrendous day."

Jackie nodded. "I know, that's why I need some ice

cream."

"Let her go, Claire," Jackie's dad said, winking at his daughter. "This is Harrisburg."

"Where an old lady was just murdered," Jackie's mother said dryly.

"Please..." Jackie whined. She gazed at her mother with pleading eyes, and clasped her hands together as if she were praying.

"Please..." Sarah copied Jackie's stance and beseeching expression.

Her mother sighed. "All right, just be home before dark."

The girls smirked at each other.

"Let's go," Sarah said.

Hinkle's stood on the corner of Main and Church, just two blocks from the police station. Cars drove up and down the street, the drivers honking and waving to people they knew. Main Street was considered the main drag to the teenagers of Harrisburg, and they called this "cruising the gut."

According to Jackie, "cruising" was the favorite pastime of the teens of this tiny burg, those that could drive anyway. It was considered a rite of passage, and Jackie couldn't wait to get her license. She had talked about it last night when she walked Sarah home. Sarah watched the cars go by, shaking her head. She didn't see much point in "cruising." The cars just went around the same city blocks for what seemed like hours. What was the point?

Sighing, her mind returned to the events of the day. "I'm so glad we weren't arrested."

"I know," Jackie said, dipping her head in Sarah's direction. She skipped ahead, and then turned to face Sarah. She walked backward as she spoke. "Do you realize we have a murder mystery right here in Harrisburg?"

Sarah nodded. "You got that right."

Jackie stopped and mused. "A major mystery in our small town."

"I thought you said nothing interesting ever happens here."

"It didn't until now," Jackie cracked a wide smile. "I wonder who killed the Cat Lady?"

"Klonsky thinks we did it." Sarah's stomach fluttered and she chewed on her nail again.

"I know." Jackie started her backward walk again.

"We've got to find the real killer before Klonsky pins this on us."

"You think so?" Jackie's eyes widened. "Why would he do that?" She stopped walking and stared at Sarah.

Sarah paused and gazed at her new friend. "I don't know. All I know is that he thinks we did it, and he's a cop."

The two girls stared at each other. Sarah saw confusion flickering in Jackie's eyes. A car honked its horn, and Sarah watched as her friend gave the driver a half-hearted wave, never taking her focus from Sarah.

"He doesn't have any evidence," Jackie said.

"Well, he could make it look like it was us even when it wasn't."

"Why would he do that?"

"I don't know, but everyone would believe him because he's a cop."

Jackie shot Sarah a skeptical look. "Are you serious, girlfriend?"

"Totally, I read about it all the time in my True Crime books. The cops go after some innocent bystander. It happens all the time."

"But we're just teenagers," Jackie protested, pulling on one of her curls. "Who would believe him?"

"He's a cop. Everyone's going to believe him. Plus, Lacey and I don't live here. No one knows us."

Sarah saw Jackie's nostrils flare, and her eyes widened as her words hit home.

"What are we going to do?" Jackie gulped as tears filled her eyes.

"We have to find the killer ourselves."

"You're right, girlfriend." Jackie wiped her eyes, and then closed the gap between them. She gave Sarah a squeeze before the girls continued their walk.

They arrived at the restaurant, and Sarah relaxed when she opened the door. It was a cheery place where all the townies gathered together to gossip and exchange family news. Hinkle's was Harrisburg's official hangout. On the walls hung Christmas lights year round and humorous plaques that brought chuckles to the patrons while they waited for their meals. As the girls walked through the door, one of these plaques caught Sarah's eye. *In life, it's not who you know that's important, it's how your parents found out.* She laughed and felt a little better, as the cold blast from the restaurant's air conditioning raised goose bumps on her skin.

"I've got to use the bathroom," Sarah said, rubbing her arms.

"Didn't want to use the one at the police station?" Jackie gave her a playful nudge.

"No way! I wanted to get the heck out of there."

The girls cracked up laughing. Now that the ordeal was over, they could laugh about it.

"I'll grab a booth," Jackie said as she turned and stopped at the hostess stand.

Sarah nodded and walked to the restroom. She glanced into the restaurant before going through the door and noticed the place wasn't busy. It was early afternoon, and the dinner rush hadn't begun yet. The hostess seated Jackie by a window. Sarah made a mental note of this, before walking through the door.

A few minutes later, Sarah slid into the booth. "We need to come up with a name."

"A name?" Jackie glanced up from her menu.

"Yeah, if we're going to be detectives. We have to have a name."

"We're going to be detectives?" Jackie dropped her menu and stared at Sarah with a perplexed expression.

"Yep."

"Why do you want to be a detective?"

"So we can find out who killed the Cat Lady." Sarah grabbed her menu and opened it, then laid it on the table.

"How about the Fashionistas?"

Sarah groaned.

"What? You don't like that name?" Jackie asked.

"Not everyone's into fashion like you are."

"What? I don't believe it."

"Believe it," Sarah giggled.

"What could be more important than being a Fashionista? I'm going to be a model, you know." Jackie flashed Sarah a smile.

"I know. Models are fashionable, but detectives keep a low profile." Sarah smirked.

"How about the Shopaholics?"

Sarah shook her head. "No, it has to be something about detectives."

"Girlfriend, you're way too serious."

Sarah rolled her eyes. "Let's focus on a name."

"How about the Crime Stoppers?"

"No, that sounds like a TV show or something. Besides, it's too late to stop the crime."

The conversation paused when the waitress came to take their order. Each girl ordered a super-size chocolate malt. Hinkle's was famous for their thick malts, and Sarah's stomach rumbled with anticipation. *Hmm*, Sarah thought, *super-size.*

Super Spies. When the waitress disappeared to fill the order, the girls leaned forward to continue their conversation.

"I know, how about The Super Spies?" Sarah asked.

"Hmm, I like it," Jackie said.

"Me too. It has a nice ring to it."

"It's like we're super heroes."

"I'm so not wearing a cape." Sarah frowned and shook her head.

Jackie laughed. "Why not? Capes are fashionable." She raised her straw and twirled it in the air.

"Detectives, not Fashionistas, remember?"

"It doesn't mean we can't be fashionable while we're being detectives," Jackie said, giving Sarah her Vanna White smile.

"The capes are out," Sarah said, with mock severity.

"Oh, come on."

"No, the discussion is closed."

"Party-pooper."

Their waitress returned with two huge malts. Sarah held her malt up in the air. Jackie followed suit. The girls raised their glasses together for a toast. Smiling at the sound of the muffled clink of their glasses, Sarah's body tingled with anticipation.

"To the Super Spies," Jackie crowed.

"To the Super Spies, without capes."

Jackie gave Sarah an exaggerated frown and then sipped her malt.

Hinkle's began filling with people, and it soon buzzed with conversation. The dinner rush had begun. Scents of cooking food wafted past Sarah's nose, and a grin spread across her face as she inhaled the delicious smells. Sounds of clattering plates and scraping silverware increased within seconds. Sarah welcomed the noise. They were less likely to be overheard.

"You know, I have a theory," Sarah leaned forward and whispered.

"Hmmm...What is it?"

"I think the Cat Lady knew her killer."

"Why do you think that?" Jackie asked, leaning forward also.

Sarah saw the glimmer of curiosity in her eyes. "You saw her house. All those stacks of papers."

"Yeah?"

"Don't you think if she were fighting for her life all those papers would be messed up?"

"Maybe."

"Oh, come on, Jack...You think the killer was concerned about being tidy?"

"Probably not," Jackie agreed. "But still, it doesn't mean she knew her killer."

Sarah raised her eyebrow and smirked at her. "Come on, Jackie!"

"How does it prove she knew her killer? Enlighten me. Bestow upon me your superior wisdom." Jackie pretended to gag on her words.

"I guess I'm going to have to teach you about the powers of deduction." Sarah sat up in her seat and pursed her lips.

Jackie cocked her head and smirked at her. "Apparently."

"Okay, first of all, the Cat Lady was a hermit, right?" Sarah held up her index finger.

"Right."

"Second of all, she never opens her door for anyone." Sarah held up two fingers.

"Right."

"Third, there was no sign of a break in, and the place wasn't messed up." Sarah held up three fingers.

Jackie's face lit up. "Oh, I get it now."

"So, it had to be someone she knew well enough to open her door and let them in." Sarah glanced over her shoulder to make sure no one heard her, and then leaned closer to Jackie and whispered, "That's why we need to sneak out tonight and look for clues in the Cat Lady's house."

Jackie's eyes widened. "What! You mean sneak into the Cat Lady's house?"

Sarah nodded.

"At night?"

"Yeah."

"Why at night?"

"Because the police are going to be there during the day and we won't be able to get in."

Jackie giggled. "Sounds like a plan to me."

"Just you and me," Sarah said, with a conspiratorial wink.

"What about Lacey?"

"You know Lacey…she's a big wimp."

"You think so?"

"Yeah, you saw her bawling on the way to the police station," Sarah shook her head.

"True," Jackie said, slurping the last of her malt.

"Let's meet at the willow tree at midnight."

"Cool beans."

"Wear dark clothes."

Jackie winked, and then swiveled to flag their waitress down. "Hey, Carla, we're ready to go."

She nodded. "I'll get your bill."

Carla returned carrying a heavy tray filled with ice cream and she struggled to keep it upright.

"She looks upset," Sarah said.

All of a sudden, Carla stumbled and the tray flew out of her hands, ice cream landed everywhere. Patrons turned their attention to the noise, and Sarah saw the red stain of embarrassment on her face.

"Are you all right?" Sarah asked, as she leapt from the booth to help her. Jackie followed behind her.

"Yeah, I'm all right. I just heard some bad news," Carla said, with a quivering lip. She began wiping up the spilled ice cream with a cloth.

"What news?" Jackie asked.

"Someone murdered Mrs. Fedewa!"

"For real?" Sarah exchanged a look with Jackie.

"What happened?" Jackie asked.

"According to my mom, the grocery delivery boy found her this morning."

"Wow."

"Yeah, I guess she was stabbed," Carla continued, with a sob in her voice.

"What a horrible way to die," Sarah frowned.

The table next to the major ice cream spill overheard Carla's story. Traveling like wildfire, the news spread through the restaurant. Sarah witnessed people's expressions changing to shocked dismay as they heard the news.

"Do you know if they have any suspects?" she asked, turning back to Carla.

"As far as I know, they don't have a clue who did it. You know, she was weird, but she didn't deserve to die that way." Carla continued mopping up the mess. "I've got to get new malts for the people at table twelve." She started to leave, then swung back around and handed the girls their bill. "Here's your bill. Have a good night."

Sarah watched Carla scurry away, while a busboy came out to finish cleaning up the ice cream with a mop and bucket.

The girls paid their bill and hurried outside. Humid air seemed to wrap around Sarah. She sighed with contentment, the atmosphere felt like a warm blanket after the frigid air in the restaurant.

"That explains why the police showed up this morning," Sarah said.

"Yeah, we must have gotten there right after the delivery boy left and called 9-1-1." Jackie fidgeted with her curls.

"I find it interesting the delivery boy found her body."

"Yeah."

"He's the one person the Cat Lady would let inside," Sarah pointed out.

"True, but why would the delivery boy want her dead?"

"Uncle Walt told me that she was one of the richest people in town," Sarah whispered.

"Are you sure?" Jackie raised her eyebrows.

"Yep."

"You couldn't tell that by the way she lived."

"I know."

Strolling down the street, Sarah noticed the early evening sun hanging low in the sky. It resembled an orange Christmas ornament suspended in the air, illuminating her world. She took a deep breath and inhaled the delicious scents of the season. The smell of freshly mowed grass, the light fragrance of summer roses, and the aroma of burgers on a charcoal grill. *This summer might be more exciting than I thought.* A grin of anticipation danced across her face, but disappeared quickly when the words *and more dangerous* flashed through her mind.

"We should probably head home," Jackie sighed.

Sarah nodded. "Yeah, probably."

"I'll meet you tonight," Jackie whispered in Sarah's ear.

"At midnight," Sarah whispered back.

Jackie tugged at a wayward curl, deep in thought. "We need a signal."

"A signal?"

"Yeah, you know, to identify each other in the dark."

"Okay, how about the hoot of an owl?"

"Cool beans."

The two girls stood on the corner and practiced their secret signal. Sarah noticed the cruisers were out in full swing. She heard strains of rock music as they drove past. Some of the drivers had turned their bass way up and their cars vibrated with the music. Shaking her head, she turned her attention back to the task at hand. After the girls perfected their signal, they exchanged conspiratorial glances and went their separate ways.

Sarah arrived home just as the sun was setting. She climbed the porch stairs and found Lacey sitting on the swing, reading in the fading light. Lacey glanced up and saw Sarah.

"Hey," Lacey greeted her.

Sarah stopped at the top of the stairs. "Hey, yourself. Feel any better after your shower?"

"Totally. I'm still freaked out about seeing a dead body."

"I know what you mean."

"How was Hinkle's?"

"It was good. I got one of their malts." Sarah walked across the porch and plopped down on the swing next to Lacey. "Jackie and I are going to solve the Cat Lady murder."

"You are?" Lacey's eyes opened wide. "I want to help."

"I don't think so… you'd be too scared."

Lacey scoffed. "I would not."

"Remember last Halloween when we went to the Haunted House at the high-school?"

"I was in seventh grade then. I'm in eighth now," Lacey said, sitting up straight in the swing and dropping her book on the porch.

"We don't need any wimps on our detective squad," Sarah grumbled.

"I'm not a wimp."

"Riiiight," Sarah said, arching her eyebrows.

"I'm not. Besides, I know someone whose dad works in the police department."

"So what?"

"He could help us."

"The only way he could help us is if his dad's involved with the investigation."

"He will be. You see, his dad is the chief of police," Lacey sat up straight as a wide grin spread across her face.

Sarah saw the triumph flash in her sister's eyes. "Awesome," she said, with a rueful smile. "Give him a call, and set something up."

"All-righty then," Lacey flashed another jubilant grin and bounced into the house.

Sarah pushed on the porch with her feet, sending the swing swaying. The cool breeze from the swing's movement felt good on her skin. Her mind drifted back to the scene the girls had stumbled on this morning. *Who would want to murder the Cat Lady?* She pondered. *There must be some clue at her house. I'll find it tonight.* She shuddered as the image of the spooky house invaded her mind.

Chapter Four

The coast looks clear, Sarah thought to herself as she peered into the darkness. With one last glance at her slumbering sister, she crawled through her window, propping it open before leaping to the ground below. Crouching motionless, she listened for any noise that didn't belong. Hearing only crickets and katydids playing their nightly music, she was satisfied everything was normal. She made her way to the willow tree.

It was the perfect night to sneak out. Humidity hung in the air and Sarah could almost feel the moisture on her skin. The full moon illuminated the night sky and reminded her of a huge glow-in-the-dark Frisbee shining high from outer space, burning so bright, Sarah didn't need a flashlight. She kept to the shadows as she made her way to the creek.

The shrill yapping of a dog made Sarah jump. He seemed close, so she dove into a thicket by the side of the road. Seconds later, she heard the dog's snuffling as it trotted by sniffing the ground, his dog tags jingling. Sarah's heart pounded against her ribcage as she waited, listening for the running footsteps of the dog's owner. When the night activity and her heart settled down, she continued her journey.

Sarah sighed with relief when she reached the path leading to their meeting place. *I made it.* She quickened her pace hoping Jackie was already there. The willow tree stood like a beacon calling her home. The moon glimmered in the sky casting a magical glow around the hardwood. All of a sudden, Sarah saw a glimmer of light and her heart lurched in her chest. She stopped.

Searching the darkness, another flash of light caught her attention, and then another. Sarah couldn't figure out what she was witnessing. She spied another burst of light. It disappeared as quickly as it had illuminated. Standing still and watching, she noticed these tiny bursts of light everywhere. One flashed right in front of her face and she saw it was a bug, *fireflies.* Realizing she had never actually seen one, Sarah watched for a few minutes as at least fifty of them lit up the night. *They have their own secret signal. I wonder what they're saying to each other.* Watching for a few more minutes, she drank in the magical glow of the moon and the tiny bursts of light. No longer afraid, she ran the rest of the way to the tree.

"Whoo! Whoo!" Sarah cooed.

"Whoo! Whoo!" Jackie responded.

The pliable branches swallowed Sarah as she slipped through them toward the sound of Jackie's voice.

"You made it, girlfriend," Jackie whispered.

"Was there any doubt?"

"Never."

The two girls laughed. Sarah put her finger to her lips, remembering it was the middle of the night, and they didn't want to be discovered.

"Our first sneaking out mission accomplished," Sarah said in a low voice and held out her hand. "Give me some skin." Jackie gave Sarah a high five.

"My turn," Jackie said. Sarah reciprocated.

Sarah gazed at Jackie, as a smile spread over her face.

Jackie giggled. "No one has a clue we're here."

Sarah saw the mischievous light dancing in Jackie's eyes. "You can say that again."

"No one has a clue we're here."

The girls cracked up, reveling in the glory of their success.

"I'm so glad I'm spending the summer here," Sarah whispered. She put her hand in her pocket and pulled out some tootsie rolls. "Want some?"

"Yeah, nothing like chocolate when you're sneaking out."

"I'm sure I wouldn't be sneaking out if I were back in Walker with my parents."

"Probably not."

"I thought small towns were boring, but it's just the opposite."

"Stick with me, girlfriend, and you'll always have fun." Jackie gave Sarah a playful punch.

Sarah snickered. "So true."

The girls stopped talking and chewed their candy. Sarah loved tootsie rolls. She stood gnawing, thinking back to when she had her first one. It had been her first time at the fair. Her father played some silly game and won the biggest tootsie roll Sarah had ever seen. From that day on, Sarah was hooked. Much to her father's dismay, she devoured the whole thing.

Closing her eyes, the midway came into view. A smile spread across her face as she remembered the fair. She envisioned the noisy rides and the carnies screaming to people walking by, enticing them to come and play their games. Sarah remembered the air around the fairgrounds smelled like a mixture of buttery popcorn and cotton candy.

Without warning, Jackie grabbed Sarah's arm, startling her. "Shh, I hear something."

"What?"

"Probably just Lacey, trying to scare us."

Sarah shook her head. "I doubt it, she's a big wimp. She wouldn't walk down here by herself."

"Watch this," Jackie giggled. She jumped out from the willow branches. "Blaaah!"

Sarah stepped through the branches looking for the source of the sound. She didn't see anything and only heard silence. All at once, the hair on the back of her neck stood up.

"Don't make any noise," Sarah muttered, ducking behind the leafy curtain.

Jackie gasped and scurried back behind the safety of the branches.

Sarah whispered, "Do you hear anything?"

Jackie shook her head, watching the darkness beyond the branches. Sarah searched the shadows with her.

"Do you see anything?" Sarah whispered.

Jackie nodded and pointed. Two figures emerged from the shadows and strolled into the moonlight's path. They were walking along the bank of the stream. The first one towered over the second man and walked with a slight limp. A shorter figure followed the tall man like a baby duck following its mother. He wore a baseball cap, shielding his face.

"Who in the world are those guys?" Sarah murmured.

"This can't be good," Jackie whispered back.

"You got that right."

Jackie grabbed Sarah's arm. "Shh. They're coming closer."

Sarah watched the two men strolling along the bank. They were so close she heard bits and pieces of their conversation.

"No one knows it was us," the guy with the limp said. He walked ahead of the man with the cap, his stride purposeful and confident.

"They don't right now, Lon, but once they start investigatin', we could be goin' to prison," the man with the cap whined.

"You know, if you would have gotten rid of this like I said, you wouldn't be so uptight right now."

"Sorry, Lon. I screwed up." The man with the cap hung his head.

"Relax, everything else is going like clockwork."

'Like clockwork' where have I heard those words before? Sarah wondered.

"I hope you're right."

"I am right," Lon laughed. "I'm always right. You worry too much."

Sarah stared at Jackie, her heart pounding and her hands slick with sweat.

"They're talking about a crime!" Jackie whispered through clenched teeth.

"Shh." Sarah grabbed Jackie's arm and squeezed.

The two men skulked past the willow tree unaware they were being watched. Sarah held her breath. She knew one wrong move, and they would be discovered.

"What are you going to do with that?" the man with the cap asked, pointing toward a bundle Lon held in his hands.

"Get rid of it."

Sarah watched as the two thugs turned on the path and walked closer to the creek.

"Are they talking about getting rid of evidence?" Sarah asked in a low voice.

"I think so."

"Let's follow them."

"Okay."

Sarah crept from beneath the safety of the willow and Jackie followed her. The girls crouched behind tall grass and shrubs, stalking the thugs silently. Barely breathing, Sarah focused on following the men. She realized her hands were wet and wiped them on her shorts.

"They're heading for the swimming hole," Jackie muttered.

Sarah nodded.

Jackie had told Sarah about the swimming hole the first day they met. It was a part of the creek, where a pool of water formed before the stream split into two separate branches, and made its way around a tiny island. The water slowed here before it picked up its pace on the other side. Local teens came to the swimming hole to cool off on hot summer days.

All of a sudden, Sarah stopped. Jackie collided with her and almost knocked her down.

"What are you doing?" Jackie hissed.

"Look." Sarah pointed.

The two men stood on the bank of the creek, talking and looking at the water. Jackie grabbed Sarah's arm and pulled her down the path, intending to hide both girls behind a thicket. They made it several yards away before the girls stumbled and slipped in the wet mud. Landing in the water with a huge splash, Sarah's heart jumped in her chest. *There's no way they didn't hear us.*

"What was that noise?" the man with the cap asked.

"I don't know, but I'll find out," Lon said, his voice a low growl.

Sarah reached for Jackie's hand, but all she found was water. Jackie had disappeared.

"Jackie, where are you?" she whispered.

Dazed from the cold water, Sarah floundered against the current. She tried swimming toward a group of cattails, but only managed to make a great deal of noise. She frantically searched for her friend. Her heart thundered against her ribs. It felt like it would burst through the wall of her chest any moment.

"There's something in the water," the man with the cap said.

"Where?" Lon asked.

"Over there."

Sarah submerged her body under the water. She kept her eyes and ears above the surface so she could see and hear what was happening. The water swirled around her pulling at her body, as the two men walked toward her. Panic gnawed at her self-control and her stomach twisted into a tight knot of fear.

I'm a goner!

Just then, she felt a strong grip around her arm. She pivoted and saw Jackie. Relief flooded through her body. Jackie was soaking wet, her curls matted to her skull.

"Where have you been?" Sarah whispered.

"Cat tails." She pointed to the opposite bank.

"We can't go back there," Sarah said as she cast a frantic glance over her shoulder. The men were twenty feet from the stream and trotting fast.

"What're we going to do?"

Sarah motioned toward the creek and mouthed the word *underwater*.

Jackie nodded.

Taking a deep breath, Sarah plunged below the surface. She allowed the current to carry her downstream, knowing it was the only way to escape.

The water transported Sarah to a shallow part of the creek. Gasping for air, she rose out of the water. She opened her eyes and saw Jackie. Another wave of relief flooded through her body and a giggle tickled her throat. Clamping her lips together, Sarah wiped water from her face and moved closer to her friend.

"That was way too close for comfort."

"No doubt." Jackie shook her curls sending drops of water everywhere.

"Who were those men?"

"I don't know."

"I've heard the big one's voice before. I just can't place it."

"Me either."

"Shh, I think I hear them coming," Sarah warned.

Jackie grabbed Sarah's arm, and pulled her toward a tree growing near the bank. The branches hung low over the water, offering cover. They ducked into them just in time. Sarah peeked between the branches and saw the shadowy figures of the men.

"Lon, did you see anything?" the man with the cap asked.

"No just some ripples in the water."

"Probably a deer."

"Let's talk somewhere else, just in case," Lon said, giving his companion a rough push forward.

The thugs continued walking downstream. Sarah and Jackie hid in the water, too scared to follow them.

"I can't believe we overheard those men," Sarah said, through quivering lips.

"They were talking about getting rid of evidence."

Sarah furrowed her brow. "Where have we heard that voice?"

"Do you think they have anything to do with the Cat Lady?"

"It's the only crime around here."

"This is huge."

Sarah grimaced. "We need some dry clothes before we go to the Cat Lady's."

Jackie nodded, her lips pressed in a tight line.

They climbed out of the water and walked toward the willow tree, clinging to each other for warmth.

"We can sneak back to my house and get dry clothes," Sarah said.

"Your clothes won't fit me," Jackie protested.

"So what, no one's going to see you."

Jackie groaned. "Your clothes aren't very fashionable."

A laugh burst through Sarah's lips. "Don't worry, you won't be infected with my lack of style."

Sarah stopped at the willow tree and pulled her friend beneath the branches.

"What?" Jackie asked.

"I just want to make sure we're not followed."

When Sarah felt safe, the girls made their way down the path. Once they hit the pavement, the teenagers abandoned the shadows for the light in the middle of the street. Sarah picked up her pace and trotted toward her home, Jackie matched her stride for stride.

Out of the corner of her eye, Sarah saw a police car turn the corner and head in their direction. "Jackie, hide!"

Jackie dove into some shrubbery growing alongside the road. Sarah was right behind her.

Flashing lights illuminated the night sky. Sarah groaned. The last thing they needed was another trip to the police station. Forgetting her damp condition, Sarah focused on staying out of sight.

"If they find us, we're in deep trouble," Jackie gulped.

"They must've seen us walking in the road."

"I so don't look good in orange."

Suddenly, a bright light shone in the shrubbery. Sarah grabbed Jackie's arm and pulled her down.

"Lie down on the ground," Sarah whispered.

The girls lay flat on the ground, their faces in the dirt. Sarah didn't dare look up. Dank earth filled her nostrils, and she willed it to hide her. Her heart pounded against her ribs. She swore she could feel it vibrate the ground below her.

The cop car stopped and two officers got out. They began searching on the other side of the road. Sarah listened to the cops talk as they searched.

"Someone reported two kids walking in the street," the first cop said.

"Yeah, I thought I saw a couple of kids in the road, but they're gone now."

"Let's keep looking. They might be hiding somewhere."

Sarah heard the policemen rustling the bushes as they searched.

"Let's go!" Sarah urged in a hoarse whisper.

"Right now?" Jackie's eyes widened.

"It's now or never."

"Where are we going?'

"The back side of Thompson's garage," Sarah whispered. "Just don't make any noise. Back up slowly."

"Riiight."

The girls got up into a crouching position, and backed away from the cover of the bushes.

Once they'd moved a safe distance, Sarah signaled to Jackie, and they broke into a sprint. They ran flat out until they'd turned the corner of Thompson's garage. As soon as they were out of sight, they stopped, gasping for breath. Sarah went weak in the knees with relief. From the safety of the garage, she peeked out and watched the cops beating the bushes.

"I can't believe we made it," Jackie whispered.

"I'm so glad one of those cops wasn't Klonsky," Sarah gasped. She held her hands against her chest as if she were preventing her heart from bursting through. "That's it!"

"What's it?"

"Klonsky."

"What?"

"The voice we heard down by the creek. It's Klonsky."

"Are you sure?" Jackie asked.

"I'm positive. Remember when we left the police station today? He said everything's gone 'like clockwork for those girls'."

Jackie grabbed Sarah's arm and squeezed. "Yeah, he did say something like that."

"Just now, the guy down by the creek said the same thing."

"Holy crap!"

Sarah and Jackie stared at each other.

Shock and fear paraded across Jackie's face. "That can only mean one thing— Klonsky's involved in the Cat Lady murder."

"He could be the murderer." Sarah slowly sank to the ground.

Both girls sat by the side of the garage, stunned into silence. Sarah rested, wet with creek water and trembling with fear. At this moment, the uneasiness she felt about Klonsky exploded into full-blown panic. Her stomach twisted into a painful knot. The Super Spies were up against a formidable foe, not only a crooked cop, but a possible murderer as well.

"Now I know why he acted the way he did," Sarah said.

Jackie nodded.

"I can't believe it—a cop involved in the Cat Lady murder." Sarah rubbed her forehead with a trembling hand.

"Yeah, but why would he want the Cat Lady dead?" Jackie asked.

"I don't know."

"And who's the other guy with him? He must be involved too."

"You're right about that," Sarah groaned. "You know what this means, don't you?"

Jackie shook her head. "I'm afraid to ask."

"This means we've figured out why Klonsky is trying to frame us."

Jackie gulped and stared at Sarah, speechless.

"Which means we've got to find some evidence linking him to the Cat Lady murder." Sarah pulled a wet tootsie roll out of her pocket. She pulled off the wrapper with trembling hands and popped the candy into her mouth.

Jackie watched her for a moment, and then found her voice. "How are we going to do that?"

Sarah turned to her and saw her trembling lips and her wide, frightened eyes. "We have to get inside the Cat Lady's house. The answer is there." Sarah's voice sounded stronger than she felt, but she had a feeling the house held the secrets they were seeking.

Jackie gave her a solemn nod.

Sarah glanced up, and noticed the sun was beginning to make an entrance at the edge of the horizon. "Uh-oh, look," she pointed to the slivers of gray and pink. "We can't do it now. We've got to get home before anyone wakes up."

"Yeah." Jackie stood and brushed off her wet shorts.

"Are the cops gone?" Sarah asked, peering down the road.

"Yeah, they're gone." Jackie pointed to the cruiser driving away.

Sarah watched the taillights disappear into the night.

After making plans to meet at the willow tree the next day, the girls went their separate ways. By the time Sarah reached home, the sky had taken on a gray hue. She felt a tiny sliver of panic as she realized her aunt and uncle would be waking soon. Sarah crept back to her window.

Peeking in the window, Sarah searched for Lily, the family cocker spaniel. Relief flooded through her body when she didn't see the excitable dog. *I've had enough excitement for one night.*

Sarah sighed. Getting back inside was the hardest part of the journey. Since her aunt and uncle's home was a tri-level, the bedroom window was four feet off the ground. She hoisted herself up into the frame with a grunt. Her wet clothes worked against her. Moaning with effort, she tried to pull herself the rest of the way through the window.

Just then, light flooded the room. Sarah glanced up and saw Lacey at the switch.

"Holy cow! You scared me half to death," Lacey scolded. There was a quiver in her voice, and she wrapped her arms around herself as if she were shivering.

Sarah groaned.

"Why are you climbing through our window?"

Sarah grimaced. "I'll tell you the whole story; just help me back inside."

"You're all wet."

"How very observant of you." Sarah held her hand out to Lacey.

"Have you been out all night?" Lacey's eyes widened, and she cocked her head. She hadn't moved from the light switch.

"Just help me back in, will you?"

"What have you been doing out all night? You freaked me out when I heard you at the window."

"Hello, I'm still hanging here." Sarah waved her hand at Lacey.

"Tsk, serves you right, sneaking out at night."

"Quit being such a goody-two-shoes and pull me in."

After Lacey helped her back inside, she scurried across the room and flopped down on her bed. Triumph flashed in her eyes and she crossed her arms over her chest. "I'm waiting."

Sarah sighed. "I'll tell you the whole story if you promise not to tell Aunt June and Uncle Walt."

Lacey pursed her lips. "I could tell and get you grounded, you know."

"True, but then I'll never tell you what we did." Sarah eyed her closely. *Take the bait.*

"All right, but the next time you sneak out, you have to take me with you," Lacey countered with a satisfied smile.

"It's a deal."

Sarah told Lacey about her night wanderings as she pulled off her wet clothes.

"You're kidding me!" Lacey's eyes widened for a second time.

"That's not all. One of the guys down by the creek was Klonsky."

"You mean the cop?"

"Yep."

"Holy cow! What crime do you think they committed?"

"Hello...didn't we just discover the Cat Lady's body this morning?" Sarah asked. "Man, you can be dense sometimes."

"Shut up."

Sarah kicked her wet clothes into the corner and pulled her favorite nightshirt over her head. It had a huge peace sign with the words *peace, love,* and *chocolate* written around it.

"Do you think Klonsky killed the Cat Lady?" Lacey asked.

"We're not sure, but we know he's involved in some way."

"Who was the other guy with Klonsky?"

"I don't know," Sarah frowned. She felt drained. The adrenaline that had gotten her through the night had dwindled away. "Jackie and I are going to start looking for clues tomorrow."

"I want to help. Remember, we have a deal."

"Yes, we have a deal," Sarah yawned. "I'm tired. I need some sleep."

"Night, Sarah," Lacey said as she walked over and flicked the switch.

Sarah heard the soft padding of footsteps as Lacey scrambled back to bed. "Night."

Exhaustion turned Sarah's body into a wet noodle. She slid beneath her quilt. As her head hit the pillow she asked herself, *why would Klonsky want the Cat Lady dead?*

Chapter Five

The obnoxious noise of a lawn mower yanked Sarah from a deep sleep. She pulled a pillow over her head, muffling the sound. It barely stifled the noise. Groaning, she swung her feet to the floor. *Time to get up.*

Sarah scratched her head as she gazed around the guest bedroom she shared with Lacey. It was a pleasant room with light green walls and flowery bedspreads, but she missed her room back home. She missed her CSI posters and her books, especially the ones about unsolved mysteries. Her favorites were the ones about the Zodiac killer. If she were given enough time, she knew she could bring the killer who terrorized San Francisco to justice. The door squeaked and Sarah turned, catching Lacey poking her head in.

"Hey, sleepyhead." She walked into the room and sat next to Sarah on the bed.

Sarah mumbled, "Morning."

"I told Aunt June you were sick," Lacey continued with a conspiratorial grin.

"Thanks." Sarah tried to pull her hand through the rat's

nest growing around her head. "Ewww, I smell creek water. I need a shower so-o bad."

"Yeah, you do kind of stink." Lacey wrinkled her nose and moved away.

"Thanks a lot!"

Lacey laughed. "Any time. Do you want me to do anything while you're in the shower?"

"Yeah, what time is it?" Sarah asked, squinting at the clock.

"It's noon."

"Okay, call Jackie, and remind her we're meeting at the willow tree at one. Tell her you're going to help us."

"I'm on it." Lacey jumped from the bed and rushed out the door.

Sarah stood and walked to the closet and gathered some clothes for the day. She chose a light blue T-shirt with a white flower pattern and denim shorts. Placing the outfit on the end of her bed, Sarah noticed her wet clothes in the corner and made a mental note to put them in the washer while her aunt was at work.

She made her way to the bathroom and turned on the shower. When it was the right temperature, she stepped into it. The hot water drummed a steady beat on her body, reviving her muscles and washing the cobwebs from her mind.

As Sarah showered, questions paraded through her brain. Who was the second man with Klonsky? Why would Klonsky want the Cat Lady dead? She finished quickly, anxious to find answers to these nagging questions. Toweling dry, she heard Lacey at the door asking if Sarah wanted anything to eat.

"I'll have a breakfast bar," Sarah called through the door.

Sarah heard Lacey bounding up the stairs. She rushed into the bedroom and dressed, fluffing her hair as she walked out of the room.

She hurried into the kitchen, where she found her sister

rummaging through the cupboard looking for breakfast bars.

"Found them," Lacey said, holding up a crimson wrapped bar.

Sarah grabbed it and sat down at the table. Glancing around the room, she saw the light pine cabinets and the yellow pineapple wallpaper. During family functions, everyone gathered in the kitchen. It seemed to be the friendliest room in the house.

Just then, Aunt June walked in. "Good morning. How are you feeling?"

"Better," Sarah mumbled, with her mouth full.

Her aunt put her hand up to her forehead. "You don't feel hot."

Just like mom, Sarah thought to herself, feeling a pang for her mother. The similarities between her mother and her aunt amazed Sarah. She doubted all sisters had so much in common. Looking at Lacey, she wondered if they would ever find common ground.

"I just didn't sleep well last night." Sarah made a point to ignore Lacey's smug grin.

"Too much excitement yesterday?" Aunt June gave Sarah a quick hug.

Sarah shrugged. "Yeah, probably."

Lacey grabbed her arm, and tugged her toward the door. "We're meeting Jackie down by the creek."

"Yeah, we've gotta go." Sarah glanced over her shoulder at her aunt.

"Be careful."

"We will," Lacey called out as the girls raced out the door.

Sarah devoured the rest of her breakfast bar as they walked. It was another scorcher, and she felt the dampness under her arms already. The sun baked the top of her head, drying her hair. She shaded her eyes with her hand and studied Lacey. "Did you talk to your friend last night?"

"Yeah, I'm going to meet him this afternoon." Lacey squinted as she glanced down the road.

"What's his name?"

"Scott."

"Did you ask him about the murder?"

"Yep."

"Did you find out anything?" Sarah frowned and gestured with her hands.

"Not a lot. I guess the Cat Lady was stabbed like six times."

"What a horrible way to die!"

Lacey shaded her eyes and glanced at her sister. "Yeah, everybody's pretty freaked out about it. The police are getting a lot of calls from neighbors. Everyone's scared."

"It's a freaky thing to happen, especially here."

Arriving at the willow tree, the girls stopped talking and strolled beneath the green canopy. Sarah was grateful for the cool shade.

Seeing Jackie made Sarah smile. "Hey, partner in crime."

"Hey, yourself," Jackie said as she clutched some of the willow branches and used them to swing her body.

"We had a couple close calls last night."

Jackie widened her eyes and gave Sarah an emphatic nod. "You are not kidding, girlfriend."

"You want a tootsie roll?" Sarah pulled some of the treasured candies from her pocket.

Jackie nodded. Sarah handed her one, then gave one to Lacey.

Sarah popped her candy into her mouth. "It blows my mind Klonsky's involved in the Cat Lady murder."

"I know," Jackie said. "How are we going to connect them?"

"The answers are inside the Cat Lady's house."

Jackie stared at Lacey. "So, you're going to help us catch the Cat Lady killer?"

"Yep."

"Awesome. Did Sarah tell you we saw Klonsky last night?"

Lacey frowned. "Yeah, I wonder what the heck he was doing?"

"Getting rid of evidence," Sarah said.

"You think so?" Lacey asked

"Yeah, that's why we're going to the Cat Lady's today."

Lacey gulped. "I don't think that's a good idea." She scuffed at the soil with her shoe and tugged nervously on her shirt.

"Why not?" Jackie asked.

Lacey started wringing her hands. "Couldn't we get in trouble?"

"Only if we get caught," Sarah said with a matter of fact tone.

"Sarah..." Lacey whined.

Sarah and Jackie exchanged a long look, then Sarah asked, "What?"

"Couldn't we get arrested?" Lacey frowned.

"Lacey, we have a crooked cop trying to blame us for the murder. We could get arrested if we don't do anything." Sarah stifled a groan and grabbed some willow branches, swaying with them. She held her breath and eyed Lacey, hoping she would jump on board with their plan.

"Yeah," Jackie nodded.

"The only way to stay out of jail is for us to find the real killer." Sarah stood still and chewed on her thumbnail.

"I guess..." Lacey wavered.

"Plus," Jackie winked at Sarah. "We have a new club. We are now the Super Spies." She opened her arms with a theatrical flourish.

"Oh, wow," Lacey brightened.

"Yeah," Sarah said, taking a step toward Lacey and putting her hand on her shoulder. "We needed a name for our club and you're in it."

"Cool. I like it. I'm glad I'm in the club."

"What time are you meeting Scott?" Sarah asked, breathing a sigh of relief.

"At four."

"We better get to the Cat Lady's."

Lacey nodded. "So who's the president of the club?"

Sarah glared at her little sister and then marched out into the blistering sunlight. Jackie and Lacey fell into step beside her. They reached the Cat Lady's, and again hid behind the oak tree growing across the street. The house sat in its yard and Sarah felt it watching the girls with its sinister window eyes. A shiver ran down her spine.

She stared at the house. "Look at all the yellow tape."

"I see it," Jackie said.

"We can't break it, or the cops will know someone's been inside." Sarah popped her thumb in her mouth and chewed on her nail.

"We're going to have to find another way in besides the front door," Lacey said.

Sarah took her thumb out of her mouth. "Let's sneak around the back. Maybe there's an open window or something."

Lacey peered up and down the street. "The coast is clear."

"On the count of three," Jackie said.

"See ya. I'm not waiting for you to count." Sarah sprinted across the street.

"Hey, wait for us!" Jackie sputtered.

"Crap!" Lacey cursed.

Sarah heard their pounding footsteps as they tried to catch her. Reaching the backyard, she spied the stump of the apple tree Jackie had told her about. It rested near the old wooden fence between two houses. She assumed the house next door was the old Farnsworth place. The house had stood vacant ever since Mrs. Farnsworth's mysterious death years ago.

The fence between the two homes had once been white, but now the rotting, gray wood peeked through the peeling paint.

"Let's look for a way inside," Sarah said.

The girls fanned out, searching along the foundation of the home.

Lacey cast furtive glances around the yard. "I hope no one sees us."

"We're lucky most people go to Hinkle's after church. They have a lunch buffet on Sundays." Jackie sounded unconcerned, but Sarah glanced up and saw her scan the neighboring houses with anxious eyes.

After a few more minutes of searching, Sarah called out, "Hey, I think I found one."

Jackie and Lacey rushed over to where Sarah struggled with a window; it had been left ajar long ago. Now it was stuck. It was a tiny basement window and it sat at ground level. Finally, with Jackie's help, the window gave way and opened with a rusty squeak.

"It's a basement window, but I think we can squeeze through," Sarah gasped.

"Cool beans."

"I don't suppose either one of you wants to go first?" Sarah asked.

Jackie beamed. "Nope. It's all yours."

"Thanks," Sarah smirked. She searched the neighborhood with a nervous glance. "Lacey, you be the look out."

Lacey nodded and continued her surveillance, looking for

any nosey neighbors.

Sarah wiggled into the tight space, and got stuck halfway down. Her heart skipped a beat when she couldn't move any further. The top of the window dug into her back and suddenly her body flooded with nervous heat. Dangling her feet below, she couldn't touch the basement floor or see it. Feeling trapped, her anxiety turned up a notch.

"Hmmm...where have I seen that before?" Lacey asked with a nervous twitter.

"Shut up."

Sarah struggled to get out of the window. Sweat formed on her upper lip. She licked it and tasted its salty residue. Finally, she admitted defeat and held out her hand to Lacey.

"Now, that looks familiar," Lacey laughed as she grabbed Sarah's hand, pulling her out of the window.

"Are you having fun?" Sarah asked, in an exasperated tone.

Lacey giggled. "Absolutely."

Sarah stood and studied the window. She noticed some weeds growing around the tiny opening and stooped to pull them out of the way. "Maybe, if I arch my back I can get down there. I can't see the floor, but it can't be too far down." Tossing the weeds into the yard, she continued to study the entrance.

"Give it a try," Jackie said, with an encouraging pat on the back.

"Do you want to go first?" Sarah glanced at Jackie. "You're pretty skinny, you know."

"True. But I like it when you go first."

Lacey grinned like a Cheshire cat. "Yeah, we like it when you go first."

Sarah grimaced. "I thought so."

She got down on her knees, and backed up to the window once more. Sliding her feet through the opening, Sarah arched her back, and then hung down into the inky darkness. Fear squeezed her throat, making it hard for her to swallow. Dangling, Sarah tried to work up the courage to let go. The pressure of her body weight made the rough window ledge dig into her hands, the pain intensified the longer she hung there. Taking a deep breath, Sarah let go.

Landing with a soft thud, light clouds of dust surrounded her, making her cough. Her eyes watered as she felt the darkness closing in on her. She drew a ragged breath and cleared her throat.

"Hey, are you okay down there?" Jackie asked, peering down into the basement.

"Yeah...I'm all right, I guess. I just don't like closed in places," Sarah croaked, then cleared her throat again.

She scuffed her shoe in the dirt making up the basement floor. Immediately, another cloud of dust rose around her feet.

Waiting for the dust to settle, Sarah peered around the basement and noticed the low ceiling and all the cobwebs. *No one has been down here in years.* She wrinkled her nose and took a few steps toward the basement stairs. Under them, she spied some large boxes. Sarah walked closer studying them. They would make great stairs. After several attempts and coughing fits, she moved some of the boxes and created a box staircase under the window. The dust swirled in the air disturbed by Sarah's activity.

"Okay, guys, come on down! You're the next contestant on the Price is Right." Sarah said with a nervous giggle. Her voice sounded unnatural to her, high and tinny. She knew she sounded anxious, but she couldn't help it—she was.

Jackie snickered as she wiggled through the window. "Tell me what I've won, Bob."

"A nice long stay at Leavenworth Prison compliments of Officer Klonsky!"

"And that's not all!" Jackie announced. "You get to make a fashion statement in that hot new color, penitentiary orange. It's all the rave these days."

The girls burst into laughter. Laughing felt good to Sarah, releasing some of the tension in her body.

As she dried her eyes, Jackie climbed down the box stairs, coughing and blinking in all the dust Sarah had kicked up. "Look at all this stuff!"

"And there's more behind door number two." Sarah pointed at the basement door at the top of the stairs.

Lacey was the last to come down. She wheezed in the dust and rubbed her eyes. "Man, look at all this crap. It's going to take us forever to find any clues."

"Let's go upstairs and look," Sarah said, walking toward the basement stairs.

"Yeah, it's too dusty down here anyway," Jackie coughed and waved her hands in the air.

Sarah led the Super Spies up the stairs. In the middle of the staircase, she put her weight down on a step and it creaked in protest. She froze.

"Boy, we're wound pretty tight," Sarah giggled.

"No doubt," Jackie agreed.

The Super Spies continued their climb to the floor above, and paused at the basement door. It had been the only barrier between the cops and the girls the previous day.

Questions bombarded Sarah's mind. *What are we going to find behind the door? Is the blood still there? Will Lacey freak out again?* Taking a deep breath, Sarah pushed the door open and walked into the cluttered kitchen. The disarray amazed her a second time. There were dirty dishes piled in the sink and newspapers and junk mail littered the countertops.

"How can anyone live like this?" she asked.

"Gross. This place smells horrible." Lacey held her nose against the offending odor of dirty litter boxes. Since the house had been sealed shut, the smell was trapped inside. She made a face. "This place is probably crawling with germs and disease."

"The smell is so bad." Sarah pulled her collar up over her nose and mouth.

"I wonder what happened to all the cats?" Jackie asked.

"I bet they were taken to the humane society."

Jackie sniffed. "I hope so."

Sarah nodded. "Me too. Let's try the living room."

The three girls walked through the kitchen into the living room. Sarah stopped just inside the door and surveyed the area. She stared at the wide arc of blood spatter on the wall closest to the front door. It started at the doorframe and then faded into the heavy drapes by the picture window.

"Lacey, why don't you go back down stairs and be the lookout," Sarah urged, twisting to block Lacey's view.

"No, I don't want to be down there by myself. Don't worry I won't freak out."

Sarah sighed and studied the blood spatter again. Her heart sank when she saw it, a grisly reminder of the violence from the previous morning. She imagined the terror the Cat Lady experienced during the last moments of her life. Shuddering, Sarah spun away.

"Don't look at the blood, Lace."

"The cat smell isn't so bad in here," Lacey observed.

Sarah nodded. She avoided the blood spatter on the wall and focused on the stacks of newspapers.

"I wish we couldn't still smell the blood," Lacey said.

Sarah turned and squeezed Lacey's shoulder. "Don't look at it and you'll be all right. Focus on looking for clues." She pivoted back toward the papers. "See, Jack, this is what I was talking about," she pointed to the piles of papers all in a row. "If the Cat Lady were fighting for her life, these piles would be all messed up."

Jackie pursed her lips. "You've got a point."

"I think the Cat Lady knew her killer and let him in."

"You know, that makes sense," Lacey said, walking toward the back of the room. "Scott said something about stabbings being personal."

Sarah nodded. "I think we're on the right track."

"Hey, guys, look at this." Lacey had moved over to the far wall, and was looking at several photographs on a shelf.

"What is it?" Sarah asked.

"I think the Cat Lady had a son."

"For real?"

"Yeah, look at these pictures."

Jackie and Sarah walked over and gazed at the photo she had in her hand. It was a picture of a young woman with her arm around a small boy. Both of them were laughing for the camera. Looking over Lacey's shoulder, Sarah studied the woman.

The picture had captured the woman's zest for life. Her wide smile invited everyone around her to join in with her laughter. Dark hair cascaded around her shoulders, contrasting with her white skin. Wow, she was pretty, Sarah realized with a start. She looked like a normal person.

"Have you ever heard of her having a family?" Sarah asked Jackie.

"No. I've only heard she was a crazy witch."

"She doesn't look like a witch in this picture, Jackie."

"Looks are deceiving." Jackie stuck her nose up in the air.

Sarah rolled her eyes. "Are you sure no one has ever mentioned a son before?"

"Nope."

"Take the picture apart, and see if there's any writing on the back," Sarah suggested.

"It says," Lacey started, "'David and me on the fourth.'"

"I wonder what happened to him," Sarah frowned.

Lacey put the picture back up on the shelf.

"Wipe off your fingerprints," Sarah instructed.

Sighing, Lacey used the hem of her T-shirt to wipe the picture off.

Jackie pulled on one of her curls. "Yeah, is he still alive, or what?"

Sarah shrugged. "Good question."

"Hey, here's another picture."

"It's the same little boy," Lacey said.

Jackie pulled the picture down off the shelf and pulled it out of the frame. "It says, 'David Fedewa August 1978'."

"He must be her son." Sarah studied the other pictures on the shelf. "Jack, wipe off your prints before you put the picture back."

"The police have already searched for prints."

"So, they might come back."

"We gave them elimination prints," Jackie reminded her as she put the picture back on the shelf.

The girls grew quiet as they searched for clues. Sarah kept returning to the pictures of the smiling young woman and compared her to the old woman she had found dead on the floor. They seemed like two different people. It wasn't just the fact the Cat Lady had grown old. She knew old people, who slowed down in their old age, but the Cat Lady seemed withered, like her life energy had been drained. What could have happened to this woman that had made her change so drastically? Pondering this for a moment, the nagging question surfaced. Why would anyone want to murder her? Rubbing her temples, Sarah hoped an answer would appear soon.

Lacey glanced at her watch. "Hey guys, I've got to meet Scott."

"Wow, time sure does fly." Sarah shook her head in surprise.

"Yeah, it does," Lacey said, as she brushed her hair out of her eyes.

"Okay. Jack, why don't you and I head down to the library and see if we can find some info on David Fedewa."

"The library?" Jackie asked.

Sarah snickered at her horrified expression.

She led the girls back down the basement stairs, avoiding the squeaky one. They scrambled out the window, and Sarah returned it to its original position. The bright sun blinded her, and she stood in the yard blinking for several seconds.

"Try and find out everything the police have on the Cat Lady's murder," Sarah instructed Lacey.

"No kidding, what'd ya think I was going to do? Ask him about Barbie dolls?"

Sarah rolled her eyes. "Whatever, just be back at the willow tree by five."

With a wave, Lacey turned and walked down the street. Jackie and Sarah watched her walk away for a few minutes, and then began their short walk to the library.

"You know, the Cat Lady looked like a normal person in those pictures," Jackie said.

Sarah smirked. "See? I told you she wasn't a witch."

"I don't know if I'd go that far."

"Oh, come on, you don't still believe in witches, do you?"

"Well, these stories have been around town...ever since I can remember."

Sarah chuckled. "That doesn't make them true."

She peered down the street and saw the heat shimmering in the distance. It appeared to turn the street into liquid metal at the horizon. *Man, is it ever hot.* Sarah wiped the sweat from her brow and noticed the street was deserted. Walking down the sidewalk, she glanced back at the legendary house. A chill ran down her spine. The house seemed to be watching the girls with its lifeless, window eyes. Her heart picked up its pace. Turning back, she focused on her journey.

Jackie's voice was a comforting sound. "I don't know, I mean, she never came out of her house." Her face had turned red from the heat.

"That makes her a freak not a witch," Sarah said, pushing her hair out of her face.

"Yeah, but what about what happened to Mrs. Farnsworth?"

"A coincidence, you know?"

Jackie shrugged. "We're almost there."

The girls turned the corner, stopping in front of the Harrisburg Public Library. It appeared old to Sarah, with its weathered bricks and cracked steps. There were places where some of the bricks had started to crumble. Someone tried to patch these areas with cement. Sarah realized the cement did the job, but didn't help the building's appearance. *Man, a strong gust of wind could blow this old building over.* Staring at the relic, Sarah tingled with excitement. She knew the library held all the secrets of the tiny burg.

"Here we are," Sarah cracked a smile.

"I don't think I've ever been to the library during summer vacation," Jackie laughed.

"For real? I go all the time."

Jackie snorted. "No doubt. You're such a bookworm."

"You say that like it's a bad thing."

The girls opened the library doors and walked into the cool air. It was dark and peaceful compared to the sunny outdoors. Blinking so her eyes adjusted to the dimness, Sarah peered down the rows of bookshelves. They went on forever and almost reached the ceiling. All at once, Sarah became aware of the scent of musty old pages, and she took a deep breath. She loved libraries. Sarah heard the quiet scrape of bindings against wood and spun toward the sound.

"There's Mrs. Parker." Jackie pointed at an elderly woman putting books back on shelves. "She's been the librarian for ages. I think she's a permanent fixture." Her new friend whispered this last statement out of the corner of her mouth. Waving as the librarian turned toward them, Jackie said in a loud whisper, "Hi, Mrs. Parker."

"Hello, girls." She patted her gray bun, and then stepped off her stool.

"Did you hear about Mrs. Fedewa?" Sarah asked.

"Yes, I did. It's a tragedy," she said shaking her head.

"We're investigating her murder," Jackie jumped in.

Mrs. Parker chuckled behind her hand. "You don't say?"

Sarah saw her blue eyes twinkle with unexpressed laughter, and her hand hid her smile. When her eyes twinkled, she appeared to be an aging sprite in hiding. Her slight build added to this image. The faded librarian smock she wore was her disguise to the world.

"Yeah, we are. We just can't figure out why someone would want to hurt her," Sarah frowned.

"I can't give you an answer. We used to be good friends before..." Mrs. Parker stopped and tears filled her eyes. She pulled a tissue out of her pocket and dabbed them.

"Before what?" Jackie asked.

"Well, her son was kidnapped." She paused to think. "Let's see...it must have been about thirty years ago."

"For real?" Sarah's heart lurched in her chest.

"Yes, his name was David. It was all over town. The family paid the ransom and everything, but David was never returned."

"What a horrible tragedy," Sarah frowned.

"Yes, it was. When David wasn't returned she just pulled away from people."

"I wonder why she did that?" Sarah chewed on her lip.

"I guess it was too hard for her to be around them, too painful." Mrs. Parker gazed down and Sarah saw sadness fill her eyes.

"Ah, maybe we should research the kidnapping then." Sarah made eye contact with Jackie.

"I'm sure there were articles in the local paper. Follow me girls, and I'll set you up on the microfiche machines."

Mrs. Parker motioned for the girls to follow her. She walked toward the rear of the library. Sarah and Jackie trailed close behind, exchanging excited glances.

The librarian stopped when she reached an alcove in the back. She had Sarah sit down, and then showed the girls how to operate the machines. The whirring of the machine broke the silence in the media center. It sounded loud and obnoxious to Sarah, an irritating noise like the unwelcome buzz of a mosquito to someone trying to fall asleep.

"Mrs. Parker, one last question," Sarah said.

"Yes?"

"Why was David Fedewa kidnapped?"

"The kidnappers never said why, but I believe it was for the money. They demanded a ransom, you know."

"Did the Fedewa's have a lot of money?" Sarah asked.

"Yes. They owned the lumber mill in town. It had been in their family for generations."

"Was David ever found?" Jackie asked.

"No," Mrs. Parker said with a catch in her voice.

"Hmmm."

The librarian cleared her throat. "Okay, you'll want to start with August sixteenth. The year would have been...1978."

"Thanks."

"Girls, if that's all, I must get back to my other duties."

"Thanks, Mrs. Parker," Sarah said.

Mrs. Parker nodded and left to finish her other tasks.

Sarah began reading through the local paper, *The Harrisburg Banner*, on the date Mrs. Parker recommended. Jackie started researching follow-up articles looking for clues.

"Hey, Jack, listen to this," Sarah whispered. "It says here David Fedewa was abducted from the community pool on August fifteenth. His dad went to use the bathroom, and when he came back David was gone."

"Was there a commotion or anything like that?"

"Nope. No sign of a struggle, and there were no strangers at the pool that day. It's like he vanished into thin air."

"Strange," Jackie frowned. "I wonder if he walked off with someone he knew?"

"A good question, detective," Sarah said in a low voice. "I'm going to print this off so we can study it later." She pressed the print key. "Did you find any follow-up articles?"

"No. They just say the police are stumped, and they're asking the public to come forward with any information."

"It might be a good idea to talk with the detective that worked on the case. His name is Detective Swift."

"What a great idea, I wonder if he's still on the force?"

"We can always call down to the station and ask for him," Sarah said.

"Yep."

Sarah glanced at her watch. "Let's get going. I'm anxious to find out what Lacey learned."

The girls packed up their papers and left the library. The heat hit Sarah as soon as she walked out the door. It baked her skin, and she felt like she was walking into an oven. It reminded her of the time she went with her father to pick up a pizza. Their favorite pizzeria stood on the corner down the block from their house. People came from miles around to devour Mr. Mancini's famous pizza pies.

Mr. Mancini was a happy Italian who allowed the Coles behind the counter that evening. He had just installed a new pizza oven and wanted to show off. With joyous flair, he demonstrated the art of pizza making. Throwing the dough high in the air, and then catching it just before it hit the floor. When the dough was stretched to the right size, the happy Italian piled it high with sauce, cheese, and pepperoni, Sarah's favorite toppings. Singing at the top of his lungs in Italian, he opened the new oven and slid the pie inside. Sarah remembered the fiery heat as it toasted her face. Every time they ordered a pizza, she insisted on going back to Mr. Mancini's pizzeria. She loved the laid back atmosphere and the sheer joy the pizza man experienced when he made a pie. Smiling at the memory, she hoped to find her passion in life, just like the pizza man.

"We've got to start riding our bikes," Jackie said, pulling Sarah from her thoughts.

"No kidding."

"We're almost there."

Up ahead, Sarah spied the willow tree. Its green leaves appeared cool and refreshing. The flimsy branches floated in the breeze, suspended in the air like a bright windsock on the lakeshore. Sarah picked up her pace, anxious to escape the sun. Jackie matched her stride for stride.

"Hey, guys," Lacey greeted them when they walked beneath the pliable limbs.

"Hey," Sarah said, and Jackie waved.

"Guys, this is Scott Johnson." Lacey introduced the slim boy next to her. His deep tan contrasted with his blue eyes and blond hair.

"Hi," Sarah and Jackie said in unison, exchanging perplexed looks.

Lacey got right to the point. "He was wondering if he could be in our club, too."

Sarah dropped her gaze and stared at her shoes. "I don't know, we don't have any other boys in our club."

Scott gave Sarah a winning smile. "I could be the first one."

"We haven't talked about new members or anything," Sarah hedged.

Scott frowned. "That's all right. Why don't you guys have a quick meeting, and I'll take a swim."

"Okay...I guess," Sarah said, giving Lacey a withering look.

"No problem, I'll be over here."

The silence grew uncomfortable as Sarah waited for Scott to walk out of earshot. She watched Lacey fidget with the hem of her T-shirt and dance from one foot to the other.

"Thanks for springing that one on us, Lacey," Sarah fumed when Scott was far enough away.

"What's your problem?"

"You can't just go inviting everyone into the club."

"He asked if he could be in the club. Besides, he could help us." Lacey pouted, and pulled her hair away from her face.

"You can't just let anyone in the club. What if he doesn't take us seriously?"

Lacey sighed. "I hadn't thought of that, but Scott seems like a good guy."

"Where'd you meet him?" Sarah placed her hands on her hips and cocked her head to the side, glaring at her sister.

"At Hinkle's. We just kind of started hanging out a couple of weeks ago."

"So, you don't actually know him, do you?"

"Sarah, knock it off. His dad's the chief of police," Jackie said.

"So what? We have a cop that's trying to pin a murder on us."

Lacey nodded emphatically. "Right, we need help. I don't want to go to jail."

"All right, guys," Jackie jumped in to referee. "We'll let Scott in, but from now on, you have to check with us before you even tell anyone about the club."

"Yeah," Sarah said peevishly. "We just started the club, and you're not in charge."

"Okay, okay." Lacey rolled her eyes. "Let's go tell Scott."

"Sarah, Scott is a good guy," Jackie whispered.

Sarah took some deep, calming breaths as the girls walked toward the creek. Out of the corner of her eye, she noticed Lacey shooting angry looks her way. She glared back at her. Jackie walked between them, oblivious to the non-verbal communication being exchanged.

"Yeow! Son of a gun!" Scott bellowed from the creek.

Sarah forgot about her anger and exchanged looks of alarm with the other Super Spies, before racing off in the direction of the brook.

Chapter Six

The girls found Scott sitting on the bank of the stream with his foot in his hands. Blood ran off of it in rivulets before dripping into the sand.

"What happened to you?" Lacey asked.

Scott's face contorted with pain. "I stepped on something sh-sharp."

Sarah noticed he shivered in spite of the heat. "Let me take a look at that."

Scott pulled his hand away from the cut. Sarah stared at it and felt sick. The wound ran from one side of his heel to the other and blood flowed freely from it.

"I think you're going to need stitches," Sarah said.

"Yeah," Scott gulped.

"How are we going to get you to the hospital?" Sarah scanned the area around her. *I wish I'd ridden my bike.*

"I'll call my dad. He'll pick me up in his cruiser." Scott scrambled for his cell phone in his pile of clothes. "I need to put pressure on this cut. Can you hand me my T-shirt?"

"Sure," Lacey said.

"You should put your foot above your heart. I remember that from health class," Sarah instructed.

"Yeah, why don't you lie back on the bank and stick your foot up in the air. We'll put pressure on it," Jackie said.

Sarah grabbed his T-shirt and pressed it over his cut. "Now push against me."

Scott pressed his foot against Sarah's thigh, and then started pushing buttons on his phone. Within minutes, she heard the sound of a siren fill the air.

"Help is on the way," Lacey said.

"I never thought I'd say this, but it's good to hear that sound," Sarah said with a sigh.

Jackie snickered and nodded.

Scott's dad pulled up and leapt from the cruiser. Sarah watched as he searched for the teens along the water's edge. In his hand, he carried a first aid kit. Spotting Scott, he rushed toward him, wearing a worried frown.

The chief ignored the girls and focused on his son. "How are you feeling?"

"Like I could puke any minute."

"Do you feel cold or faint?"

"Cold."

"Can one of you girls grab the sweatshirt in the back of the car? And bring the water bottle too." The chief opened the first aid kit and rummaged around inside.

"Sure," Lacey jumped up and ran to the cruiser. Returning with the sweatshirt, she draped it over Scott, and then handed him the water bottle.

"Thanks."

"Let's take a look at this cut," Chief Johnson pulled the blood soaked T-shirt away from his son's injury.

Scott winced.

"What in the world did you step on?"

"I have no idea," Scott said. He draped his arm over his eyes to block out the sun.

The chief bent down and grabbed some gauze out of his kit. "I'm going to bandage this foot up, then we'll get you to the hospital. Are you feeling any better?"

"No."

"We need to get you out of the sun."

The chief went to work on Scott's foot. Scott grimaced, but kept silent, letting his dad labor.

Sarah watched the chief dress Scott's wound. She noticed he worked efficiently like he'd bandaged a cut this deep a million times.

She realized Scott was the spitting image of his father, same blond hair and blue eyes, the same deep tan.

Jackie whispered in Sarah's ear, "You can tell Scott's going to be a hottie when he's older."

"Tsk. Only you would think about that when we've got someone lying on the ground bleeding."

"What's wrong with that?"

"It's an emergency, and all you can think about is whether or not he's going to be cute. Who cares? We've got an emergency here."

"It's not a life threatening emergency," Jackie scoffed.

"You would say the same thing even if he was dying." Sarah shook her head and rolled her eyes.

"Girlfriend, you're way too serious. Lighten up."

"Scott," the chief said, bringing the bickering to a halt. "That was one deep cut. Do you have any idea what you stepped on?"

"I don't know. I was walking in the water and lost my balance. When I tried to get it back I felt this huge pain in my foot."

"Where were you walking?"

"Over by that tree." Scott pointed toward a sapling hanging over the water's edge.

His father squinted as he gazed toward the water. "You girls better stay out of the water until we find whatever Scott stepped on. We don't want any more injuries like this."

Sarah made a mental note of the sapling, and then nodded in agreement with the other Super Spies.

"Okay, let's get you to the hospital." Chief Johnson helped his son to a standing position, and then draped his arm across his shoulders. He chuckled. "You're going to have to ride in the back. Can you imagine the gossip down at Hinkle's? The chief of police had to arrest his own son."

"Yeah, but Dad, you don't have to use your lights and siren, you know."

"Oh, but I do," he said, laughing at Scott's horrified expression.

The cruiser pulled away from the cul-de-sac with its sirens blaring and lights flashing. Jackie and Lacey stood at Sarah's side. They stayed there until the sound of the siren disappeared.

"Let's look for whatever Scott stepped on," Sarah said.

"You heard the chief. He doesn't want us going in the water," Lacey protested.

"I know, but I'm going anyway."

"You have a problem with authority," Jackie snickered.

Sarah laughed. "So what?"

"So...nothing, let's look."

"You guys," Lacey pouted.

Sarah rolled her eyes. "You don't have to look. Jackie and I will."

"Come on, Sarah."

"Lacey, what is your problem?"

"The chief of police told us not to go in the water." Lacey crossed her arms over her chest and glared at her sister.

"So what?." Sarah gave her sister a dismissive wave. "Do you think he's going to arrest us for going in the water?"

"We were arrested yesterday when we didn't do anything."

Sarah shook her head. "We weren't arrested."

"We were handcuffed and put in a police car. That's sounds like being arrested to me." Lacey stamped her foot to make her point.

"That's because you had blood all over your shirt."

"Guys, knock it off," Jackie said, waving her hands in the air. "Sarah, let's look. Lacey, if you don't want to help then stand on the bank until we're done."

"Don't say I didn't warn you guys," Lacey said, sticking her nose in the air.

Sarah made a face at her sister. "Don't worry, we won't."

The water swirled around Sarah's legs as she searched, rushing past her as it made its way downstream. Feeling the strong pull of the water, she braced herself against the current. It was hard to see anything at the bottom of the creek bed with the water surging past, but she didn't give up. At first, the cold water had been a shock but now Sarah enjoyed its briskness. Walking through the frigid water drained the heat from her body, making the sweltering sun bearable.

A half an hour went by before Sarah caught a glint of something shiny in the creek. She plunged her hand into the icy current, only to find the object out of reach. Taking a deep breath, she dove under water. Opening her eyes, she saw the glint of metal. It was hard to see through the churning water, but Sarah persisted. Her lungs ached for air, so she surfaced, gasping for breath. Diving down again, she used a tree root to pull herself closer to the shiny object. Her heart almost burst through her chest when she realized what it was. Wedged between two rocks was a knife with its jagged edge sticking straight out into the creek. Shooting to the surface, she gasped for air one more time, before plunging below and prying the knife free.

Jackie shrank back in horror when Sarah pulled the huge knife out of the water. It sported a leather handle with an eight-inch blade and jags at the end.

"Holy crap!" Jackie gulped as she stared at the knife. "That is one nasty knife."

"You can say that again." Sarah examined the knife in her hands. "Scott's lucky he didn't get hurt worse. This could have gone all the way through his heel."

"Holy cow!" Lacey shrieked from the creek bank. "Is that what I think it is?" She danced from one foot to the other.

"What's the matter? Gotta go to the bathroom?" Sarah smirked.

"Shut up."

"Just stop freaking out, would you?" Sarah grumbled.

"Look at this." Jackie pointed to the spot where the tip of the knife should have been.

"It must have broken off," Sarah said.

"Yeah, it looks strange."

"We better show this to the chief," Sarah told Jackie.

"No doubt," Jackie said as she made her way to the bank.

"They're probably still at the emergency room," Lacey pointed out.

"Let's go." Sarah rushed toward the bank, splashing water everywhere.

"We need to put the knife in a backpack or something," Jackie said.

"You're right." Sarah pursed her lips and blew air through them. "We can't go walking into the hospital with a knife. Let's stop at home and I'll grab my backpack."

The girls sprinted back to the house. Sarah dashed in the back door and flew downstairs. She changed out of her wet clothes and grabbed her backpack. Rushing out the front door, she found Jackie and Lacey in the yard.

"It will be faster if we ride bikes," Jackie suggested.

"True. You can ride on the back of mine," Sarah said.

The Cole girls grabbed their bikes and pedaled to the emergency room. Lacey took the lead, and Sarah and Jackie wobbled behind her.

"For a beanpole, you sure are heavy," Sarah puffed.

"Wimp."

"Cork it." Sarah grunted as she leaned forward and pushed down on her pedal.

"Just keep pedaling."

"Man, I'm out of breath already."

"That's because you keep talking. Shut up and pedal."

"Maybe you should pedal and I should ride."

"I don't think so," Jackie snickered.

They reached the hospital and locked their bikes to a lamppost standing outside the emergency room door. Sarah brushed her hair away from her sweaty temples and sighed.

"What's the matter, girlfriend? Are you all tuckered out?" Jackie teased.

"Shut up."

"Make me."

"I can't. I'm too tired from hauling a beanpole on the back of my bike."

The girls looked at each other and laughed.

"Come on you two," Lacey groaned, holding the door for them.

Walking down the corridor, Sarah was surprised to find the hospital so quiet. Whenever she saw a hospital show on TV there was always a flurry of activity. Doctors rushing to the emergency rooms, nurses screaming down the halls for doctors, and orderlies pushing bodies covered with blood on gurneys. This hospital contrasted sharply with the image

Sarah had of them. It seemed peaceful to her, as she took in the shiny waxed floors and the subdued conversations at the nurses' station. She spied a sign reading 'Emergency Room' and motioned for Jackie and Lacey to follow her.

The Super Spies walked into the brightly lit waiting area. Chairs lined the walls of the room with wooden tables in the corners. Plants and magazines sat on the tables, giving the area a comforting atmosphere.

Sarah saw the chief first as he paced in the waiting area. He was the only one in the room. She noticed he kept glancing at his watch as he walked.

"Hi, Chief," Sarah greeted.

"Hello, girls."

"How's Scott?" Lacey asked.

"He's getting stitched up. He's going to be okay."

"We found something in the creek, after you left." Sarah opened her backpack.

"I thought I told you girls to stay out of the water?" The chief stopped pacing and frowned.

"I didn't go in the water," Lacey said, crossing her arms across her chest and giving Sarah and Jackie a superior look.

"Good for you," he winked at Lacey.

"I think you should arrest them."

The chief laughed. "I can't arrest them for going in the water."

Sarah smirked. "Told you."

"You should, they didn't follow orders." Lacey put her hands on her hips and gave Sarah and Jackie a reproachful look.

Chief Johnson chuckled and shook his head.

Sarah ignored her and pulled the knife out of her backpack. "This is what we found." She held it up with a flourish.

The chief pursed his lips and let out a low whistle. "You found this in the water?"

Sarah nodded. "Yeah, is it a hunting knife?"

"I'm not sure, but you better let me have that."

Chief Johnson took the knife out of Sarah's hands and turned it over in his own, examining it.

"What kind of knife is it?" Lacey asked.

"It's a dangerous one," he said, not taking his eyes off of it.

"I wonder how it got into the water?" Sarah wrinkled her brow.

"I don't know, but I'm going to find out. You girls run along now. I'll have Scott call you when he's done here."

"Bye, Chief."

"You girls be good," Chief Johnson winked as they were leaving.

The Super Spies left the emergency room and walked toward the doors leading outside. Sarah noticed again the peaceful atmosphere and the cleanliness of the hospital. Even though it appeared stark, with its white walls and white tiled floors, she felt comforted and safe. It hummed with the hushed tones of efficient care. Pushing open the door, Sarah walked outside.

The heat hit her as soon as she walked out. It was like walking into a wall of hot jello. Her movements required more effort. Heavy moisture hung in the air, and Sarah's lungs worked extra hard to suck in oxygen. Sarah stopped when she reached her bike, deep in thought. Jackie and Lacey paused beside her.

Sarah squinted in the sun. "Man, we need to meet and pull all of our info together."

Jackie fussed with her curls. "You're right. Maybe we can meet tonight?"

"Yeah, I'll ask Aunt June if you can spend the night. Maybe we can camp out."

"Awesome," Jackie beamed.

"I want to camp out, too," Lacey piped up.

"Only if you help put up the tent."

"Deal."

The girls pedaled their way to Jackie's house and dropped her off. Her house stood on the corner of Broadway and Walnut. Surrounding the dignified home was a stone fence with an iron gate. A manicured lawn grew within the boundaries of the fence, whispering of a forgotten era of garden parties and croquet games. Sarah wondered about the history of the house and the many secrets of the small town.

"Thanks for the ride." Jackie climbed off the back of the bike, pulling Sarah from her thoughts.

"Be at my house at seven." Sarah pushed her hair away from her sweaty forehead and took some deep breaths.

"Do you think you're up for a campout?" Jackie teased.

"Be there or be square, Beanpole."

Jackie laughed. "See ya at seven." She waved and hurried inside.

Gliding through the streets of Harrisburg, Sarah felt the breeze cool her skin. She couldn't remember ever feeling so free. At home, her family had to schedule a biking excursion and take the bikes to a bike trail in order to ride. The trail was always busy with bikers and people on roller-blades—it wasn't as carefree as this small town. *I might like growing up here,* Sarah mused, as she steered her bike onto her street.

The girls turned into the driveway and dropped their bikes on the front lawn. Racing inside, Sarah asked their aunt if Jackie could spend the night. She said it was okay, so Sarah called Jackie while Lacey helped with dinner.

After a dinner of spaghetti and meatballs, Sarah and Lacey dashed off to put up the tent. Both girls were excited about camping out in the backyard. Sarah couldn't wait for Jackie to spend the night, and her heart danced with anticipation. *We go together like peanut butter and jelly.* A smile burst out on Sarah's face. Even though the threat of Klonsky lurked in the background, she was enjoying her summer and her new friend.

Sarah and Lacey managed to get the tent up without too much trouble, and they brought out sleeping bags and a cooler full of soda. While her sister was in the house gathering more camping supplies, Sarah opened the flaps to air out the tent. It smelled musty from being stored away all winter.

Joining her sister in the backyard, Lacey carried a flashlight and a radio in her hands. "Looks like we're ready."

"It sure does."

Lacey searched the cooler, counting cans with her index finger. "I'm going to get some more, just in case."

"Good idea, you can never have too much."

While her sister ran back into the house, Sarah's thoughts turned toward their investigation. A chill ran down her spine when Klonsky came to mind. What possible reason could he have for killing the Cat Lady? As she pondered this question, a police cruiser turned the corner and drove slowly down the street. Sarah saw Klonsky at the wheel. He glared at her from inside his car. Sarah's blood ran cold. She sucked in a breath and stared back, refusing to be intimidated. Scowling and shaking his finger at her, he yelled and sped away. Sarah took several deep breaths; she hadn't understood what he shouted, but she knew it couldn't be good. With trembling hands, she pushed her hair out of her face. All of a sudden it hit her.

Klonsky knows where I live.

Chapter Seven

Jackie arrived at seven. After she said hello to Sarah's aunt and uncle, Sarah and Lacey whisked her outside. They ambled through the yard enjoying the slight breeze blowing in with the twilight.

The air was still thick with humidity—Sarah took a deep breath and let it out slowly. Her chest felt heavy as if the moisture in the air was too thick for her lungs. This feeling brought back the memory of the family camping trip last summer. They had gone to Colorado and hiked through the Rocky Mountains.

On one of their hikes they discovered a river. While sitting on the edge cooling their feet, a herd of elk walked near the Cole family and drank from the water. At that moment, Sarah realized she loved nature. These wild animals just accepted her family as a part of the world, there was no fear or aggressiveness.

She felt at peace as she watched the herd. It was one big family. The older elk kept an eye out for predators, while the calves played in the water. Watching the elk, Sarah realized how important her family was to her. *Even my sister,* she admitted to herself. All of a sudden, gratitude for her family overwhelmed her, and she couldn't help but compare her life to the Cat Lady's.

Tears welled in Sarah's eyes and her heart swelled with sorrow as she thought about the Cat Lady's tragic life. The idea she had been haunted until her dying day by the disappearance of her son struck a chord deep in Sarah. A grave injustice had been done, and she felt compelled to rectify it.

Reaching the tent, Sarah stepped inside. Her thoughts turned to Klonsky and apprehension flowed through her body like a raging river. The teens sat in the center of the tent in a circle. Sarah took a few minutes and told the girls about her sighting of the crooked cop.

Jackie's eyes widened when she heard the tale. Lacey whimpered but didn't make any other sound.

Jackie took a shuddering breath. "There's something wrong with that guy."

"You got that right," Sarah said.

The girls squirmed for a few minutes getting comfortable on the floor, then Sarah held up a notebook she carried with her. "This is going to be our spy-book."

"Okay, I'll bite, what's a spy-book?" Jackie asked.

"It's the book we're using to keep track of all our clues," Sarah said.

"Cool beans."

Sarah scrawled the words 'spy-book' across the front of the notebook.

"Anyone want a soda?" Lacey asked.

Sarah and Jackie both nodded.

Lacey handed the girls their soft drinks, and they all popped the tops and drank.

Huddling together in the middle of their new shelter, the teens leaned forward as if they were planning a conspiracy. Setting her soda off to the side, Sarah turned on the flashlight and set it in the center of the tent. The light shone on the ceiling. It cast a warm glow, creating a cozy atmosphere.

Sarah grabbed the spy-book. "Okay, this is what we know so far." She began writing. "The Cat Lady opened her door for her killer. That means she knew Klonsky."

"Or felt comfortable with him because he's a cop," Jackie said, pulling on a curl.

Sarah nodded. "Yeah, that's right, and we heard him down by the creek last night getting rid of evidence."

"Scott stepped on a knife," Jackie pointed out.

"Right, and the Cat Lady was stabbed." Sarah scribbled frantically in the spy-book.

"Wait a minute, guys," Lacey said, holding out her arms as if she were stopping traffic. "When I talked to Scott, he said the police have a suspect already."

Sarah shook her head. "No way."

"Way...I guess there's been a rash of murders in this state."

"Are you serious?" Sarah frowned.

"Yeah, it's some guy posing as a delivery man. That's how he gets in the door, then he goes after them, kills them, and robs them blind. Scott says this is called a blitz attack."

"It can't be true," Sarah shook her head.

"It's true," Lacey insisted. "The cops have a nickname for him. They're calling him the Death Messenger."

"Then what were Klonsky and the other guy doing last night?" Jackie asked.

Lacey shrugged. "I don't know."

"Remember what he said about us when we were leaving the police station? He said we killed the Cat Lady."

"That was probably before they found out about the Death Messenger." Lacey pulled on her shoelace.

"I don't know." Sarah shook her head and put the spy-book down.

"Yeah, what about the knife we found today?" Jackie asked.

Lacey raised her hands in agesture of confusion. "Beats me, maybe a hunter lost it."

"Remember, the evidence tells the story," Sarah frowned and fiddled with her pen. "I think it's strange we heard Klonsky down by the creek last night getting rid of evidence, and then the next day we find a knife in the water."

"You've got a good point," Jackie said.

"Plus, the Cat Lady was stabbed to death. It's all pointing toward Klonsky."

Jackie nodded. "We just don't know why."

"We've got to get back inside the Cat Lady's house." Sarah furrowed her brow and doodled on the spy-book.

"Yeah, we do," Jackie said as she shifted her weight.

"What about the Cat Lady's son?" Lacey asked. She suddenly leaned forward and whispered. "Maybe he's the Death Messenger." Her eyes widened as she stared at Sarah.

Sarah stared back at her sister—she could tell images of the Death Messenger were running rampant through Lacey's brain. "He couldn't be. We found out he was kidnapped when we were at the library."

"No way."

"Yeah, and the Cat Lady paid the ransom and everything," Jackie added.

"Did they ever find his body?" Lacey asked.

"Nope."

"How much was the ransom for?" Lacey fiddled with her shoestring.

Sarah fumbled in her backpack and pulled out some of the photocopied articles. She quickly scanned one of them, looking for the ransom information. "It says here... one hundred thousand dollars."

"She paid it, huh?" Lacey asked, pulling harder on her shoelace and untying her shoe.

"Yep."

"I wonder if he's still alive?" Jackie speculated.

"At this point anything is possible." Sarah scribbled in the spy-book. "We need to find more evidence, guys."

"Yeah, we do," Jackie said.

"You know what that means?" Sarah cracked a smile.

"We're sneaking out tonight?" Jackie asked, matching Sarah's grin with one of her own.

"We are?" Lacey gulped.

"Yep. We need more evidence to put Klonsky away."

"But what if it's not Klonsky? What if it's the Messenger?" Lacey asked, wringing her hands.

"More evidence will tell us," Sarah said firmly. "I have a hunch it's Klonsky."

Jackie tugged on her curls. "I think Klonsky is looking for a fall guy, someone to blame the murder on."

Sarah's stomach fluttered. "You know, I just had a thought."

"You had a thought? What'd it feel like?" Jackie teased.

"I'll tell you later," Sarah snorted. "I'll describe it in great detail. In fact, I'll even write it down for you. I know you've never had one, so you don't know what they feel like."

"Ooooh, you're soo funny."

"Why, yes...yes I am," Sarah laughed.

"A regular comedian."

Sarah laughed again and then grew serious. "What if Klonsky heard about this other guy and tried to copy him. He murdered the Cat Lady to make it look like the Death Messenger."

"You mean like a copycat?" Jackie asked.

"Yep." Sarah doodled on the spy-book.

"He's smart." Lacey grimaced. "He's going to get away with it, isn't he?"

"Not if we can help it," Sarah said.

"You guys, this could get dangerous," Lacey whimpered.

"We laugh in the face of danger," Jackie crowed. She lifted her hand in the air, and pretended to swing a sword.

"It's already dangerous." Sarah gave Lacey a long look. "Klonsky is trying to pin this murder on us. The only way out of this mess is to find more clues." Sarah placed her elbow on her knee and leaned her head against her fist. Her brow wrinkled as she thought about the Cat Lady.

All of a sudden, she heard an odd snuffling noise from outside the tent. Jackie gazed at her with a confused expression.

"It's Lily. Uncle Walt must be walking her." Sarah answered the question lurking in Jackie's eyes.

"Hi, girls," he said from outside the tent.

"Hi," they chorused.

"I just thought I'd see if you girls need anything before I turn in."

"We're okay," Sarah said.

"I think Lily would like to sleep out here with you."

"Awwww, she's going to bark at every little noise," Sarah complained.

"Just keep her in the tent. She'll be okay."

"All right," Sarah grumbled.

Uncle Walt unzipped the tent, and Lily trotted in. She went to work sniffing the far corners of the tent, her coppery nose intent on finding any long forgotten morsel.

"Don't stay up too late, girls."

"We won't," all three girls said in unison.

Sarah giggled. This was the universal warning given by parents at all sleepovers, along with the universal reply by teenagers.

"Night."

"Night."

Sarah put her fingers to her lips, telling the other girls to be quiet. She listened as Uncle Walt made his way back to the house. Minutes later, she heard the squeak of the screen door, and then the loud bang as the taut spring pulled the door shut. Secrets were being shared, and uncles were not allowed.

"What are we going to do now?" Jackie asked.

"Looks like we can't sneak out tonight." Lacey sighed with relief.

"We'll think of something." Sarah furrowed her brow. "We won't let Lily ruin our plans."

"We might as well unroll our sleeping bags and get comfortable," Jackie suggested.

The girls stood and unrolled their sleeping bags. They put the tops of the bed rolls in the center of the tent, so when they were asleep their heads would be close. All three Super Spies proceeded to lie on top of their sleep sacks.

Lily lay down on Sarah's bag, with her chin on the teenager's leg. Sarah stared at the ceiling of the tent. She played with the flashlight, moving it back and forth.

Watching the shadows dance on the side of the tent, Sarah planned the night's adventure. "We'll wait until everyone's asleep and then put Lily back in the house."

"Okay," Jackie agreed.

"I don't know if it's a good idea to go to the Cat Lady's at night," Lacey said, chewing on her lip.

"We can't go during the day, Klonsky and the other cops will be there," Sarah reasoned.

"I just can't figure out why Klonsky would murder the Cat Lady?" Jackie frowned.

"I keep going back to what Uncle Walt said about her being one of the richest people in town." Sarah continued to play with the flashlight as she spoke.

"Do you think this is about money?" Jackie sat up and scratched Lily's head.

"I don't know, but it's one of the oldest reasons in the book."

All of a sudden an offending odor engulfed the girls. They wrinkled their noses and scrambled out of the tent.

"Gross, Lily farted!" Sarah grimaced and covered her nose.

"Man, that was bad." Jackie took several deep breaths of fresh air.

"You can say that again," Sarah said.

"Man, that was bad." Jackie snickered and gave Sarah a playful nudge.

The girls burst into laughter.

"But that does give us an excuse to put Lily back inside the house," Sarah beamed.

"It sure does," Jackie giggled.

Sarah grabbed Lily. She squirmed in protest, but Sarah kept her under control. "I'm taking her in."

With Lily squirming in her arms, Sarah walked toward the back door. She stopped when she noticed the stars were out in full force. They littered the sky with their twinkling lights. For a moment, Lily stopped struggling as if their beauty mesmerized her too. After a few seconds, Lily put her cold nose on Sarah's arm, bringing her back from the heavens. Sarah hurried the rest of the way to the house. Uncle Walt came to the door, and Sarah explained to him why Lily had to sleep inside.

"What did Uncle Walt say?" Lacey asked when Sarah returned to the tent.

"He just laughed. He said he would put her in her kennel for the night."

"So sneaking out is still on?" Jackie asked.

"You bet. Let's just wait until Uncle Walt falls back to sleep."

After checking to make sure there were no more fumes, the girls crawled back into the tent.

"Boy, Lily sure has stinky farts," Sarah said.

Jackie rummaged around in her backpack and pulled out a small bottle of perfume. She began spraying it in the corners of the tent.

Sarah laughed at her. "What are you doing?"

"Making sure the fart smell is gone." Jackie continued spraying the perfume until the tent was filled with the flowery aroma.

"Knock it off, you're making my eyes water," Sarah protested.

All three girls laughed until tears came to their eyes. Wiping her eyes, Sarah sat down on her sleeping bag; the other girls followed her lead.

The Super Spies lay on their sleeping bags talking, the stories turning to the town of Harrisburg. Sarah and Lacey sat wide-eyed as Jackie regaled them with tales about the quirky characters in the tiny burg. There was Mr. Copinski, a shrunken old man who walked around town sweeping the sidewalks and the streets. Jackie said he wasn't right in the head, and on a number of occasions he appeared drunk and had to be taken to jail. She giggled as she stood and imitated his hunched, drunken walk.

Sitting back down, her expression turned serious and her eyes darkened when she told the Cole girls about Mr. Dewilde. If the Cat Lady was the town's crazy lady, then Mr.

Dewilde was the town's crazy man. According to Jackie, he came home from work one day and found his family brutally murdered. The police investigated, but the mystery remains unsolved to this day. Mr. Dewilde locked up the house and left it just the way he found it and has never returned. *Another True Crime mystery,* Sarah thought to herself.

"Wow, there sure are a lot of crazy people in this town," Sarah said.

Jackie flopped down on her sleeping bag. "Tell me about it. This town is full of crazy people. It's amazing that I'm as sane as I am."

"You're sane?" Sarah laughed.

"Are you questioning my sanity?" Jackie sat up and put her hands on her hips, pretending to glare at Sarah.

"Okay, okay." Sarah put her hands up in mock surrender. "What time is it?"

Jackie placed her wrist in the beam of the flashlight. "It's midnight."

"It's time to go."

"Are you sure we should do this at night?" Lacey whimpered.

"We have to move fast," Sarah said, casting a sideways glance at Lacey as she sat up.

"You don't have to go, if you don't want to," Jackie said.

"I'm just nervous."

"Then don't go," Sarah said.

"I don't want to miss anything, either."

"Here, have some tootsie rolls." Sarah handed Lacey a handful of the treasured candies. "It'll calm your nerves."

"Okay." Lacey grabbed the candy and pulled it out of its wrapper with trembling hands.

"Let's head out." Jackie pulled her curls into a fuzzy ponytail. "Grab a flashlight."

Armed with flashlights and backpacks, the Super Spies left the safety of the tent and began their journey to the Cat Lady's.

Sarah sighed as she walked, the moon lighting her way. Listening to the crickets and katydids, Sarah's mind wandered to the nagging questions haunting her. *Why would Klonsky want the Cat Lady dead? Who was the man that was with him by the creek? What is the connection between the Cat Lady and Klonsky?* No answers came to her.

Shaking her head, she focused her attention on the streets of Harrisburg. They were different at night. The moon hung in the sky like a half-eaten lollipop minus the stick. Moonlight hit the giant trees and houses, throwing eerie shadows everywhere. A chill ran down Sarah's spine, and she shivered in the heat. Finally, the girls reached the Cat Lady's house and once again hid behind the oak tree across the street.

"Cross your fingers, girls. Let's hope we find some answers tonight," Sarah whispered.

She peeked out from behind the tree and stared at the house. It sat dark and forbidding. No lights shone in the windows, and the worn out look it had by day turned sinister at night. Sarah's stomach clenched into a tight knot.

"Are you sure you want to do this?" Lacey gulped.

"We have to. We can't let Klonsky get away with murder," Sarah said. Her voice sounded braver than she felt, but she was more determined than ever to put the crooked cop away.

"We don't even know if it's Klonsky," Lacey argued.

"What about the knife we found?" Sarah whispered.

"We don't even know if it's the murder weapon." Lacey peered at the house as she spoke.

"We don't know it's not, either." Sarah rolled her eyes, refusing to believe anything but her own theory.

Lacey sighed. "I don't think this is a good idea."

"Then stay here, wimp."

"No way! I'm not staying here by myself."

"Guys, we're wasting time," Jackie said, drumming her fingers on the tree trunk.

"Jackie's right. Let's get going." Sarah peered out from behind the tree again. "Well, here goes nothing." She took a deep breath, and sprinted across the street.

Jackie and Lacey caught up with Sarah at the basement window. She sat hunkered down in the dark, waiting for them.

"What took you so long?" Sarah grumbled.

"You do that every time," Jackie groused.

"I suppose I'm going in first?" Sarah whispered.

"Yep." Jackie peered into the dark window.

Sarah pushed her backpack through the window, and then backed up and went in feet first. She remembered to arch her back. Once inside she took a deep breath, working up the courage to go down the box stairs. It was so dark she couldn't see her hand in front of her face. Nervous sweat broke out under her arms; she felt swallowed by the inky darkness.

Her heart raced as she fumbled for her backpack. Images of the Cat Lady's ghost invaded her mind. Her hands trembled and she willed them to stop. Sarah swallowed her fear. It was a huge lump that didn't go down easily. Reaching into her pack, she pulled out her flashlight. Turning it on, she took several ragged breaths, easing her panic. Finally, she descended the makeshift stairs, the beam of her light casting eerie shadows on the walls and ceiling.

"Okay, it's safe. Come on down," Sarah whispered when she reached the floor.

She heard Lacey mutter in a strangled voice. "I want to go next."

"Hurry up."

Finally, all three girls were together at the bottom of the box stairs.

"It's a lot different being here at night," Lacey whispered.

"You can say that again," Sarah answered as she watched Jackie come down the box stairs.

All of a sudden Jackie shone her flashlight under her chin and contorted her features. "Blaaaah."

Lacey shrieked and jumped back, tripping over the box stairs. She landed on her rear and clouds of dust erupted around her. "Knock it off," she sputtered.

"It wasn't me, it was the Cat Lady's ghost," Jackie snickered.

"Shut up."

Jackie laughed at Lacey sprawled in the dirt. Sarah's lips twitched, but she stifled her laughter and took a deep breath. She felt some of the tension leave her body.

"You guys are total freaks!" Lacey snapped.

She coughed spastically. Standing, she brushed the dirt off her sweatpants and adjusted the waistband. Glaring at Jackie, she stepped closer to her sister.

"Okay, you guys, let's start looking for clues," Sarah said.

The girls climbed the stairs to the basement door. Sarah opened it and shone her flashlight into the inky darkness of the kitchen. Repugnant air hit Sarah as soon as she stepped into the room. She pulled her collar up over her nose, hoping it would mask the smell.

"What are we looking for?" Jackie asked, covering her nose with her sleeve.

"We're looking for anything connecting Klonsky to the Cat Lady. Let's look in the living room." Sarah walked through the kitchen, her flashlight cutting through the murkiness.

The house was stifling. It had been closed up since the murder, and the foul stench of cat urine polluted the air. Sarah pulled her collar tighter around her nose and mouth. Jackie and Lacey followed her, covering their noses. Taking a deep breath, Sarah stopped between the kitchen and the living room.

"Okay, guys. Let's look for more pictures, a photo album, or better yet a diary," she said, in a muffled voice.

The girls fanned out, and aimed their lights on the shelves. Sarah avoided shining her light on the blood spatter and concentrated on the pictures sitting on the far wall. She hoped to find some answers in the faces of the photographs.

"There's not much down here," Jackie said after a few minutes. "Just piles of newspapers."

"Let's go upstairs." Sarah gestured for the other girls to follow her.

She tiptoed toward the staircase beginning in the living room. Climbing slowly, she focused on finding clues. The air grew warmer as Sarah ascended. Sweat broke out on her brow, and she wiped it away. All of a sudden, the stairway seemed to narrow. Sarah's heart beat rapidly, and her breathing came in shallow gasps. Relief flooded through her when she reached the top of the stairs and found a wide hallway. Stopping, she bent down and took huge gulps of breath. The panicky, closed in feeling went away. Turning, she noticed the stairway appeared normal again. Jackie and Lacey were staring at her, both of their faces shiny with sweat.

"It's hot up here, let's hurry," Jackie said.

Sarah nodded and opened the first door at the top of the stairs. It was a boy's bedroom. She flashed her light around and then stepped inside.

Shining her light around the room, Sarah noticed the airplane wallpaper was peeling away from the walls. A twin bed sat across the room near the window. It had been made, but by a child's hands. Sarah could tell because the bedspread draped the bed in a haphazard fashion. On one side, it hung all the way to the floor. Perched on top of the bed was a well-loved teddy bear. Its brown fur had been worn away in spots, and one button eye hung by a thread. Strewn about on the floor were toy soldiers, along with a baseball and glove. The closet door stood open, and Sarah caught a glimpse of clothes hanging on hangers. In a heap on the closet floor were clothes that had been hastily discarded, as if the young boy hadn't had time to re-hang them. Sarah's throat constricted as it dawned on her this room hadn't been touched since the day David disappeared.

Her eyes welled up. "The poor Cat Lady, she must have been so sad. Losing her son just ruined her life."

"She must have been totally grief-stricken," Jackie sniffled.

Lacey nodded. "Yeah, can you imagine, waking up every day, not knowing where your kid is?"

The girls stood in silence as Lacey's words washed over them. Sarah felt a deep sense of loss and her heart went out to the weird old woman. Tears threatened to spill down her cheeks, but she forced them back. She cleared her throat. "Let's go down the hall. I don't think we'll find anything in here."

Jackie wiped her eyes on her sleeve. "Okay."

The next room appeared to be the master bedroom. Where the rest of the house was cluttered and dirty, this room had been well maintained. There was very little dust on the shelves, and a single baby picture of David sat on the bureau.

"I think the Cat Lady spent most of her time here," Sarah said.

"It looks like it. Jackie pursed her lips and wiped the sweat from her brow.

"There's only one picture of David?" Lacey said, raising her hands in a gesture of confusion.

"It might have been too hard to have a bunch of pictures around." Sarah peered around the room, wondering where to start.

"Yeah, I think this poor woman was tormented by grief."

"You're right about that. Why don't you guys start looking over there on the shelves, and I'll start going through the night stand."Sarah's fingers tingled as she rummaged through a drawer. *We're close. I can feel it.* "I so want to get Klonsky, you guys," she said, closing the drawer. "We have to get justice for the Cat Lady."

"Absolutely," Lacey said in a determined voice.

"Guys, I found a photo album," Jackie whispered. She opened the cover, looking for clues.

"Great, we'll take that back to the tent, and check it out." Sarah walked over and grabbed the album. "We don't have time to look at it now." She stepped back and placed it in her backpack.

"I can't seem to find anything," Lacey complained.

"I can't either." Sarah brushed her hair out of her eyes. "You would think the Cat Lady would've kept a diary or something."

"You hide your diary between the mattress and springs," Lacey pointed out. "Maybe the Cat Lady did the same thing."

"Have you been reading my diary?" Sarah asked, placing her hands on her hips and glaring at her sister.

"Not at all," Lacey feigned innocence. "I just know where you keep it."

"I'm definitely moving it now." Sarah walked over to the bed and reached between the mattress and springs. Her efforts were rewarded and she felt the leathery binding of a book. "Hey, I think I found it," Sarah beamed as she pulled the book from its hiding place.

"What is this?" Jackie knelt and pried something from the carpet.

"What is it?" Sarah walked over to where Jackie knelt. She carried her backpack with her, placing the diary inside.

Jackie aimed her flashlight on it. "It's some sort of tie tack or lapel pin. It has the number ten on it. I think it's got blood on it!"

"It's a clue! Wrap it in this tissue and put it in my backpack." Sarah handed Jackie a tissue and her knapsack.

Jackie wrapped the pin in the tissue, and put it in Sarah's pack next to the diary. She had just zipped it close when a loud thump came from the rear of the house. Sarah clicked off her flashlight and dropped to the floor. Her companions followed her lead.

"What was that noise?" Lacey whispered. Sarah heard the tension in her voice.

"I don't know," Sarah replied in a low voice. Sweat rolled off her forehead and down the side of her face.

The girls stayed frozen in their crouched positions. Sarah listened for more thumping noises.

"I don't hear anything else," Jackie whispered.

"I think it's time to go," Lacey whined.

"Yeah," Sarah agreed. "Let's go."

Sarah led the girls into the hall. She stopped just outside the bedroom door and listened. The hair on the back of her neck prickled, but she heard no other noise.

"Let's go already," Lacey insisted.

Sarah moved forward again. She made it as far as David's bedroom before the sound of voices startled her.

"Crap."

She opened the door to David's room and scrambled inside. Jackie and Lacey were right behind her. Sarah shut the door once her companions were out of the way.

Heavy footsteps thumped up the stairs. "I don't think it's a good idea ta be here," a man whined.

Sarah recognized the voice as one of the men from the creek. Klonsky had called him D.W. Her stomach tightened into a painful knot, and her heart pounded against her ribs.

"I lost something, and I want to make sure I didn't lose it here."

Sarah shuddered at the sound of Klonsky's snarling voice. Pressing her ear against the door, she listened. Jackie followed suit. Grabbing Jackie's hand, she squeezed as she strained to hear more of the conversation. Her throat constricted and she had a hard time swallowing. Lacey huddled next to Sarah as if she were cold.

"What did ya lose?" D.W. complained.

"My service pin. You know, the one I got when I had ten years on the force."

"That's jus' great," D.W. fumed, showing a rare spark of anger. "You're a cop and you lose somethin' at your own crime scene."

"Calm down," Klonsky grumbled. "The lady could have grabbed it in the struggle."

Sarah heard the two criminals as they reached the top of the stairs. They were right outside David's door.

"Come on," Klonsky exhaled an irritated sigh as he stomped further down the hall. "It could have her print on it… even a partial would be bad."

Sarah couldn't hear the conversation anymore, but she'd heard enough. Her heart lurch in her chest and goose bumps rose on her skin.

"We found his pin," Sarah whispered.

"We've got to get out of here," Jackie muttered.

Lacey's breath was hot and quick on the back of Sarah's neck, as she grabbed Sarah's shirt and held on for dear life.

"If we're going to go, we've got to go now," Sarah said.

She turned the knob on the door and slunk out into the hall. Pausing, she listened to the two men rummaging around in the Cat Lady's bedroom. Sarah crept toward the stairs— Lacey and Jackie were right behind her.

Sarah held her breath as she tiptoed down the stairs. Her heart pounded against her ribs. She was sure the men would hear it and come searching for the source of the noise. She wanted to get down those stairs as fast as she could. Lacey still clutched the back of her shirt, slowing her down. Jackie took up the rear.

They reached the living room when the sound of a door opening from above stopped the girls dead in their tracks. Sarah searched frantically for a place to hide. She heard heavy footsteps as the criminals moved toward the stairs.

"Over here," she muttered.

The girls dashed behind a couple piles of newspapers just as Klonsky and D.W. came down the stairs.

"It's not here. So, we're fine," Klonsky said.

"'Less the cops found it already."

Klonsky laughed. "No problem, I'm heading up the investigation, so I know what they have. Everything's going like clockwork."

Sarah heard the arrogance in his voice, and it turned her stomach. The villains' footsteps grew fainter as they turned toward the kitchen.

Suddenly, Lacey sneezed against Sarah's back. Sarah's breath caught in her chest and her throat tightened. She turned and grabbed Lacey's head, forcing it down into the carpet. Lacey struggled against her and whimpered in protest. Sarah let her up only to keep her quiet. Clamping her lips together, she stifled the groan that was about to escape. *I can't believe my sister's bad timing.* Clapping her hand over Lacey's mouth, Sarah pressed down tightly. She could feel Lacey's teeth against her lips. Her sister struggled against her. Sarah was pressing too hard. Reluctantly, she eased the pressure off of Lacey's mouth.

"What was that noise?" D.W. asked from the kitchen.

Sarah heard footsteps coming back into the living room. All of a sudden, a beam of light flashed around the piles of newspapers. Her heart lurched in her chest and her spirits sank. *We almost made it. What will Klonsky do if he catches us?* A chill ran down her spine and she held her breath, praying they wouldn't be discovered.

"Probably one of those cats," Klonsky said.

"Yeah. You know there's somethin' familiar about this here house," D.W. said.

Sarah watched the beam of his light as it roamed around the room. She heard him amble through the maze of newspapers coming closer to where they hid. Her heart thundered in her chest. *I wish I could disappear into the floor.*

"You don't say?" Klonsky asked.

"Yeah, I'm thinkin' I've been here afore."

"You were here before, with me, the other night."

"No, I mean afore that."

"I doubt that." Klonsky dismissed him. "Come on, let's get out of here."

"Lon, I thinks I been here," D.W. insisted.

"Let's go."

Sarah watched as D.W., in a moment of independence, took a step toward the shelves. He shone his light on the photos and took several more steps to get a better look at them. By doing this he stepped directly on Jackie's hand. Jackie grimaced in pain as his full weight crushed her hand.

D.W. shone his flashlight on the ground. "What the heck?"

"Yeow!" Jackie howled. She tugged at her hand trying to pull it out from under D.W.'s foot.

D.W. shrieked and dropped his flashlight. He stumbled back against a pile of newspapers. They cascaded to the floor.

"Run!" Sarah shouted.

She grabbed Lacey's hand and pulled her away from the carnage. Turning toward the kitchen, Sarah saw Klonsky looming in the darkness. He blocked the only way to escape.

All of a sudden, Lacey tripped and pushed Sarah from behind — she stumbled, stopping inches away from Klonsky. She couldn't see his face, and hoped he couldn't see her.

"What the heck..." he snapped. He brought his light around to see.

Sarah swung her backpack and knocked his flashlight to the floor. She could hear it rolling away out of reach. Klonsky staggered back and lost his balance. Next, she heard a loud thump as he crashed to the floor. *He must have tripped over a kitchen chair.*

Thinking fast, Sarah reached around Lacey and grabbed Jackie's strap on her backpack. She tugged it, trying to pull it off her shoulders. Jackie seemed to understand what she was doing and dropped the backpack to the floor.

"Perfume," Sarah whispered.

Jackie rummaged around inside and pulled out the bottle and handed it to Sarah. Meanwhile, Klonsky floundered in the dark, looking for his flashlight.

Spying her opportunity, Sarah dashed by the crooked cop, pulling Lacey with her. She heard Jackie fumble with her backpack and hoped she was right behind them.

Sarah made it to the basement door before Klonsky had recovered his flashlight. She heard Jackie yelp and her gut twisted into a tight knot. The dirty cop had just captured her friend.

Clutching the perfume bottle, she pushed Lacey toward the stairs.

Sarah turned and saw Klonsky struggling with Jackie. She dashed toward them and sprayed Klonsky right in the face with the perfume. He yowled in pain. Dropping Jackie's arm, he balled his hands into fists and rubbed his eyes, then stumbled back against the kitchen counter.

"Got him," Jackie said in a low voice.

Sarah grabbed Jackie's hand and raced down the basement stairs. She heard the satisfying bang as Jackie slammed the door behind her. Reaching the box stairs, Sarah was relieved when she found Lacey there. Scrambling to the top of the stairs, she pulled Lacey behind her. Her hands shook as she climbed. Throwing the perfume bottle to the side, she struggled out the window. Glancing back, she saw Lacey and Jackie right behind her.

Once outside, Sarah took several gulps of the cool night air as she stood trying to bring her shaking hands under control. She waited for her two companions to come through the tiny window.

Just as Lacey wiggled out of the casement, the back door burst open and Klonsky lurched into the night.

"Run!" Sarah shrieked.

Sarah pulled Jackie out of the window, and then grabbed Lacey's hand. She took off sprinting through the Cat Lady's back yard. The tall grass gripped her ankles as she ran, slowing her down. Jackie ran behind her, and Sarah heard her gasping for breath. Forging ahead, she saw the fence separating the Cat Lady's yard and Mrs. Farnsworth's. Turning toward it, she ran, hoping to scramble over it before the crooked cop caught them.

Sarah reached the fence and dropped Lacey's hand. She placed her hands on the top horizontal board. Putting all of her weight on the board, she pulled her legs to one side. Up and over like a gymnast leaping over the pommel horse. Landing, she turned and helped Lacey over. Jackie imitated Sarah's move and all three girls were over the fence.

Sarah spied Klonsky running toward them. She hoped he couldn't see the fence. It was dark and the fence was a rotted gray color, too dark for someone to detect at night. Grabbing

Lacey's hand again, she ran through Mrs. Farnsworth's yard. Jackie was right behind them.

Sarah stopped when she heard the splinter of wood and a sharp cry of pain. Looking back, she could just make out the image of Klonsky on the ground and D.W. hovering above him. *Yes!*

Turning, Sarah let go of Lacey's hand and ran as fast as she could. She could hear Jackie and Lacey behind her, gasping for breath as their feet pounded the pavement. They sprinted blindly down the streets of Harrisburg. Sarah heard strangled shouts as they ran but she didn't stop. Finally, the girls reached their tent and scrambled inside. All three teens collapsed on the floor and lay there with their chests heaving.

"I can't believe we almost got caught by the killers," Lacey gasped, and then started to cry. "I'm not sleeping out here. I'm going inside."

"Calm down," Sarah said.

"Don't tell me to calm down. We almost got caught by the killers!" Lacey looked like she was about to hyperventilate.

"Take it easy." Sarah patted her on the back. "I'm sure they didn't get a good look at us."

"You hope," Lacey retorted.

"They didn't. I knocked the flashlight out of his hands before he could shine it on us."

"Yeah, and Sarah got him with my perfume," Jackie snickered. "He didn't see anything."

Sarah couldn't help but smile at the memory. "Yeah, we got him good."

"You think so?" Lacey sniffled.

Jackie put her arm around Lacey. "Absolutely."

"I never thought I'd say this, but your fashion sense saved us this time." Sarah snickered.

"There. You see, girlfriend, being fashionable is an asset."

Sarah and Jackie giggled. The laughter felt good to Sarah and she relaxed.

"I'm still going to sleep inside," Lacey said. She pulled her sleeping bag around her and jogged toward the house.

Sarah heard the screen door slam behind her sister. She sighed and flopped down on her bed roll.

"That was too close for comfort," Sarah said.

"You can say that again, girlfriend."

"I need a soda." Sarah opened the cooler and pulled out a can, popped the top, and took a long drink. It fizzled down her parched throat, almost burning it with carbonation, but she continued to drink.

"Hey, hand me one of those."

Sarah pulled another can from the cooler and tossed it to her. Jackie opened her can and guzzled.

"Ah...that hit the spot," Jackie laughed, and then quickly grew serious. Her expression turned grave as she said, "Now we know Klonsky killed the Cat Lady."

Sarah frowned. "Yeah, but we don't know why, and we still have to prove it."

"We found his service pin at the crime scene with blood on it. Isn't that our proof?"

"Yeah, but I don't think it's going to be as easy as you think." Sarah gazed out at the night sky, deep in thought.

"Why not?"

"He's a cop. It will be our word against his."

"So?"

"Who are the police going to believe, us or one of their own?" Sarah sighed, suddenly bone tired.

Jackie set her pop down. "He's going to get away with it, isn't he?"

"No." Sarah shook her head. "We'll think of something."

"You know, I'm trying to figure out this D.W. guy."

"What do you mean?"

"Well, who is he? And did you see what he was wearing? Overalls and a baseball cap."

"So what? Oh wait, overalls aren't fashionable, right?" Sarah smirked.

"When have you seen a grown man wear overalls?" Jackie pulled her hair out of her rubber band and shook her curls. They looked like a sea urchin waving its arms in the ocean.

"Maybe he's a farmer," Sarah suggested. "This is a farm town, you know?"

"Farmers are in bed early during the summer. That's when they're the busiest. The guy's no farmer."

"So what do you make of it?" Sarah asked, chewing on her thumbnail.

"I don't know, I just think it's strange." Jackie's brow furrowed as she concentrated. "There's just something weird about him. Did you hear him talking?"

"Yeah, I did. He didn't seem smart."

"No, he didn't."

The girls sat together in a grim silence, drinking their soda. Sarah welcomed the quiet, after the tension of the last few hours it felt good.

"Hey, what about the detective?" she asked.

"Which one?"

"The one who investigated the kidnapping thirty years ago."

"Yeah," Jackie said, sitting up and grinning. "He could help us."

"Let's call him tomorrow and see if we can meet with him." Sarah took another swallow of her soda.

"Why don't we have Scott call him? He might know him, since his dad's the chief."

"Good idea. We'll have Lacey call Scott in the morning."

"I don't know about you, but I'm whipped," Jackie yawned.

"Yeah, me too." Sarah unzipped her sleeping bag, and crawled inside. "Night."

"Good night," Jackie mumbled.

Sarah snuggled deeper into her sleeping bag. She shivered as she thought about their narrow escape. Her muscles tensed as she replayed the events of the night in her head. Thinking back, she was sure Klonsky hadn't seen their faces.

All of a sudden, Sarah heard the sound of a car. It seemed to slow down and sit idle as if it were at a stop sign waiting for traffic to clear. Crawling out of her bed roll, she crept to the entrance of the tent. With a pounding heart, she pulled the flap back just far enough for her to look out. She glanced at Jackie and noticed she watched her with wide eyes.

Just as she was about to look at the car, the driver revved its engine and peeled out. The car's screaming tires destroyed the peaceful night. It left the bitter scent of burning rubber. Sarah sighed with relief when she no longer heard it. Without a word, she crawled back into her sleeping bag and snuggled closer to Jackie.

Chapter Eight

Sarah woke and found herself alone in the tent. Sitting up, she rubbed her eyes and shook her head. She felt groggy. She hadn't slept well after her run in with Klonsky. Stretching, Sarah glanced around the tent and spied the photo album in the corner. She grabbed it and started turning the pages.

She studied the pictures, hoping to understand the Cat Lady a little better. There were photos of David and his mother hugging. Another captured David and his first fish, according to the caption below, and both mother and son seemed proud. The next picture showed David and his mother throwing their heads back in laughter. Across from that picture was one showing both of them sleeping in a hammock, the Cat Lady on her side and David curled up next to her, his mother's arm thrown around him in a protective gesture. Looking at these pictures, Sarah realized David and his mother had been close.

Sarah caught another glimpse of what the Cat Lady had been like before the kidnapping. She saw a mother who loved her son without measure, unconditionally. A lump rose in her throat and tears welled in her eyes, as she imagined the pain the Cat Lady must have endured when her son disappeared. Wiping away her tears, she focused on her search for clues. As she turned the page, Sarah gasped. Shock ran through her body like a bolt of lightning.

"Holy cow," Sarah said out loud. She carried the album with her as she dashed from the tent. Opening the screen door, she found Lacey and Jackie in the kitchen making breakfast.

"Hey," Jackie greeted her.

"Hey, you guys, take a look at this." She opened the photo album and pointed at a picture of two young boys in baseball uniforms—she read the caption below. "'David and his friend LONNY KLONSKY before their first baseball game.'"

Jackie's eyes widened. "I don't believe it. Klonsky and David Fedewa were friends."

"Don't you find that odd?" Sarah asked.

"Very strange." Jackie nodded emphatically, sending her curls into a frenzy.

"These crimes are connected." Sarah pounded the table with her fist.

Jackie patted Sarah on the back. "You are a brainiac."

"What do you mean?" Lacey asked.

"Klonsky was involved in David's kidnapping, I just know it. And we found out last night he murdered the Cat Lady." Sarah's brow furrowed as she concentrated. "I just haven't figured the whole thing out yet."

"Don't you think Lonny was a little young to be kidnapping anyone? I mean he was only five or six," Jackie said and she paged through the photo album.

Sarah rubbed her forehead. "Good point. We need to talk to that detective."

"I'm already on it," Lacey said, taking pancakes off of the griddle. "I called Scott this morning and he's calling the detective now. He's retired, so he has lots of free time."

"Hey, Sarah, who took these pictures?" Jackie asked.

"I don't know. I wondered that, too."

"And why isn't David's dad in any of these?"

Sarah shook her head. "I have no idea." She turned to Lacey. "What time is it?"

"It's noon," Lacey answered as she glanced at the pineapple clock hanging above the sink.

"Man, I'm starving."

"Here, eat these." Lacey set a plate of pancakes in front of Sarah.

"Hey, what about mine?" Jackie protested.

"Don't get your undies in a bunch—there's more," Lacey giggled, and put a plate of pancakes in front of Jackie.

The shrill ring of the phone filled the room, making Sarah jump.

"I'll get it. It's probably Scott." Lacey picked up the phone and walked into the den.

Sarah and Jackie devoured their pancakes.

After a few minutes, Lacey walked back into the kitchen, placing the phone on the counter. "We've got a meeting with Detective Swift at two this afternoon."

"Cool beans!"

"I need a shower," Sarah declared as she finished her pancakes.

"Jackie, you can use my aunt and uncle's bathroom," Lacey said.

"All right." Jackie dashed off to grab her bag and take her shower.

Sarah pushed her plate away and stood up from the table. "Thanks, Lacey."

"No problem."

"I'll be done in fifteen."

"Okay."

Sarah hustled down the stairs. She quickly chose a pair of khaki shorts and a white tank top to wear to the interview. Jumping in the shower, she tingled with anticipation. It felt like her nerve endings had been turned up a notch, and she was super sensitive to everything. The Super Spies were getting closer to finding answers. She could feel it.

After the girls showered, they cleaned the kitchen, and then grabbed their bikes. They set off for the detective's house and Sarah could still feel the tingles. She was relieved Uncle Walt decided to go into the city for the day. He often left the girls to their own devices, which worked just fine for Sarah. She enjoyed her new freedom and knew she'd have a hard time giving it up when she returned home. Sarah sighed; living in the city had a lot of advantages, but nothing compared to the freedom of a small town. Pedaling faster, she turned her attention back to the task at hand.

"Did Scott tell you where he lives?" Sarah asked.

"He lives on Green Street. Three blocks from the Cat Lady's house," Lacey said.

The Super Spies glided through the streets of Harrisburg. Sarah was anxious to find the next piece of the Cat Lady puzzle. She felt the breeze on her skin as she pedaled. It lifted her hair off of her neck, and when she pushed down on her pedals her hair flapped in the wind like a pair of golden wings. Feeling the sun's toasty warmth on her skin, Sarah beamed. *We're getting closer.*

"Do you have everything?" Jackie asked.

"Yeah, it's all right here in my backpack." Sarah shifted the backpack so it fit better on her shoulder. "I left the photo album in our bedroom, though. It was just too bulky to carry."

"Just as long as you have the pin."

"Here we are," Lacey said as she glided to a stop in front of a beige house.

The detective's house stood in the middle of the block. It sat back from the road, giving the impression of a vast yard. On the porch sat an antique wooden bench.

Scott sat on the bench with his crutches to the side. A white bandage encased his foot.

"Hey, guys," Scott greeted.

"Hey," Lacey said with a shy smile.

"How's your foot?" Sarah asked.

"It's been better, that's for sure."

Sarah dropped her bike on the lawn and walked up to the porch. Jackie and Lacey followed her.

"What do you have in the folder?" Sarah asked, scuffing her sandal on the sidewalk.

"I've got a copy of the file on the Fedewa murder," Scott said, grinning broadly.

"How did you get that?" Lacey asked.

"I waited for my dad to fall asleep, and then I made a copy."

"You have a copier at home?" Lacey twirled her hair with her finger.

"No way. I made it with our fax machine." He beamed again and puffed up his chest.

Sarah smirked. *He looks like a rooster getting ready to crow.* "Can I read it?" she reached for the folder.

Scott pulled it away. "Let's wait until we're inside."

"All right," Sarah frowned.

"It's just...I'd feel more comfortable inside. Besides Detective Swift is a family friend. Our secrets are safe with him."

"Well, then, what are we waiting for?" Sarah bounded up the stairs and knocked on the door.

The tallest man Sarah had ever seen opened the door.

"You must be Detective Swift. I'm Sarah."

The detective dazzled Sarah with a wide smile. His deep tan contrasted with his snow-white hair. Wrinkles surrounded his bold blue eyes. He would have intimidated Sarah if his eyes hadn't been so kind. Winking at her, he scanned the rest of the teens in his yard.

His gaze rested on Scott. "Hey, champ. How are you?"

"I'm doing all right."

"Come on in, and let's see how I can help you." The retired detective opened the door wide, motioning for everyone to come inside. "Why don't we go sit out on the back porch? Does anyone want some lemonade?"

"Yeah," the Super Spies cried in unison.

"I can show you the way." Scott hobbled forward. "Follow me."

"I'll be back in just a few minutes." Detective Swift pivoted toward the kitchen.

The Super Spies followed Scott through a long hallway. The walls were covered with antique tools, and Sarah heard the loud tick-tock of a grandfather clock that stood in another room. It was a comforting sound, and she relaxed. She suddenly realized she had been nervous about meeting the detective.

They reached the screened-in porch. It ran the length of the house and was furnished with tasteful wicker furniture. The teenagers fanned out looking for seats. Scott sat on a wicker sofa standing against the inside wall. He propped his foot on a glass-topped coffee table. Lacey sat at the opposite end of the sofa. There was a rocker in the corner across from the couch with a matching end table. Next to the table was an oversized chair. Sarah rested there and Jackie plopped down on the floor, reserving the rocker for the detective.

Sarah suppressed a giggle when she caught Lacey casting shy glances toward Scott. *Lacey's in love.* A song breezed into her brain. *Scott and Lacey sitting in a tree, K-I-S-S-I-N-G. First comes love, then comes marriage, then comes Scott and Lacey pushing a baby carriage.* She averted her gaze so she wouldn't laugh. Just then, Detective Swift appeared, carrying a tray of lemonade.

After passing out the lemonade, the detective sat in the rocker and took a long drink, then set his glass down on the table next to him. "Well, Scott. Why don't you start from the beginning?"

"Okay." Scott licked his lips. "This all started when Lacey called me, asking if I had any info on the Cat Lady murder."

Lacey blushed and stared at her hands.

"The Cat Lady?"

"Ahh…Mrs. Fedewa."

"Okay, go on," Detective Swift gestured with his hand.

"The reason Lacey called him is because we stumbled on the Cat-er-Mrs. Fedewa's dead body," Sarah said, unable to control herself.

"That must have been a big shock."

"It was," Lacey chimed in, crossing her arms over her chest.

Sarah rolled her eyes. "Then later that night we heard two men down by the creek. They were talking about covering up a crime and getting rid of evidence."

"I see, and you think the two men were talking about the Fedewa murder?" Detective Swift reached for his glass and took another drink.

"They didn't say that, but it's the only crime in Harrisburg," Sarah said.

"I see. Do you have any idea who these two men are?"

"We know one of them is Officer Klonsky." Sarah balled up her fist and pounded her knee with it.

Detective Swift chuckled. "You think one of the murderers is a cop?"

"Yes, we do," Sarah glared at the detective and squared

her shoulders while sitting up straight in her seat.

"Sorry," he said, trying to control his laughter. The detective scratched his cheek, deep in thought. "But why would Klonsky murder Mrs. Fedewa?"

"We haven't figured that out yet," Sarah said, relaxing back against the seat cushion.

The detective placed his glass back on the table. "Do you have any evidence he did it?"

"When we went back to the Cat Lady's last night, we found this." Sarah pulled out the balled up tissue and thrust it at the detective.

"What is it?"

"It's some sort of lapel pin. It has blood on it, and we think the killer dropped it."

Detective Swift carefully opened the tissue and stared at the pin. "Do you know what this is?"

Sarah shook her head.

"It's a service pin. Patrolmen receive this after ten years of service. Where did you say you found this?" The detective leaned forward in his chair.

"In the Cat Lady's bedroom," Jackie said.

"How did you girls get in?"

"We climbed through a window." Jackie gulped some of her lemonade.

"Did you see any yellow crime scene tape?"

"Yeah, we were careful. We didn't rip it," Sarah said.

"Do you girls know it's against the law to remove evidence from a crime scene?" He gave Sarah a long level look and frowned.

"It's against the law?" Lacey gulped.

"Yes it is. It's called tampering with evidence."

"Could we go to jail?" Lacey whimpered.

"That's something for the chief to decide."

"I so don't look good in orange," Jackie groaned.

"That's the least of your worries." Detective Swift eyed the girls with an angry glare. "We're going have to report this to the police."

"We were trying to help," Sarah said.

Detective Swift shook his head. "This is a real mess."

"Wait a minute," Jackie frowned. "Lon Klonsky came back looking for it while we were there."

"Are you sure it was Klonsky?"

"Yes," Sarah said.

The detective stared at Sarah with a grim expression. He stood and walked into the kitchen. "I'm going to put this in a plastic bag."

"We kept it safe," Sarah said.

"I'm sure you did." Detective Swift strolled back out onto the porch. "But we don't want to contaminate it any further." He sighed as he sat back down. "You kids should have never gone back into the Fedewa home."

"We were looking for clues," Sarah explained.

"You girls aren't detectives, you've had no training. Do you realize you put your lives in danger?" Detective Swift gave Sarah a severe look.

Sarah stared down at her feet, unable to meet the Detective's gaze.

"We need to get this down to the police station."

"But, Klonsky's a cop," Sarah protested.

"You're going to have to tell the chief what you've done," the detective said, ignoring Sarah.

Sarah scowled at him. "We didn't have a choice. Klonsky's trying to blame us for the murder."

"What?"

"That's right," Jackie nodded. "This cop is trying to frame us."

"So you see?" Sarah leaned forward and made eye contact with the detective. "We didn't have any other choice but to find the murderer on our own."

Detective Swift leaned his elbows on his knees and put his face in his hands. "Are you sure about this?"

"Yes," Sarah gave him and emphatic nod.

"We have to get this to the chief," Detective Swift sighed.

"But Klonsky *is* the police," Sarah argued.

"I know," the retired detective sighed. "But what other choice do you kids have?"

Sarah opened her mouth to speak, but no words came out. The detective was right. They didn't have any other choice. She could only hope the chief would believe their story.

"Right now?" Scott squirmed.

"Yes. Now." The detective stood and walked toward the kitchen.

Sarah exhaled a heavy sigh, and then stood and followed him. The rest of the Super Spies fell into step behind her.

Climbing into the detective's Chevy, Sarah sat in the backseat next to Jackie and Lacey. Scott sat in front. Sarah chewed her thumbnail and stared at the back of Detective Swift's head, her mind going a million miles a minute. She felt the motion of the car as it backed up and then roared down the street.

On the way to the station questions paraded through Sarah's mind like a worn-out song. Would the chief believe them? What would he do when he found out they trampled through his crime scene? She groaned as the enormity of her predicament finally hit her like a ton of bricks.

Detective Swift pulled into the parking lot and parked the car. Leaning over the backseat he handed Sarah the plastic bag containing Klonsky's pin. "Take this to the chief, and tell him what you've done."

"You're not coming with us?" Scott asked, licking his lips.

"No, I think it would be better if they didn't know I was involved. I'll wait for you here."

"Why?" Sarah asked, as alarm bells went off in her head.

"Just in case things don't go well."

"What do you mean?" Sarah leaned forward to get a better look at the investigator.

"Well, I think it's better if Klonsky doesn't find out you kids have talked to me."

"Why is it better?"

He gave Sarah a patient smile. "Trust me, Sarah. I'm on your side. This is like playing poker. We're not going to show Klonsky all your cards, okay?"

"All right," Sarah said, grudgingly.

Trudging toward the station, Sarah chewed her thumbnail. She lagged behind the other Super Spies, thinking of a way out of their predicament.

Reaching the door, Scott pulled it open and walked into the reception area. The girls followed behind him. Sarah marched like she was on her way to the gallows. Each step felt heavier than the last. She turned her attention to an officer sitting at the front desk.

"Hello, kids. How can I help you?"

"Hi, Jim. We're here to see my dad. Is he around?" Scott asked.

"Let me check." The officer got on the phone and spoke into the receiver.

After a few minutes of conversation, he hung up the phone and said, "He's in his office. You know the way." He waved Scott down the hall.

"Thanks, Jim."

"Hey, how's your foot?"

"Better."

"Glad to hear it."

Scott turned the corner and started down a narrow, dimly lit hallway. Sarah and the rest of the Super Spies followed him. She felt the walls closing in on her and the hair on the back of her neck prickled. Her mouth was dry as cotton and her throat scratchy.

"Boy, I could sure use some water," she whispered to Jackie.

"No doubt."

Scott stopped in front of a door. He took a deep breath and then knocked.

From inside Sarah heard a voice yell, "Come in."

Scott opened the door. "Hi, Dad."

The Super Spies found the chief sitting at his desk, going through some files. He glanced at the teenagers. "Hi, son. What are you kids doing inside on such a beautiful day?"

"We have some things we need to tell you." Scott gave his dad a hesitant smile.

"I'm pretty busy here, son. Can't this wait until I get home tonight?"

"No, it can't."

"All right, I'm listening." He frowned.

Scott stepped through the door, and the rest of the group followed him. He waited until everyone was inside and then closed the door.

Sarah glanced around the office—it was just as cluttered as the desk. There were a few boxes on the floor with case numbers written on the sides. Awards hung on the walls, along with pictures of the chief with various people in the community. Turning her attention to Scott, she noticed he fumbled with his crutches. *He's stalling.*

"I'm not sure where to start," Scott said with a sheepish look.

"How about at the beginning?" Chief Johnson said as he organized his desk.

"Okay."

"This all started when we stumbled on Mrs. Fedewa's dead body," Sarah jumped in. Scott gave her a grateful smile.

"Go on," the chief said.

Sarah told him the whole story. He listened attentively and didn't interrupt once. She took a deep breath, and then told him about the pin they'd discovered in the Cat Lady's bedroom.

"You mean to tell me you trespassed on my crime scene?" Chief Johnson asked with a grave expression.

Sarah winced. "We didn't know it was against the law. We're sorry."

The chief stood and began pacing.

"This is the evidence we found." Sarah held the plastic bag up for the Chief.

He grabbed the bag with an angry swipe. "Let me see that."

He examined the pin through the plastic. "This is an officer's service pin. It could have been dropped by an officer investigating the crime." His face turned a dangerous shade of red.

"Yes, it could have been, but it wasn't," Sarah said in a voice that sounded braver than she felt.

"How do you know?"

"Because when we were there looking for clues, Klonsky came in looking for it," Sarah said while pointing at the plastic bag.

"He's investigating the murder. It's his job to look for clues at the crime scene," Chief Johnson scoffed.

"At night?"

The chief stopped, and studied Sarah. "Are you trying to tell me you think Klonsky murdered Mrs. Fedewa?"

"Yes." Sarah held her breath, hoping for a pat on the back.

"You kids don't know what you've done." The Chief clenched his fists.

"What do you mean? We just solved the murder for you."

"No, you didn't." The Chief shook his head and paced. "First of all, if this were evidence and you removed it from the crime scene, you would've created a chain of custody issue."

"I don't understand," Sarah frowned. She stared at the rest of the Super Spies. They appeared confused, just like her.

"You kids aren't police detectives. If this were evidence, which I highly doubt, you've opened the door for a defense attorney to exclude it from trial."

"But," Sarah sputtered.

"No buts. Never under any circumstances should you remove anything from a crime scene. It's against the law." The chief glared at Sarah. "You shouldn't even be at a crime scene."

"Klonsky murdered the Cat Lady, and he's going to get away with it." Sarah said as she glared back at the chief.

"Klonsky's the lead detective on this case. He probably lost this when he was investigating the crime."

"But we heard him down by the creek. He was talking about a crime," Sarah argued.

The chief shook his head.

"He was getting rid of the murder weapon," Jackie burst out.

"Did you actually see him with the murder weapon?" Chief Johnson asked.

"No, but I bet a million dollars that the knife we found in the creek is the knife that killed the Cat Lady," Sarah said.

"Where is the knife?" Jackie asked.

The chief sighed. "I sent it to the State Police. They're testing it to see if it was involved in some other crimes."

"So, it *was* the weapon used to kill the Cat Lady, wasn't it?" Sarah put her hands on her hips and stood in a defiant stance.

"Yes, it was." The chief rubbed his eyes as if he were suddenly tired.

"Does Klonsky know you have the murder weapon?"

"No, I haven't briefed him on that yet. I just found out this morning."

"Don't tell him," Sarah implored.

"You kids are wrong. Klonsky has been on the force for ten years! He's a highly decorated officer."

"What if we're right?" Sarah pleaded, her fists clenched into tight balls. "If we're right and you ignore our evidence, you'll be letting a killer go free."

"You're not right. There's no way that Klonsky did this."

"But what if I am right? Just think about it. Why would Klonsky investigate at night?"

"He may have been thinking about the case and decided to look at the crime scene again."

"At night?" Sarah asked, putting her hands on her hips in exasperation.

"Yes, at night."

Sarah sighed in frustration. She stood, pondering what the chief was telling her. "Would he go to the crime scene with someone who wasn't a police officer?"

"What do you mean?"

"Yeah," Jackie piped up. "He was at the crime scene with someone named D.W."

The chief stared at the kids. "He let this person walk through the crime scene?"

Sarah nodded. "Yes, he did, and he wasn't an officer."

"Well, I'll have to talk to him about that." The chief moved back behind his desk. He tapped his fingers on the files and gazed out the window, deep in thought.

Sarah's shoulders slumped in defeat. Tears of frustration filled her eyes. "He's going to get away with murder!"

"No one's getting away with anything."

Sarah could no longer hold back her tears. Crying for the Cat Lady and little David Fedewa, she also cried for herself and her friends.

After a few minutes, Sarah felt arms around her. She knew it was Jackie, because she could smell her flowery perfume. Sarah snuffled and dried her eyes. Taking several ragged breaths, she cleared her throat. "Maybe you could keep the fact that you found the murder weapon a secret."

"What?" Chief Johnson asked, turning to face the teens.

"If he's innocent, then there's no harm in keeping this information from him."

He shook his head. "This isn't a game."

"I'm not playing games. Just think about it. What if Klonsky is the murderer? Are you going to let him get away with it?"

"Of course not," the chief sputtered. "But there's no way Klonsky did this."

"You might be right, but what if you're not? Just give us some time to prove our case."

"I don't want you kids anywhere near this investigation." His face turned a deeper shade of red, and his eyes blazed with anger.

Sarah held up her hands in surrender. "We won't go near the Cat Lady's house. I promise."

"That's right." The chief leaned on his desk and pointed a finger at Sarah. "You kids stay away from my crime scene." His eyes blazed at Sarah again. "I could arrest you kids for what you've done! I should arrest you!"

"Please don't," Lacey pleaded.

"Why would you do that?" Sarah asked.

"Because you kids went through my crime scene and removed evidence from it. It's against the law! You should be punished!"

"What about Klonsky?"

"What about him?" the chief asked with an angry wave of his hand.

"Are you going to tell him about the murder weapon?"

"I don't want to hear any more about Klonsky. You kids get out of here, before I arrest you."

"But, Dad," Scott protested.

"Out!"

"Dad!"

"We'll be talking at home, young man," the chief said with a frosty glare.

The Super Spies scrambled out of the chief's office and trudged down the long corridor.

Sarah's shoulders sagged. "That didn't go so well."

"It sure didn't." Jackie frowned.

"Now, we are going to jail," Lacey whimpered.

Sarah rolled her eyes. "If he were going to arrest us, he would have done it by now."

Lacey let out a relieved sigh. "I hope you're right."

"You guys, we've got to do something." Sarah frowned and bit her lip.

"We can't let Klonsky get away with this!" Jackie said, raising her voice.

Just then Lon Klonsky loomed around the corner. He stood larger than life, glaring at the Super Spies as they met in the middle of the hall.

"What are you kids doing here?" He scowled.

"None of your beeswax." Sarah crossed her arms over her chest and stood defiantly in the middle of the hall. Lacey clutched the back of her shirt and held on for dear life. Sarah felt her trembling like a leaf in the wind.

Klonsky glowered at Sarah. Looming above her, his face wore a ferocious sneer. He probed her with his eyes looking for weaknesses, Sarah was sure. They were still red from their battle with the perfume last night. A small scar ran from his eyebrow to the corner of his eye. It gave him a more sinister appearance. *As if he needs any help in that department,* Sarah thought wryly.

"Are you kids in trouble again?" Klonsky's voice was an angry rumble.

"No." Sarah glared at him.

"Were you kids in the Fedewa home last night?"

"No," Sarah lied. She met his gaze with an unwavering stare, but her stomach twisted into an apprehensive knot.

"Then what are you doing here?"

"We're leaving."

Klonsky leaned down and whispered in a dangerous voice. "I'm going to put you behind bars for the murder of that old lady."

A flash of anger erupted in Sarah's belly, and she gave the crooked cop a withering look. *Not if we get you first.* Sarah bit her tongue to keep the words from escaping her mouth.

"You know we didn't do it," Sarah said, instead.

"I don't know that. Now, get out of here." Klonsky gave them a dismissive wave and proceeded down the hall.

"No problem," Jackie said, giving his back a mock salute.

"You got that right." Sarah glared at his back as he walked away, her hands clenched into angry fists.

"Let's get out of here," Lacey whimpered.

The Super Spies continued down the hall, but Sarah suddenly stopped and turned. "Hey Scott, is he going to see your dad?"

He paused, and peered down the hall. "Yeah, I think he is."

"Let's go listen." Sarah took a step toward the chief's office.

Scott grabbed her arm. "I've got a better idea. Let's go around to the front. We can listen through the windows."

"Were the windows open?" Lacey asked.

"I didn't notice, but I know my dad. He would choose fresh air over air conditioning any day of the week."

"Good idea, your dad's back will be facing the windows. He won't even see us," Sarah said.

The Super Spies hurried outside, turning the corner to the back of the building.

"Hey, the windows are open," Sarah said.

"We can hide between the bushes and the wall of the building," Jackie pointed out.

The teens scrambled to their hiding place. Sarah made sure everyone ducked down, hiding from anyone on the street and the police officers inside. She breathed a sigh of relief; the shrubs were green, thorn free, and thick with leaves.

The Super Spies listened as Klonsky and Chief Johnson talked about the annual police golf outing. Within minutes, the conversation turned toward the Cat Lady murder.

"So Lon, any new developments on the Fedewa case?"

"Not yet. The MO appears to be the same as the Messenger every way you look at it, though."

"Did you find any other clues?"

"We found vomit at the crime scene, and we think it belongs to the perp. I've sent it to the lab for testing."

Sarah's heart lurched in her chest and she put her arm around her sister. She felt Lacey tremble and squeezed her tight.

"Any suspects?"

"No, not yet, but I'm still suspicious of those kids we found at the crime scene."

"You think those girls were strong enough to stab Mrs. Fedewa?"

"There were three of them."

"You think those three girls are the Death Messenger?" the chief asked.

Sarah heard the shock in his voice.

"They're probably copycats."

"Yeah, but what was their motive?"

Sarah's blood boiled as she listened. Looking at Jackie, she saw her friend's eyes widen until they were as big as saucers. She dared a peek through the window. The chief sat behind his desk and Klonsky lounged in a chair facing him.

"I don't know yet," Klonsky frowned. "But they're from the city...lots of violence in the city."

Chief Johnson rubbed his neck and paused as if he were considering what Klonsky was saying. "Yeah...but let's stick to the evidence for now. Did you find the murder weapon yet?"

"No, sir."

"Well, I came across a new development."

"You did?" Klonsky asked. Sarah heard the surprise in his voice. She ducked down, hoping she wouldn't be discovered.

"Yep. Some kids went through our crime scene and found this," the chief said.

Sarah heard the sound of a drawer opening and the rustling sound of plastic rubbing against plastic. She knew the chief was showing Klonsky the service pin. Standing on tiptoes, she peeked inside. The policemen were focused on each other and didn't notice her peeping in the window.

"No kidding."

"Yeah."

"What is it?"

"A service pin."

"One of our service pins?" Klonsky sat back in his seat and crossed his legs.

"Yep," Chief Johnson said.

The chief seemed to study Klonsky as if he were trying to gauge his reaction. "These kids claim they found it at the crime scene. They said they were there at night and ran into you."

"Are you kidding me?" Klonsky sat up straight and shifted in his seat. He uncrossed his legs and bounced them as if he were suddenly full of nervous energy.

"No, I'm not kidding." Chief Johnson rubbed the back of his neck. He seemed to be waiting for Klonsky to tell his side of the story. When he didn't take the bait, the chief continued. "Yep, they said you were there with someone who wasn't a cop."

"Who was I supposedly with?" He rolled his eyes as if the mere mention of this incident was preposterous.

"Someone named D.W."

Sarah saw Klonsky turn white at the sound of the name. He shifted uneasily in his chair and cleared his throat. "I was not near the Fedewa home last night with someone named D.W."

"These kids say you were and they found this." The chief tossed the plastic bag containing the service pin toward Klonsky. "Does that look familiar to you?"

Klonsky caught the bag and studied the pin.

"It's your service pin," the chief said.

Klonsky squinted at the pin. "You're right, it is my pin. I probably dropped it when I walked the scene."

"Yeah, that's what I told those kids." Chief Johnson glanced down and rifled through some files on his desk. Faking a laugh, he opened a file as if he were studying it. He kept his face hidden from Klonsky, but Sarah witnessed the red stain of anger creeping up his neck and ears.

"I'm going to need that pin back," Chief Johnson said.

"Why?"

"Well, these kids trespassed on a crime scene, and I need it as evidence against them."

"Oh, yeah. Sure thing, boss." Klonsky stood and put the plastic bag down on the chief's desk.

Sarah quickly ducked down so she wouldn't be seen. After a few seconds, she raised her head and watched the scene before her. Klonsky was slouching in his chair again.

"By the way, who were the kids in the house last night?"

"Didn't get a good look at them, huh?" Chief Johnson tossed the question out into the air so casually he could have been asking Klonsky about the weather.

Klonsky caught himself. "Wh-What?" He sat up straight in his chair.

"Just checking," Chief Johnson joked. "I need you to make sure the Fedewa home is locked up tight."

"Sure, boss." Klonsky cleared his throat. "Who were the kids that got in?"

"I'm handling that. Don't worry about it." The chief gave Klonsky a dismissive wave of his hand.

"I just thought I could help you out with that. You know, bring them in for you." Klonsky gave the chief a winning smile.

Sarah gasped and then held her breath. Klonsky didn't get a good look at them last night! She prayed the chief wouldn't spill their names. Her heart hammered against her chest. Grabbing Jackie's hand, she squeezed tight. Jackie squeezed back.

Lacey let out a low whimper.

"Shhh," Sarah warned.

"I said I'm handling the situation." He began writing in a file on his desk. "You just worry about solving the Fedewa murder."

"Yes sir." Klonsky cleared his throat. "It wasn't those kids that just left, was it?"

"I said, don't worry about it. Just focus on the Fedewa murder."

"Sure, boss."

"Make sure the Fedewa house is locked up tight, Take

Wilson with you."

"Yes sir."

"I think we need to bring the State Police in on this one. I'm going to set up a task force, and I want you involved."

"You think we need the Staties?" Klonsky leaned forward in his chair and put his hands on his knees.

"Yes, I do."

"With all due respect, boss, I think we can handle this on our own."

"I don't agree, and I'm running the show. You're dismissed, Detective."

"Yes sir."

Klonsky stood and walked out the office door.

The Super Spies gaped at each other. Sarah put a warning finger to her lips.

"Shhhh."

She heard the chief pick up the phone.

"Watson, how are ya? It's Chief Johnson, I was wondering if you could do me a favor?"

There was a pause as if the chief were listening to Watson's response.

"I was wondering if you could get me the logs and the inventory on the Fedewa murder? Yeah, that's right. I need to take a look at it."

"Follow me," Scott whispered, gesturing with his hand.

The girls crept from their hiding place and followed Scott to the parking lot. Detective Swift had parked against a fence with the motor running. Piling in his car, the Super Spies all spoke at once.

"Hold on!" Detective Swift yelled above the din. "One person at a time."

Everyone was silent.

"Well, how did it go?" he asked.

Jackie made a face, pretending to vomit. "It was horrible."

"You can say that again," Sarah said.

"It was horrible."

Sarah giggled in spite of the dire circumstances.

"Well, what happened?"

"My dad didn't believe us." Scott scowled.

"Yeah, he gave Klonsky back his service pin," Jackie complained.

"Yeah, but he took it back, and he didn't tell Klonsky our names," Sarah beamed.

"So what?" Jackie said.

"Soooo, Klonsky still doesn't have proof it was us last night."

Jackie gave Sarah a satisfied smile. "Cool beans."

Sarah beamed at her friend. "And...He didn't tell Klonsky he found the murder weapon."

Lacey leaned forward and draped her arm over the front seat. She listened to Scott tell Detective Swift about the conversation between Klonsky and his father.

In the back seat, Jackie leaned closer to Sarah and asked, "What do we do now?"

"Well," Sarah said, leaning close to Jackie and whispering, "I've got an idea."

"Oh," Jackie winked at Sarah, and then mouthed the words. "What is it?"

"Later," Sarah whispered. She turned her attention to the front seat. "Detective Swift?"

"Yeah?"

"When the police don't have any evidence, but they know who the criminal is, what do they do?"

"Do you still think Klonsky murdered Mrs. Fedewa?"

Sarah ignored his question. "So, what do they do?"

"You still believe he killed Mrs. Fedewa?" Detective Swift glanced at Sarah in the rear view mirror as he spoke.

"Yeah."

"You mean if there's no evidence to link him to the murder?" His eyes darted to the road in front of him and then back at Sarah.

"Yeah."

"The only other way is to get him to confess."

Jackie stared at Sarah. "Uh-oh."

Sarah gave her a cocky smile.

Detective Swift drove the car into his driveway and turned off the engine. The old Chevy sputtered and knocked before it died. Everyone poured out of the vehicle and stretched.

"You kids should let the police handle the investigation from here," Detective Swift warned. He gave Sarah a long look. "This is a dangerous situation."

"You're right," Sarah agreed.

The retired detective studied Sarah; she gave him a disarming smile, and he turned his attention to Scott.

Sarah sighed. The detective seemed satisfied his warning was enough to keep her from investigating any further. She suppressed a smile. *Good thing he doesn't know me very well.* A giggle escaped her mouth, and she covered it with her hand. Suppressing another giggle, she took a jaunty step toward her bike. Jackie and Lacey followed her. They clustered together in the driveway, while Scott and the detective talked.

"You guys, we need to read the Cat Lady's diary," Sarah said. She sat astride her bike, ready to pedal away.

"Why?" Lacey asked.

"Because we have to find the link between her and Klonsky."

"I thought the link was her son David," Jackie said.

"It is, but there's more to it than that."

"What do you mean?" Lacey asked.

"Just because Klonsky and David were friends, doesn't explain why he murdered the Cat Lady," Sarah reasoned.

"That's why we need to read her diary, to find out about their friendship."

"Why don't we do that right now?" Jackie asked.

Lacey glanced at her watch. "It's dinnertime. Why don't we do that tomorrow?"

"How about tonight?" Sarah asked.

"I need to sleep," Jackie said, dropping her shoulders. "Two nights of sneaking out has me whipped."

Sarah sighed. "Okay, first thing tomorrow morning then."

"Cool beans."

After waving goodbye to Scott and Detective Swift, the Super Spies jumped on their bikes and rode off. At Walnut Street, Jackie split from the Cole girls and waved goodbye. Sarah watched her pedal away. The wind blew Jackie's hair back, revealing her stem-like neck and her muscles flexing as she gripped the handlebars and pushed down on her pedals.

At that moment, a wave of gratitude washed over Sarah. She was glad she had met Jackie. A truer friend couldn't be found, and she was thankful Jackie was the one helping her investigate the Cat Lady murder. The thought of the Cat Lady yanked Sarah back to reality. With her mind back on target, she increased her speed.

Lacey kept pace with Sarah as she flew toward home. Anxiety made Sarah pedal even faster. She had the sinking feeling time was running out for the Super Spies. A chilling question suddenly burst through to the surface of her mind, twisting her gut into a painful knot. *Now that Klonsky knew the chief was suspicious, what was his next move going to be?*

Chapter Nine

Sarah woke to the sound of Lily snoring. She nudged the dog with her leg, and Lily shifted in her sleep, and then grew quiet. Snuggling deeper under her covers, Sarah tried to fall back to sleep. Instead, thoughts of the previous night danced through her brain.

Since the Super Spies agreed to take a night off from the Cat Lady mystery, Sarah decided to spend her downtime watching her all-time favorite movie, "To Kill a Mockingbird." Curling up on the couch with a bowl of popcorn, she snuggled with Lily and pressed play on the remote. She loved the characters and never tired of watching them. Her favorite was Atticus Finch. She admired him because he wasn't afraid to stand up for what he believed, even when it made him a target.

Soon after the movie started, Lacey joined her on the couch. She too became engrossed in the movie, and the two sisters enjoyed the evening together. It surprised Sarah that Lacey liked the same movie. Sarah was even more surprised when they were able to get through an evening without arguing once. In her mind, Lacey was her polar opposite. Feeling a pang of guilt, Sarah realized she'd been so busy with her own life she hadn't spent much time with her sister. *Maybe we're not so different after all.*

After the movie, the two sisters talked about it. Sarah had read the book for a school assignment, and she told her sister "To Kill a Mockingbird" was the only book Harper Lee had published. Intrigued, Lacey wanted to borrow it. A new bond was forming between them, and Sarah liked it. *We don't go together like peanut butter and jelly, but maybe that was okay. Maybe relationships are as unique as people are, and maybe I shouldn't expect to have the same relationship with my sister as I do with Jackie.* Satisfied that she had just uncovered a universal truth about life, Sarah fell fast asleep.

She opened her eyes when she heard the bedroom door opening. She beamed, expecting to see her sister.

"Rise and shine, sleepyhead," Jackie crowed from the door. With a running start, she pounced on Sarah's bed. Lily dove to the floor with a yelp and rushed out the door.

Sarah protested the intrusion with a loud groan. "What are you doing here already?"

"You said to be here first thing in the morning. So here I am. You know me, I always do what I'm told," Jackie snickered.

Sarah snorted. "You picked a fine time to follow directions."

"Rise and shine." Jackie pulled on Sarah's quilt.

"Who let you in?"

"Lacey did."

"Where is she?"

"In the shower."

Sarah heard the whine of the blow dryer and tried to pull the quilt closer around her. "It's not even light out, yet."

"Come on. We've got to read the Cat Lady's diary."

Those words got Sarah moving. She gave Jackie a bleary-eyed scowl before she jumped out of bed. "Just let me take a quick shower, first."

"Sounds like a plan. I'll start breakfast." Jackie headed toward the door.

"You haven't eaten breakfast yet?"

Jackie stopped and pivoted toward Sarah. "No, I wanted to eat with you guys."

"Jack, you are definitely a freak." Sarah shook her head with a smile.

"My freakiness is what you like about me."

Sarah raised her right eyebrow and smirked at her friend. "Says who?"

"Says me." She gave herself an emphatic thump on the chest.

"You've had way too much sleep."

"So true. Now get in the shower, time's a'wastin'."

Sarah stumbled toward the bathroom while Jackie dashed off to make breakfast. She met Lacey in the hallway.

"You let the beanpole in, huh?"

"Yeah, I figured I'd let her wake you up. I didn't want to put my own life in danger," Lacey giggled.

Sarah laughed. "Jackie's making breakfast. You might want to supervise."

Lacey snorted. "No kidding."

After a quick shower Sarah joined the girls in the kitchen. She wanted to read the diary immediately, but the smell of pancakes caused her stomach to rumble.

"I'm starving!"

"They're almost done," Lacey said with a smile.

"I brought the diary to read after we eat."

"Cool beans," Jackie crowed.

Lacey set two plates of steaming pancakes on the table, and Jackie carried her own.

"Dig in."

Sarah scarfed down her breakfast, anxious to explore the secrets inside the Cat Lady's diary. The other two girls dug into their pancakes. For a while, the only noise in the kitchen was the sound of silverware scraping plates.

Sarah finished first and licked the syrup from her fork. She grabbed the diary and opened it. She searched the entries for anything that would put Klonsky behind bars.

"Where should we start?"

"How about the day David disappeared," Jackie suggested.

"Umm, let's see. Yeah, here it is." Sarah cleared her throat.

"'*August fifteenth. The police have searched everywhere for him. I am so worried that I can't think straight. Where could he be? I've racked my brain for hours and still come up with nothing. Doctor Mahoney wants to give me something to make me sleep. Who wants to sleep? Where is David?'*"

"So this entry was written after David disappeared," Lacey said.

"Yep."

"What happened the next day?" Jackie asked.

"I don't know, there's no other entries after that day." Sarah flipped through the pages of the diary.

"Okay, go back a couple of weeks. Let's find out what was going on in the family," Jackie suggested.

Sarah cleared her throat. "'*August first. I have finally worked up the courage to tell John we were through. He took it hard, but said he would not contact me again. I am grateful for his promise. However, I am afraid of his anger. It would devastate Russell if he knew, and it would tear my son apart. David is the reason there will be no divorce.'*"

"The Cat Lady was having an affair," Jackie said as her mouth formed a perfect O. "She must have been so unhappy."

Sarah nodded. "Yeah, she only stayed in the marriage because of David."

"Who's John?" Jackie asked.

Sarah wrinkled her brow. "Let's find out." She turned the pages of the journal back a couple of weeks. "July twentieth."

"*'John and I met at the cabin again. It is so peaceful there—I can forget my problems while I'm with him. I know we cannot go on like this much longer. For just awhile, though, it is a great escape.'*"

"Go back a few more weeks," Lacey instructed.

Sarah glanced at her sister, a smile spread across her face. She could tell Lacey was engrossed in the story.

"Okay." She turned the pages.

"*'July fifth. It is the day after the Fourth of July party. No one could tell. I feel like I have a large red A on my blouse. I hope Russell never finds out about this. He would never understand.'*"

"The poor Cat Lady," Lacey said as her eyes welled with tears.

"We still don't know who John is."

Sarah felt sorry for the Cat Lady stuck in an unhappy marriage. The only reason she stayed in the marriage was because of her son, and then he vanished. *Major bad karma for the Cat Lady.* Sarah felt tears prickle in her eyes, and she blinked rapidly to keep them at bay.

"Go further back," Jackie said.

"*'June second. I have finally given in to John's aggressive advances. Afterwards, I felt horribly guilty, but at the same time it felt so good to be wanted. Sadly, the good feelings overpowered my guilt. I am sure I will see him again. He has pursued me for months and has been quite relentless—he wants us to run away together. It is such a wonderful fantasy, to run away from problems, and then the reality of the situation comes crashing in. How will this effect Lonny and David I wonder? What would happen if they ever found out? The Klonskys have been such good friends, I fear this could destroy the friendship. Especially since I will never leave Russell. He is David's father, and I will not break up our family. In time, John will see I am right.'"*

"The Cat Lady had an affair with John Klonsky!" Sarah's jaw dropped.

"That must be Lonny's dad!" Jackie said.

Sarah's heart skipped a beat. An affair with John Klonsky! She knew they had found a huge piece of the puzzle. Staring at Jackie and Lacey, she saw a mixture of shock and dismay dance across their faces.

"I bet a million dollars John Klonsky didn't take it too well when the Cat Lady told him it was over," Sarah said. She still couldn't believe it. Shock ran through her body as she grappled with this new information. "This is the link we've been looking for."

Jackie stared at Sarah and nodded. "You're right."

"We have to find out everything we can about the Klonskys and the Fedewas."

"How are we going to do that?" Lacey asked.

"We have to go back to the library and talk to Mrs. Parker."

"Why?" Lacey asked.

"Where else are we going to get the information?" Sarah picked up her plate and silverware and put them in the dishwasher.

Jackie walked her plate over to the dishwasher and handed it to Sarah. "Let's get our bikes and go down there, right now."

Just then, Uncle Walt shuffled into the kitchen wearing his bathrobe. His wispy hair was standing on end. He stared at the girls with a bleary-eyed expression.

"Morning, girls."

"Morning," they responded.

"Boy, this is a surprise to see all of you up so early. Especially during summer vacation." He stopped in front of the refrigerator, opened the door, and pulled out a pitcher of juice. "What's gotten you girls out of bed so early?"

"We're being detectives," Sarah said with a wide smile.

"You don't say?" he asked, walking to the cupboard and searching for a glass.

"Yes, we're on our way to the library right now."

"Going to the library during summer vacation. I like the sound of that." He poured juice into a glass and took a sip.

"See ya, Uncle Walt."

"Bye."

The girls rushed out the door, and hopped on their bikes.

The day was already hot. Sarah stood on her pedals and glided through the streets of Harrisburg with the wind in her hair. She enjoyed the movement of the air as it cooled her skin. It felt wonderful, a nice reprieve from the suffocating humidity.

She heard the sounds of the neighborhood as it awoke. The slamming of screen doors and yells of children as they played outside before the day grew too tropical.

Taking in the neighborhood as she pedaled, Sarah couldn't help but think about the Cat Lady and her tragic life. *Did she have mornings like this? Watching David run through a sprinkler, or taking him for ice cream?* Tears filled her eyes. *What right did anyone have to take that away from her?*

A spark of anger started in her belly, then traveled through her body until it consumed her. She clenched her teeth to keep from screaming. Gripping her handlebars, Sarah took several deep breaths, hoping to calm the raging fire inside. *Klonsky.* The fire whispered.

The girls parked their bikes in the library bike rack just as Mrs. Parker unlocked the doors for the day.

"Perfect timing," Jackie giggled.

"Looks like we're the only ones here," Lacey said.

"Does that surprise you?" Jackie asked.

Sarah giggled in spite of the smoldering fire inside. "You'd be surprised, Jack, how many people come to the library during summer vacation."

"You mean you're not the only one?"

"Nope."

"I don't believe it."

"Believe it, beanpole."

Jackie and Lacey followed Sarah up the stairs. Her nerve endings prickled with anticipation; she knew they were close to putting all the pieces of the puzzle together. Opening the door, they found Mrs. Parker at her desk.

"Mrs. Parker," Sarah called out from the door.

"Shhh. You're supposed to be quiet in the library." Mrs. Parker put her hands on her hips in protest.

"There isn't anyone else here."

Mrs. Parker shook her head. "How can I help you girls?"

"We're still investigating the Fedewa murder," Sarah started.

"Yeah, and we need to find out everything we can about the Fedewas and the Klonskys," Jackie blurted out.

Mrs. Parker walked out from behind her desk. "Well, girls," she said taking a breath. "The Klonskys and the Fedewas were good friends. In fact, John Klonsky worked for Mr. Fedewa at his mill."

"Wow, are you sure?" Sarah asked, casting a sideways glance at Jackie. "What about Lonny and David?"

"They were close. In fact, they were inseparable."

"No kidding?"

"No kidding," Mrs. Parker nodded her head emphatically.

"Did you know Mrs. Fedewa and John Klonsky had an affair?" Jackie blurted out.

"Where did you girls hear that?"

"From a very reliable source," Jackie said, acting mysterious.

Sarah snorted. Jackie should be a movie star instead of a model.

"I don't know anything about that."

"We need to find out everything we can about the friendship between the two families," Sarah said.

"Yeah, please help us find Mrs. Fedewa's murderer. She was your friend," Lacey pleaded.

Mrs. Parker frowned. "I don't know anything about an affair between Frieda Fedewa and John Klonsky."

Sarah studied the librarian. "Are you sure?"

"Yes, I'm sure," she insisted, but gazed at the floor and sighed. "It wouldn't surprise me if it were true, though."

"Why do you say that?" Sarah asked.

Mrs. Parker sighed again. "Because, Russell worked all the time, and Frieda was lonely. Her only companion was her maid."

Jackie snapped her fingers. "The maid must have been the one taking all those pictures."

"What pictures?" Mrs. Parker asked.

"Ahh—nothing," Sarah said quickly, staring at Jackie with a 'shut your mouth' look. "I wonder if we could talk to her maid?"

"Her maid died about five years ago…You know, you need to talk to Scoop Davis." Mrs. Parker shook her index finger in the air.

"Who's Scoop Davis?" Sarah asked.

"He's the investigative reporter who covered the kidnapping for the paper. If anyone knows anything about the two families, it would be him."

"Does he still work for the paper?" Sarah felt a ray of hope and wiggled her tingling fingers.

"No, he's retired, but I do have his home phone and address. Would that help?"

"Yes!"

Mrs. Parker walked back to her desk and searched for a pen and paper, and then thumbed through her rolodex. She jotted down the information, and handed the paper to Sarah.

"Thanks," Sarah said.

"Yeah, thanks," Jackie chimed in.

Armed with the new lead, the girls left the library. They trotted down the stairs and stopped on the sidewalk. Sarah studied the paper and then pulled her cell phone out of her pocket.

"What are you doing?" Lacey asked.

"Calling Scoop Davis." Sarah held the phone to her ear. "It's ringing."

"Hello," a male voice answered.

"Hello, ah...my name is Sarah Cole," Sarah began, realizing she hadn't rehearsed what she was going to say.

"Yes?"

"Ah...my name is Sarah Cole, and my friends and I are investigating the Fedewa murder. We were wondering if we could ask you a few questions about the kidnapping thirty years ago."

"I'm retired," Scoop replied abruptly.

"I know, but we think there's a link between the two crimes, and Mrs. Parker told us you were the person to talk with about the kidnapping."

"Did you know the kidnapping has never been solved?"

"Yeah. We think there's a link, but we need more information to prove it."

"You said you think there's a connection between the two crimes?" Scoop asked. Sarah could tell he was interested.

"Yes, there is." Sarah scuffed the sidewalk with her sandal.

"What's the connection?"

"If we could meet... we could explain the whole thing to you." Sarah crossed her fingers and held them up in the air for Jackie and Lacey to see.

"Well, I was about to go fishing...but," Scoop wavered. "I guess I could meet you first. Where do you want to meet?"

"How about Hinkle's?" Sarah beamed and gave the girls the thumbs up.

"That would work."

"How about twenty minutes?"

"Make it fifteen."

"Sounds good. Um... what do you look like?"

Scoop's laugh boomed through the phone. Sarah winced and pulled it away from her ear for a second. "I'm a balding Santa minus the beard."

"Okay, there's three of us, and we're called the Super Spies."

"The Super Spies, eh? I'm certainly intrigued. I'll see you in fifteen."

Sarah disconnected the call. "He's meeting us at Hinkle's."

"Cool beans!"

"Let's get moving," Sarah said, taking a step forward. Lacey and Jackie fell in step beside her.

Reaching Hinkle's with minutes to spare, the girls sauntered in the door. Sarah welcomed the cold blast from the air conditioning. It dried the sweat on her brow and the back of her neck.

A hostess appeared and escorted them to a table. The girls ordered sodas while they waited for Scoop.

Looking around, Sarah noticed the restaurant wasn't busy. There were a few stragglers who were leisurely finishing their coffee or reading the local paper. It was the lull of inactivity just after the breakfast rush and right before the lunch crowd came bustling through the doors. The wait staff was gearing up, getting ready for the next surge of customers.

"You guys, we're so close to catching Klonsky," Sarah said, stirring her soda with her straw.

Jackie nodded. "We are."

"But how are we going to prove he did it?" Lacey asked.

"I've got an idea, but I just need a little more information before I can tell you," Sarah winked.

"Tell me now," Jackie demanded.

"Yeah, tell us now."

"I can't. I think Scoop Davis just walked in." Sarah pointed to a balding man who stood at the hostess stand.

Sarah saw the short, stocky man gaze around the restaurant. She caught his eye and gave him a tentative wave.

He ambled over. "The Super Spies, I presume?"

"That's us," Sarah said.

Scoop grabbed a chair and pulled it up to the booth.

Sarah studied him as he sat down; what was left of his hair was snow-white and curled around his ears. "You're right, you do look like Santa without the beard."

Scoop shook with laughter, his blue eyes watering.

He's even jolly like Santa. Sarah stifled a giggle tickling the back of her throat.

The waitress came by to take Scoop's order. He dried his eyes while he ordered a soda.

"So, how can I help you young detectives?" he asked.

"We think there's a link between the Cat Lady murder and the Fedewa kidnapping," Sarah said.

"Who's the Cat Lady?" Scoop stroked his chin.

"Mrs. Fedewa."

"I see…well, explain the connection to me." He turned toward Sarah and gave her his full attention.

Sarah took a deep breath, and told Scoop the whole story. She even told him about Chief Johnson and the threat of arrest.

Scoop chuckled. "Well, you girls certainly stepped into a hornets' nest."

The waitress brought Scoop his soda. He thanked her and waited until she was out of sight, and then pulled a flask from his pocket. Casting furtive glances around the restaurant, he poured a brownish liquid into his drink.

The smell of alcohol burned Sarah's nostrils. She wrinkled her nose and stared at Scoop, amazed by his brazen behavior. Sarah noticed the other girls gawked at him too.

Scoop glanced up and caught Sarah's eye; he seemed to notice he was the center of attention and winked. "A little hair of the dog." He chuckled and took a long drink from his straw, then smacked his lips appreciatively.

"It's not even noon," Sarah protested.

"Hazards of the profession." He took another long drink.

"But you're retired." Sarah crossed her arms over her chest and flashed a disgusted look at Scoop.

He cleared his throat. "Some habits die hard."

Sarah gazed at Jackie and shook her head.

"Now, let me get this straight. You found Klonsky's pin at the crime scene in a place where he shouldn't have lost it, right?"

"Right."

"It had blood on it, right?" He stared at Sarah.

"Yep."

"The chief told him you found it at the crime scene?"

"Yep."

"Well, there's only one conclusion we can draw from this," Scoop said in a matter of fact tone of voice.

"What's that?" Sarah held her breath.

"You girls are definitely up a creek without a paddle." He took another long drink of his cocktail and smacked his lips.

"What?" Sarah crossed her arms over her chest and glared at Scoop, annoyed with his unconcerned air and his drinking.

"Yeah, what about seeing him down by the creek and finding the knife?" Jackie asked.

"Number one, you didn't actually see him throw the knife in the water. There's no way to prove he was the one getting rid of it."

"Crap," Sarah groaned.

"Number two, finding his pin at the crime scene can be explained, and number three, what was Klonsky's motive?"

"The money. He was going to inherit the Cat Lady's money," Sarah blurted out.

Scoop gazed at her, pulling on his ear. "Why would Klonsky believe he was going to inherit the money?"

Sarah's spirits sank as she realized there was a flaw in her logic. "I just think it's strange David Fedewa was friends with Lonny Klonsky and he's kidnapped. Then thirty years later David's mother is murdered, and Lon Klonsky is investigating the crime." She refused to believe she was wrong.

"Yeah," Jackie nodded. "What about the fact he was friends with David…"

"Yeah," Sarah interrupted. "I bet a million dollars Klonsky was there at the pool when David disappeared."

Scoop opened a folder, and consulted some notes. He nodded. "Yes, Lonny was at the pool with David and his father."

Sarah slapped the table and pointed her finger at Scoop. "I bet Lonny Klonsky lured David away from the pool and helped kidnap him."

Scoop scratched his head. "Why would John Klonsky and his son want to kidnap David Fedewa?"

"Because John Klonsky had an affair with Mrs. Fedewa and knew she would never leave David's father."

"Yeah," Lacey said, finding her voice.

"Did you know John Klonsky and Frieda Fedewa had an

affair?" Sarah leaned forward and stared at Scoop.

Scoop sighed. "Yes, I found out about it when I investigated the kidnapping."

"Were the Klonskys questioned about the kidnapping?" Jackie asked.

Scoop consulted his notes. "They were, but as witnesses, not as suspects."

"You see!" Sarah raised her voice and gestured with her hands.

He snorted. "Hold on, now. It doesn't prove your theory."

"It doesn't disprove it either." Sarah gave Scoop an unwavering look. She knew her stubborn streak showed, but she didn't care. The puzzle pieces were beginning to fit.

Scoop chuckled. "Okay, okay. All I can do is give you information... you're going to draw your own conclusions."

"What other information do you have?" Jackie asked.

Scoop consulted his notes again. "Well, I know what happened when the Fedewas tried to give the money to the kidnappers."

"What happened?" Sarah sat straight up in the booth, her body rigid with anticipation.

"Let's see. First of all, Russell Fedewa wanted John Klonsky to go with him to the drop."

"The drop?"

"That's the place where the kidnappers meet the family to pick up the ransom."

"So, what happened at the drop?"

Scoop frowned. "It was a mess. Mr. Fedewa was jumped from behind, and they used chloroform to knock him out. They took the money and ran."

"What happened to John Klonsky?" Sarah asked.

"The same thing."

"Was he there when Mr. Fedewa woke up?" Sarah stared

at Scoop, trying to read his mind.

"I don't know. I just assumed that he was." Scoop took his straw out of his glass and set it on the table, then gulped his drink.

"Is Lonny's dad still around?"

Scoop shrugged. "I don't know, shortly after the kidnapping he moved with Lonny over to Bingham County. They bought some land way out in the boonies."

"Where's Mrs. Klonsky?" Jackie asked.

"She died from cancer when Lonny was three."

"What happened to Mr. Fedewa after the drop?" Sarah asked.

"Well, he felt responsible for his son being kidnapped, and then when the delivery failed… he fell into a depression."

"Where is he?" Sarah clenched her hands, anticipation ran through her body like a runaway train. *We're so close.*

"He left town, and drank himself to death. He died a few years after the kidnapping."

"What a horrible tragedy. I feel so sorry for the Cat Lady." Tears prickled in Sarah's eyes, and she blinked fast to stop them.

"I do too, but how are we going to get Klonsky?" Jackie asked.

"The only way we can." Sarah leaned back in her seat and looked away, deep in thought.

"Enlighten me, oh wise one." Jackie pretended to gag.

Sarah stuck her tongue out at her friend. "We're going to have to get a confession from him."

"Hold on, what are you talking about?" Scoop protested.

"That's the only way we can catch him." Sarah crossed her arms over her chest.

"This is a matter for the police to handle," Scoop said with a stern look.

"But Klonsky is the police. The Cat Lady isn't going to get justice, and he's going to get away with murder."

"Not only that, he's going to get the Cat Lady's money," Jackie added.

"The only way Klonsky would inherit the money is if Mrs. Fedewa left it to him in her will," Scoop argued.

"What if she didn't have a will, what happens then?" Sarah asked.

"Well, the estate would be divided among her heirs."

"The only heir was her son, right?" Sarah asked.

"Yeah, and he's presumed dead."

"But, a body was never found," Sarah said.

"Did you say there were two men down by the creek?" Scoop asked.

Sarah nodded, as questions danced in her mind.

"Did Lon ever call the other man by name?" Scoop leaned forward in his seat and gave Sarah an intent look.

"Not down by the creek, but at the Cat Lady's, he called him D.W.," Jackie jumped in.

"D.W.?"

Sarah stared at Scoop. She saw the glimmer in his eye. *Who was D.W.?*

"Yeah," Jackie said. "What does that mean?"

"I'm not sure, but I've got to do some research. I don't want you kids doing anything until you hear back from me." Scoop stood and pushed his chair back.

"Where are you going?" Sarah asked.

"I'm going to find out if Mrs. Fedewa had a will."

"How are you going to do that?"

"I have my ways." Scoop cracked a wide smile. "My name's Scoop Davis, I used to be a star reporter, you know." He leaned on the table and gave Sarah a warning look. "I don't want you kids doing anything until you hear from me."

"Okay," Sarah said with a smile.

Scoop paid for his drink and left the restaurant. Sarah watched him march through the door, his stride long and purposeful. *He's a man on a mission.*

"What should we do now?" Jackie asked, blowing bubbles in her soda.

"We need to get a confession from Klonsky," Sarah responded.

"You heard Scoop. He doesn't want us doing anything until we hear back from him," Lacey protested.

"So, Scoop isn't the boss of us," Sarah giggled.

"You so have a problem listening to authority figures, girlfriend."

Sarah snickered. "Scoop's not an authority figure, he's just an adult."

The girls burst out laughing.

"How in the world are we going to get a confession?" Jackie asked.

"Let's head back to the tent and brainstorm," Sarah suggested.

The Super Spies paid for their sodas and left. They strolled out of the restaurant into the muggy heat. Walking back to their bikes, Sarah obsessed about Klonsky. How were we going to get a confession from him? Mounting their bikes, they began to wind their way home. No answer came to her, just more questions. *Who is D.W.? Why would he want the Cat Lady dead?*

Chapter Ten

Sarah glided into the front yard, standing on her pedals, the wind fanning her hair out behind her. Slowing when she hit the grass, she waved to Uncle Walt as he pulled out of the driveway. Jackie and Lacey stopped on the sidewalk before the driveway and waited for him to back out into the street.

Sarah dropped her bike as the other two girls coasted up beside her. "Man, riding made me thirsty all over again. I'm going to grab a soda." She bounded up the steps and opened the front door. "Does anyone else want one?"

"I do," Jackie said, dropping her bike.

Lacey nodded.

"Okay, I'll meet you guys at the tent." Sarah dashed inside and met an excited Lily. She ruffled the dog's fur affectionately and then grabbed the sodas. On the spur of the moment, she ran down to her bedroom and snatched the Cat Lady's photo album.

"There might be more clues in here," she muttered to Lily, who trotted behind her.

After making sure Lily was secured in the house, Sarah jogged out to the tent. She found Lacey and Jackie inside rolling the sleeping bags out of the way.

Sarah handed out the drinks, and then popped the top on hers. She took a long swallow. "That hits the spot."

"It sure does," Jackie nodded.

The air in the tent felt hot and sticky. Sarah opened the flap and secured it, hoping some fresh air would circulate. While she did that, Jackie and Lacey finished moving the bed rolls to the side of the tent.

The girls sat in a circle in the middle of their shelter, their knees touching. Sarah's stomach clenched. Her intuition told her answers lay inside the faded pages of the photo album. She just had to look. Opening the book, her brow furrowed as she concentrated.

"What are you looking for?" Lacey asked.

"I feel like we missed something the first time we went through it."

Sarah fell silent as she turned the page. On the next page they found a portrait of young David Fedewa. The picture was taken when he was just a year old. A photographer had done an excellent job catching his joyous expression. *He looks like his mother,* Sarah realized with a start. It surprised Sarah how much he resembled the Cat Lady. David had the same dark hair and expressive brown eyes. Written below the picture in his mother's neat handwriting was the caption, *David William Fedewa, one-year-old.*

"Look how happy he is," Lacey said with a catch in her voice.

"Yeah, this whole thing makes me so sad." Sarah's eyes filled with tears.

"Can you imagine being five years old and someone taking you away from your parents?" Jackie asked.

"This is such a tragedy." Sarah wiped a tear from her eye. "Imagine never seeing your parents again." She put the photo album down on her sleeping bag and took a couple of deep breaths. "I've been thinking about the confession."

"Uh-oh, that can only mean trouble," Jackie giggled.

Sarah gave Jackie her raised eyebrow smirk. "Well...the chief didn't mention the murder weapon to Klonsky. So, I thought we could send him an e-mail."

"Why?" Lacey asked.

Sarah stifled a groan. "To tell him we found the murder weapon."

"Why?" Lacey picked nervously at her shoe.

"So he'll meet with us."

"Why do you want to meet with him?" Lacey squirmed.

"To tape his confession." Sarah exchanged a look with Jackie and sighed.

"We don't know his e-mail address," Jackie said.

"Yeah...but Scott might." Sarah glanced at Lacey.

"Yeah, he might." Lacey frowned and fidgeted with her shoelace.

"Okay, so we send him an e-mail and tell him to meet us," Sarah continued.

"Can't we just call him on the phone?"

Sarah shook her head. "We don't have his phone number. Besides he's a cop, he's not going to say anything over the phone."

"What are we going to say in the e-mail?" Jackie asked.

"We're going to tell him we know about the knife he threw in the creek."

"What makes you think he's going to believe us?" Jackie asked.

Sarah sighed. "Because, we're going to tell him we saw him throw it in the water."

"So?" Jackie stared at Sarah, her expression suggesting Sarah was on her way to crazy town.

She rolled her eyes. "So-o, the only people who know about him throwing it in the creek are him and D.W."

"Yeah?"

"So, he'll know we're telling the truth."

Jackie nodded. "Okay...but we don't want him to know the e-mail came from us."

"True." Sarah took another drink of her soda. "I think we can open a junk e-mail account and only use it this one time."

"All right, but won't he be able to trace it back to the computer we use?" Jackie asked as she attempted to tame her curls.

"You're right, so we're going to use one of the library's computers."

"Oh man, that's the third time I'll be at the library during summer vacation. My reputation is ruined." Jackie flung herself down on the tent floor with her arm draped across her forehead.

"It's a small price to pay to avenge the Cat Lady's death." Sarah cracked a wide grin. "Besides, you might just want to take a look at a book. It's amazing what you can learn."

"So-o lame."

Sarah rolled her eyes. "Let's call Scott and see if he can get Klonsky's e-mail address."

"I'll do it," Lacey volunteered. She scrambled from the tent.

"I hope this works." Jackie frowned.

"Yeah, me too."

"My reputation is on the line."

"Don't worry, you can go shopping after this is all over," Sarah said, giving Jackie a playful nudge.

"I'm just kidding about that." Jackie gave Sarah an affectionate smile, and then sat up. "I'm just worried something might go wrong."

"Like what?"

Jackie shrugged her shoulders. "I don't know."

Sarah sighed. "Jack, we have to do something." She started pushing grains of sand on the floor into a pile.

"I know. I know. It's just risky."

"True, but it's even more risky to do nothing. Remember, Klonsky's trying to frame us," Sarah said as she brushed her hair away from her face. "Besides, if we don't avenge the Cat Lady, who will?"

"You've got a point," Jackie said with a solemn nod.

Just then Lacey scurried back into the tent. "Scott wants to meet us at the library in twenty minutes."

"We just left the library." Jackie flung herself back down on the floor.

"Do you want to send the e-mail or not?" Lacey frowned.

"Definitely." Sarah nodded.

"Another trip to the library?" Jackie groused.

Sarah snorted. "Let's go. It's worth it just to see the beanpole walk in there again."

For the second time that day, the Super Spies hopped on their bikes and pedaled their way to the library.

As Sarah pumped her pedals, she enjoyed the wind in her hair. It cooled her skin, drying the sweat on her neck and brow. All of a sudden, she realized she hadn't thought about her friends at home since she met Jackie. It dawned on her she didn't miss them as much as she thought she would. She thought back to last summer, about the soccer games and pool parties she had attended. They seemed so important then. Now, the only thing Sarah could think about was catching Klonsky. Her stomach fluttered; she knew once they sent the e-mail it was the beginning of the end.

The flutter in Sarah's stomach suddenly twisted into a tight knot. Her emotions were all mixed up, a combination of anticipation and fear. One minute she was flying high at the thought of actually solving the Cat Lady mystery. The next minute she felt the huge weight of dread when she realized the Super Spies must face Klonsky one more time.

Sarah coasted to a stop in front of the library, banishing the crooked cop from her mind. She decided to focus only on the task at hand. Jackie and Lacey drifted to a stop beside her. The girls found Scott sitting on the steps. They parked their bikes in the rack and walked over to him.

"Hey," Scott said.

"Hey," the girls responded in unison.

"So tell me this crazy plan of yours, Sarah."

Sarah took a deep breath and explained the e-mail plan.

"Where are we going to meet Klonsky?" Scott asked.

"I don't know." Sarah scratched her head. "Probably down by the creek."

Jackie nodded. "Yeah, we know the area like the back of our hand."

"We'll just meet at the willow tree."

"I don't know." Scott pursed his lips and shook his head. "Are you sure he doesn't know about the knife, already?"

Sarah frowned and gnawed on her thumbnail. "I don't know. Where are they in the investigation?"

"Last I heard they were bringing in the Staties."

"Man, we need to find out if Klonsky knows about the knife," Sarah said.

"Let me call my dad. I'll try to get the info out of him." Scott pulled his cell phone out his pocket.

"Try walking over there, you'll probably get better reception." Lacey pointed to the corner.

Scott walked to the corner with his phone against his ear. After a few minutes, he frowned and began talking. Sarah noticed he wore regular tennis shoes and walked with a slight limp.

A pickup truck rumbled past, and Sarah watched Scott plug his opposite ear as he listened to the person on the phone. She realized they were lucky; traffic was light at this time of day.

Sarah paced, waiting for Scott to get off the phone. It all boiled down to this one detail. If the chief told Klonsky he had the murder weapon, all was lost. He would get away with murder. Scott closed his phone and walked back, wearing an uneasy expression.

"Well?" Sarah asked.

"It's weird...I didn't talk to my dad, because he's out of the office, but I talked to Officer Wilson," Scott began.

"And?"

"I don't think they know about the knife."

"Why do you say that?" Sarah stopped pacing and studied Scott.

"Because Klonsky brought in a knife today, saying he thinks it's the murder weapon."

Sarah took a few steps toward Scott. "Who brought in a knife, saying it was the murder weapon?"

"Klonsky."

"That is totally weird."

"What does that mean?" Jackie asked.

Scott shook his head. "It's just strange because my dad ran tests on the knife we found, and it came up one hundred percent positive it was the murder weapon."

Sarah started pacing again. She gazed down at the ground as she walked, deep in thought. "So, Klonsky doesn't know they have the real murder weapon."

Scott shook his head. "It doesn't look like it."

"How can they tell which knife killed the Cat Lady?" Lacey asked.

Scott walked over and sat next to Lacey on the steps. "Remember when you found the knife in the creek?"

Sarah stopped pacing and listened to Scott.

"Do you remember the tip was missing?"

"Yeah," Lacey nodded.

"Well, this is kinda gross, but the knife broke when Klonsky stabbed the Cat Lady."

"So…what does that mean?"

Scott cracked a smile. "Well, the tip was found when they did the autopsy on the Cat Lady, and it fits the knife we found perfectly."

"Wow."

"Okay this is great news," Sarah said.

"It is?" Lacey asked.

"Yeah, that means our plan will work," Jackie said.

"So what are we going to say in the e-mail?" Scott stood and brushed his shorts off.

"We're going to say we know he killed the Cat Lady, and we found the murder weapon down by the creek." Sarah brushed a wayward strand of hair out of her face.

"Yeah, we'll have to ask for money," Jackie blurted out.

"Why?" Lacey asked.

"Because, why wouldn't we just take the knife to the police? We have to have a reason for returning it to him." Sarah went back to chewing her thumbnail.

"Oh."

"So we'll tell him we want ten thousand dollars," Sarah continued.

"Okay, do you guys have an e-mail address to send this from?" Scott asked.

"We were going to set up a junk e-mail address just for this reason," Sarah said.

"I've already got one. We can use mine," Scott replied.

"Do you think that's a good idea?" Sarah asked.

"Maybe not." Scott sighed. "It can probably be traced because I've already used it once before."

"Okay, we'll just create a new one while we're here. Let's do it.'" Sarah turned toward the stairs.

"Are you sure this is the only way to get a confession?" Lacey gulped.

"Absolutely."

Sarah climbed the stairs to the library. She chewed on her thumbnail as she climbed, and the knot in her stomach twisted tighter. *This is it.* There was no turning back once they sent the e-mail. Looking back at the rest of the Super Spies, Sarah noticed Jackie pulling on her curls and Lacey fidgeting with the hem of her T-shirt.

"I don't know about this," Lacey whimpered.

"You don't have to come with us." Sarah put her arm around her sister.

"I know, but I don't want to miss anything, either."

"Just take it one step at a time." Sarah gave her a squeeze.

Pulling open the doors to the library, Sarah squared her shoulders and took a deep breath, before walking into the dimly lit entryway. The rest of the Super Spies walked behind her.

Giving Mrs. Parker a wave, Sarah walked past the librarian's desk. The familiar scent of old pages filled her nostrils. It was a dry musty smell, but it calmed Sarah's nerves.

"The computers are usually in the back," she said.

"Only you would know that information," Jackie giggled.

"Careful, you might learn something."

"Not if I can help it."

Sarah felt grateful for the easy banter she shared with her friend. She realized their jokes were their way of dealing with the stress of catching the crooked cop. Her pulse quickened as she walked to the computer area. The Super Spies were alone in the library, and the silence seemed deafening to Sarah.

"At least we don't have to wait in line," Jackie said as the group stepped up to the computer.

"Scott, do you know Klonsky's e-mail address?" Sarah asked.

"I know my dad's. It's his name with Harrisburg Police.gov after it. I'm guessing Klonsky's is the same."

"Let's find out." She motioned toward the chair in front of the computer. "Scott, do you want to send the message?"

"Sure." Scott sat down at the computer and began typing. "Okay, I've got a new junk e-mail account all set up. Now let's see if Klonsky's e-mail address will work." He typed the address. The rest of the Super Spies watched over his shoulder. Sarah held her breath. *Work, work ,work,* she prayed.

"Yes! It works!" Scott exclaimed

"How do you know?" Lacey asked as she pushed her way to Scott's side.

"Well, if it's a bad address the software will highlight it in red," Scott answered with a shy smile.

"Okay, now type our message," Sarah urged, rolling her eyes.

Scott typed the message and then stopped. "Do you want me to say who it's from?"

Sarah shook her head reading the message over his shoulder.

We saw you get rid of the knife that killed Mrs. Fedewa. You threw it in the creek and we found it. If you don't give us ten thousand dollars we'll go to the police. Meet us at the big willow tree by the creek at midnight tonight to make the exchange.

"No, we don't want him to know who's sending it," Sarah said.

Scott pressed the SEND button. The message disappeared. No turning back now. Sarah sighed as her stomach fluttered again. "Okay, guys, let's go down to the creek and make up the rest of our plan."

"I'm hungry," Lacey said.

"Yeah, me too," Jackie piped up.

Sarah groaned. "All right, let's eat at Hinkle's, and then head to the creek."

After a quick lunch of Hinkle's famous cheeseburgers and fries, the Super Spies made their way to the willow tree.

When they reached the cul-de-sac, they dropped their bikes in the long grass and walked to their secret meeting place. Sarah noticed the sun had burned away the humidity of the day, leaving dry heat.

Walking under the willow branches felt cool, and Sarah took a deep breath, enjoying the shade. She relaxed and plopped down on the ground. The others followed her lead.

"Okay, guys," Sarah began. "I've been thinking on the way over here... and when we meet Klonsky, I don't think we should all come out."

"Yeah," Lacey agreed.

Sarah saw relief wash over her face. "I think it should be just me and Jackie."

"Yeah, Lacey and I can hide and tape everything. Where should we hide?" Scott asked.

Jackie glanced around. "Why don't you hide behind the willow tree branches?"

"How about up in the tree?" Sarah suggested.

"Up in the tree?" Lacey squirmed.

"Great idea," Scott said. "We won't be seen by Klonsky and his partner."

Sarah noticed Lacey grimacing, but she didn't say anything.

"You think D.W. will come with him?" Sarah pulled at the grass beside her.

Scott nodded. "Yeah, I don't think he'll come alone."

"You're probably right," Sarah nodded.

"What if something goes wrong?" Lacey asked.

"We can run and jump in the creek. It worked before."

Jackie grimaced. "Yeah, let's just hope Klonsky can't run."

"Are you worried?" Sarah asked, tossing a handful of grass at her.

"Kind of, he's a big guy." Jackie threw a twig at Sarah.

"Yeah, but he's hurt, remember the fence?" Sarah sounded more confident than she felt. She chewed on a blade of grass, giving her thumbnail a reprieve.

"Hey, I could bring some of my dad's pepper spray if you want," Scott offered.

Sarah's spirits lifted. "Awesome idea."

"Okay, so we get him talking and get his confession." Jackie placed her hands on her hips. "What are we going to do after that?"

"What do you mean?" Sarah turned toward Jackie.

"Hello, we don't have a knife to give him." Jackie gestured wildly with her hands.

Sarah shoulders sagged. "Holy cow! I totally forgot about that. What are we going to do?"

"I've got a hunting knife that's just like the one you guys found in the creek. I'll bring it," Scott said.

"You actually have a knife like that?" Lacey asked.

Scott nodded. "Yeah, they're pretty common."

"Thanks, Scott." Sarah beamed at him as relief coursed through her body. "Beanpole, I'm so glad you thought of that." She laughed and shook her head.

"Hey, what can I say?" Jackie held out her hands and gave the thumbs up sign.

"All right, let's meet down here around eleven, so we can all get into position," Sarah said.

"Cool beans."

"Tonight's the night, guys." Sarah sighed and noticed the tension on their faces. "Everything's going like clockwork."

She stood and brushed off her shorts. Everyone chuckled politely at the use of Klonsky's catch phrase. Using his words tasted bitter in her mouth. It didn't get the laugh Sarah expected.

Sarah walked from beneath the green canopy. Visions of the Cat Lady killer in cuffs filled her mind, and a shiver ran down her spine.

"Tonight is for the Cat Lady," Sarah said.

Jackie nodded. "For the Cat Lady."

"For the Cat Lady," Lacey and Scott said in unison as they walked.

Reaching her bike, Sarah lifted it upright and studied her friends. She noticed their grim expressions. They were scared, just like she was. Suddenly, anger at Klonsky ran through her body like a raging river. *How dare he put us in such a horrible position. Who does he think he is?* Her anger at the crooked cop dimmed her fear.

"I can't wait to see Klonsky behind bars for the rest of his life," Sarah said through clenched teeth.

"Me either," Lacey said with a grimace.

"And when he starts whining about being innocent...," Sarah began.

"That's when we're going to say, 'That's what all the criminals say,'" Lacey finished.

Sarah burst into laughter, surprised by Lacey's sudden spunkiness. The tension eased from her body, and she took a deep breath. Smiling at her friends, she climbed on her bike. "Knuckle bump."

The Super Spies mounted their bikes and knuckle bumped. Sarah wondered for the first time, *what happens if Klonsky wins? What happens to her friends?* A chill ran down her spine and a lump of fear formed in her throat. She took a deep breath and expelled these thoughts from her mind. *He won't win, he just won't.*

Sarah swallowed the huge lump and managed to smile before turning her bike toward home. She began pedaling and struggled to keep her bike upright in the long grass. Reaching the pavement, pedaling grew easier.

Tonight's the night. Sarah clenched her teeth and gripped her handlebars so tight her knuckles turned white. *This is the most dangerous thing I've ever done. I hope it's not the last.*

Chapter Eleven

Sarah paused and listened for a moment before she crawled through her bedroom window. It was quarter to eleven, and she was mentally preparing for the night's adventure. She tried to get Lacey to stay behind, but her sister was determined to see this through. *She's getting braver.* Sarah smirked at this thought, but quickly frowned when she thought about what they planned to do.

"We can go. The coast is clear," Sarah whispered. She leapt to the ground and scrambled out of Lacey's way. Her pulse raced as she waited for her sister in a crouched position. It seemed to take her forever.

"Come on. Jump," Sarah whispered.

Lacey whimpered, and then plummeted to the ground below. She rolled into Sarah, knocking her over.

Sarah stifled a groan and righted herself. "We should've just camped out."

Lacey stood and brushed off her sweat pants. "Yep, that's definitely easier than sneaking out of the window."

Sarah ignored Lacey's reproachful tone. "We'll plan better next time."

"I hope there won't be a next time."

"Let's go." Sarah led the way and Lacey followed close on her heels.

The moon hid behind the clouds, throwing mysterious shadows everywhere. Sarah's anxiety intensified. Her palms were already slick with sweat, and they hadn't even left the back yard. *I hope everything turns out all right tonight,* Sarah thought to herself as she took several deep breaths.

Lacey grabbed her by the back of the shirt and held on tight. "I'm getting the weebeejeebees."

Reaching behind her, Sarah squeezed Lacey's trembling hands. "Yeah, it's creepy tonight."

Sarah's pulse quickened as the girls made their way to the cul-de-sac. A slight breeze rustled the leaves on the trees. Stopping when they reached the path, Sarah took a deep breath and let it out slowly. She peered into the gloom, looking for anything out of place.

Searching through the murkiness, Sarah spied the willow tree. It stood on the bank of the creek, casting a forbidden shadow. In the dark it loomed like a wicked troll waiting to gobble the girls up.

The first flare of fear ignited in the pit of Sarah's stomach. "It's now or never."

Lacey twisted Sarah's shirt tighter in her hand. "I'm right behind you."

The Cole girls crept toward the hardwood. Sarah felt the hair on the back of her neck rise and a chill ran down her spine.

"Whoo! Whoo!" Sarah called.

"Whoo! Whoo!"

Sarah walked through the branches, feeling slight stings as they slapped her face. She found Jackie first, her eyes wide with fright, and her face sickly pale. Scott stood next to her, his breathing shallow, and his face shiny with sweat. Suddenly, dread coursed through Sarah's body.

"Hey, guys." Sarah frowned.

"Hello, girls," a deep voice snapped in the darkness.

The flare of fear in Sarah's belly exploded into a raging fire.

Klonsky loomed from the shadows. "I got your message."

Silence. Sarah saw the mixture of fear and frustration on Scott and Jackie's faces.

D.W. followed Klonsky out of the shadows and stared at the teens.

Jackie finally found her voice. "I guess we weren't the only ones who decided to come early."

"That's right," Klonsky said, and took a menacing step toward Sarah, brandishing a gun. "Now where's the knife?"

Sarah stared at the gun and gulped. Thoughts ran through her brain like a runaway train. She couldn't seem to focus on any one thought, just the gun pointed at her.

"Where's the knife?"

"In a safe place," Sarah stalled, trying to pull her thoughts together.

"You don't have it with you?" Klonsky glared.

"No. Do you think I'm that stupid?" Sarah returned his glare with a defiant stare of her own. *Avenge the Cat Lady! Don't let him see you're scared!* She stood in a rebellious stance, hiding her trembling hands. Her heart pounded her chest with a ferocious beat. "You can't shoot us, because then you'll never find the knife." Sarah's mind still spun a mile a minute, trying to come up with a get away plan.

"If you're dead, it won't matter."

"We gave it to some friends and told them if they don't hear from us within an hour to call the police," Sarah lied.

"You're lying."

"Maybe, maybe not." Sarah shrugged. "Are you willing to take that chance?"

"Shut your pie hole," Klonsky snapped.

He stood in a threatening pose, but Sarah could tell by the look on his face that her words had hit home.

"What are we gonna do now?" D.W. whined.

"We'll get the knife, and then we'll take 'em back to the crime scene." Klonsky stared at Sarah. "Where's the knife?"

"I'll take you to the knife," Sarah lied. "But first I want to hear why you killed the Cat Lady."

"That's none of your concern," Klonsky said, with an arrogant sneer.

"So you admit you did it?" Sarah pounced.

"Don't try and get smart with me, kid. I'm a cop."

"What are we gonna do?" D.W. whined.

The crooked cop sighed. "Let's take them back to the house. I'll think of a plan by the time we get there." He pushed Sarah forward. "Move it."

Sarah walked with Lacey behind D.W.; Jackie and Scott followed them, and Klonsky took up the rear. Walking forward, Sarah racked her brain for an escape route. *We outnumber them,* the small but brave voice inside her head whispered.

"I've got to pee," Sarah complained.

"Too bad," Klonsky snapped with a dismissive wave of his hand.

Sarah ground her teeth in frustration. She continued to walk. Lacey whimpered beside her.

Sarah put her arm around her. "It's going to be okay." *I wonder if I could get the pepper spray from Scott.*

Suddenly, Sarah pulled Lacey to the ground, tripping Jackie and Scott. They fell in a heap, all tangled up.

"Pepper spray," Sarah muttered to Scott. As if by magic, the can appeared in her hand.

"Get up!" Klonsky yelled.

Sarah concealed the pepper spray in her pocket. She prayed the crooked cop and his partner wouldn't notice the bulge.

"Quit screwing around," Klonsky said. His voice sounded like the growl of an angry dog.

The Super Spies picked themselves up and brushed the leaves and grass from their clothes.

Klonsky pushed Sarah and Lacey ahead of him. "Keep moving."

Stumbling forward, panic gnawed at Sarah's self-control. She knew if they were going to escape they would have to go now. Putting her arm around Lacey as if to comfort her, Sarah whispered, "Run." Using her body as a shield, she pointed toward the field, which lay in the opposite direction of the creek.

Lacey sniffled and wiped her nose on the hem of her T-shirt. She made eye contact with Sarah and nodded. In a flash, Lacey took off through the field and Sarah ran toward the creek.

"Run!" Jackie screamed.

Sarah glanced over her shoulder and saw Jackie and Scott running in different directions. The criminals reacted by taking up the chase.

Sarah heard Klonsky behind her, his footfalls hammering the earth, heavy and unrelenting. She imagined the land trembling every time one of his feet pounded the ground. Her heart raced. The creek was her only hope. If she made it to the water, she would escape. A relieved sob burst through her lips when she heard the bubbling waters of the stream. Lengthening her stride, she prepared to jump. *I'm almost there.*

All of a sudden, Sarah was yanked to the ground. Agony erupted around her head. Klonsky had grabbed her hair and pulled. She was airborne. Landing, she screamed in anguish as all of her weight came down on the pepper spray can in her pocket. Pain radiated from her head, but it was no match for the misery shooting down her leg.

Sarah moaned. Panting, she opened tear-filled eyes and saw Klonsky looming above her. She saw fire in his eyes, and anger radiated from every pore. He grabbed her by the arm and pulled her to a standing position.

"Don't try that again," he said in a menacing voice.

Sarah shrank away from him, her knees buckling from the pain. She almost went down, but Klonsky supported her by pulling her against him. Smelling his after-shave sickened her; it was a heavy musky scent.

She pushed away from him. "I can walk on my own."

"Just don't try anything funny," he said with a sneer. "Remember, I have a gun."

She took several unsteady steps. Her leg throbbed, and her head pounded. Sucking air through clenched teeth, Sarah willed herself not to puke.

"This way," Lon commanded. He pushed her forward.

She stumbled. Righting herself, she took several deep breaths and swallowed the wave of saliva flooding her mouth. Nausea wormed its way up her throat again. Fighting it, she kept it down. She limped forward, searching for an escape route.

Out of the darkness, D.W. appeared with Scott in tow. "Lon, I gots this one, but the girl got away."

Scott tottered forward. His injured foot hindered him, causing his capture.

Klonsky grumbled in frustration. "Let's get these two back to the house." He pushed Sarah and Scott ahead.

"What are we gonna do?" D.W. whimpered. "Those other two are going straight to da cops."

"Stop your sniveling. I'll think of something. Don't forget I'm a cop."

The criminals and the captives walked in silence. Sarah gazed down as she limped—praying Klonsky would stumble, or fall—anything that would allow her to get away.

"Lon, what are we gonna do?"

"Shut your pie hole. I'll think of something."

Klonsky's mood darkened as they walked. He kept nudging Sarah from behind with the gun.

Sarah sighed and dared an angry glare at the crooked cop. Escape was not an option at this point. She searched the darkness looking for signs of Jackie and Lacey, hoping they were following close behind. Her efforts were not rewarded, and she knew their prospects were grim.

After what seemed like hours, they reached the Cat Lady's house. Sarah stopped and stared at the infamous dwelling.

It stood dark and uninviting. The sagging porch seemed to match Klonsky's sinister sneer. Sarah shivered as she stared at the dark windows; she felt like the house was alive and watching them. It seemed to be laughing at her predicament, and Sarah's heart skipped a beat.

All the stories about the Cat Lady flew through her head. She wished they were true; then the Cat Lady's spirit would swoop down and save them with her magical powers.

Sarah watched as Klonsky pulled something out of his pocket and walked up the steps. She realized it was a key when she heard the door unlock.

"Get in here," he said, his voice nothing more than a growl.

Sarah and Scott hobbled up the front steps. Her heart raced as she tried to think of a get-away-plan.

"Hurry up!" Klonsky demanded as he pulled a flashlight from his back pocket and turned it on.

Picking up her pace, Sarah limped through the front door, and stopped. Scott followed behind her. Sarah noticed the usual cat smell in the air and quickly pulled the collar of her shirt over her nose and mouth.

"Where are we supposed to sit?" she asked.

She surveyed the room, looking at the stacks of newspapers. Tears of compassion for the Cat Lady filled her eyes, and she forgot about the pain in her leg. Sarah knew she would heal, but the Cat Lady never got that chance.

"Right here," Lon said as he brought in two chairs from the kitchen. He dropped them right in front of the bloodstain, glaring at the teenagers.

Staring at the dark stain, Sarah fought back her tears as rage coursed through her body. She clenched her teeth and moved her chair away from the bloodstain. Scott followed suit. Sarah eased into her chair, struggling to keep her swirling emotions under control.

"He's such a creep," she whispered, feeling powerless. She was no match for Klonsky, and this made her even angrier.

Scott glanced around, and then gave Sarah a slight nod.

It was eerie sitting in the living room with the Cat Lady killers, and Sarah shivered in spite of the heat. She'd never been in this situation before, and it finally dawned on her she was in over her head. Sarah's shoulders slumped as she realized even if she had been injury-free she would still have difficulty escaping.

The hammering in her head subsided, but her leg still throbbed. A groan burst through her lips as she moved it. Heat seemed to radiate from her injury and another wave of nausea engulfed her. Beads of sweat broke out on her forehead, but she managed to keep the nausea down. Sarah pressed her lips together, keeping any more sounds from escaping.

Wiping the sweat from her brow, Sarah peered at Klonsky from beneath her hand. He disappeared from view behind a stack of papers, but she could hear him pacing in front of the staircase leading to the second floor.

"Lon," D.W. whimpered, walking over to where Lon marched.

"Shut up, and let me think."

He continued pacing,growing more agitated with each step.

"Where's the knife?" the crooked cop demanded, stopping with an abrupt turn and peering over a stack of papers.

"Relax, I've got it right here in my backpack," Scott said.

"Give it to me." He walked around the papers and stood in front of the teens with his hand out.

Scott reached into his backpack and pulled out the knife. It was bundled in a rag. Klonsky snatched it from Scott's hand, and quickly opened the bundle to see for himself.

Scott and Sarah exchanged an apprehensive glance.

"All right." Klonsky expelled a deep breath.

"What now, Lon?" D.W. asked.

"Shut up, and let me think."

Sarah exhaled a deep sigh of relief. *The substitute knife worked. It bought us some time.* She sighed a second time, as the room grew silent and the tension thicker with each passing minute. Klonsky took up his pacing again, clenching and unclenching his hands.

Sarah tried to come up with a get-away plan, but the cop's constant movement was driving her insane. Sweat formed on Sarah's brow again. She didn't want to draw Klonsky's attention, so she let it run down her face. It dropped off the end of her chin onto her T-shirt.

She glanced at Scott. His face was shiny with sweat, and his eyes were wide with fear.

"What should we do?" Sarah whispered

"I don't know," Scott answered.

"Lon," D.W. whined.

"I know, I know."

"We gots the knife…let's just get out of here."

Leaving would be good. Sarah exchanged a glance with Scott and gave him a nudge.

"We can't do that, these kids know too much."

Those words shot sparks of anxiety through Sarah's system. Her stomach clenched as a new fire of fear ignited. She squirmed in her seat. Scott put his hand on her arm and squeezed, telling her to be still.

"What do you mean?" D.W. asked.

"We'll have to make it look like an accident."

"What?" D.W. protested. "What about the other two kids?"

"We'll be all right. I'm a cop. It'll be my word against theirs."

Sarah heard the arrogance in his voice, and the bile rose in her throat. What a total creep. She swallowed, refusing to puke.

"I don't know," D.W. wavered.

"Do you have a better plan?" Klonsky asked.

"No."

"All right, then it's settled. We'll make it look like an accident." The crooked cop strode around the stack of newspapers and stood before the teenagers, glaring at them.

Following, D.W. asked, "How are we gonna do that?"

Klonsky sighed. "I haven't got that far yet."

"Lon, they's just kids."

"I know, but they should've kept their noses out of my business." He pivoted and walked back toward the kitchen.

Fear wrapped its fingers around Sarah's throat, making it hard to breathe. Her heart pounded in her chest. The sound seemed deafening, and she couldn't believe no one else heard it.

"We've got to do something," she whispered to Scott.

"Pepper spray," Scott whispered back.

Sarah let out a strangled sob. Pepper spray! She'd forgotten about the can in her pocket.

"Hey," she called out. "What are you going to do with us?"

Sarah heard Klonsky's heavy steps, and then he loomed over the stacks of paper glaring at the teens. "Shut your pie hole."

He disappeared into the kitchen. Sarah could hear him rummaging around in the drawers.

"Make him come all the way in here," Scott whispered.

Sarah nodded. She put her hand in her pocket and grasped the can of pepper spray.

"Why'd ya do it, Klonsky?" Sarah yelled out. Her voice sounded high and tinny. She cleared her throat and took several deep breaths. She could hear him coming into the living room. The house shook with his thundering steps. "Why'd you kill poor Mrs. Fedewa? What'd she ever do to you?"

Klonsky stood directly in front of her, glowering from above. She could hear D.W. shuffling into the room behind him.

"Lon, what'd she say?"

"Nothing." He glared at Sarah. "Shut your pie hole."

"Why'd you do it? Murder Mrs. Fedewa?"

"Lon...that lady...she has the same last name as me," D.W. said.

D.W. is David Fedewa!

"Uh...uh...uh," Lon stammered, turning toward his partner.

Now! Sarah made her move. She sprang from her seat, bringing the pepper spray forward as she stepped toward the crooked cop. At the sound of her movement, Lon spun toward Sarah, and she sprayed the pepper spray in his face.

Stumbling back, he fell to his knees. His hands balled into fists, and rubbed his swelling eyes. He coughed uncontrollably, and tears streamed down his cheeks.

"Lon, are ya all right?" D.W. wailed.

"I can't see! Stop those kids!"

Screaming, Sarah rushed D.W., pushing him aside. He stumbled against a stack of newspapers. Scott lurched from his chair and slammed into D.W., knocking him to the floor. D.W. grabbed Scott's injured foot.

Sarah grabbed Scott's arm and tried to pull him toward the door.

"Stop them!" Klonsky bellowed.

"I gots his foot!" D.W. shrieked.

Scott pulled a can of pepper spray from his pocket and sprayed it in D.W.'s face. The criminal howled in pain and fell to the floor.

Sarah pulled Scott to the door. The teens burst through it, just as two police cruisers pulled up in front of the house.

"You kids get back behind the cruisers!" one officer yelled as he bolted toward the front door. Sarah and Scott hobbled behind the cruisers, both of them gasping for breath.

"I'm glad that's over," Sarah gulped. She clenched her hands to stop them from shaking. She took huge gulps of air and kneeled down on the ground, hoping she wouldn't faint.

"Me too." Scott's voice sounded thin and far away.

"I didn't know you had another can of pepper spray."

"I brought two. I always have a backup, just in case," Scott said with a weak smile and leaned against the cruiser.

"We didn't get our confession, though."

"Yeah." Scott scuffed the pavement with his shoe. "I wonder how the cops knew we were here?"

"I'm guessing Jackie and Lacey had something to do with that." Sarah stood and leaned against the cruiser next to Scott. She clasped her hands in front of her to stop the trembling.

"Where are they?"

Sarah and Scott searched the crowd forming around the cruisers. The flashing lights and sirens had disturbed their sleep, and they were gathered together, wearing pajamas and robes. She spotted Lacey and Jackie across the street behind the oak tree in front of the church. Smiling, she hobbled across the street with Scott behind her.

"Thanks for calling the cops," Sarah said with a quivering lip.

"We called Detective Swift. He called the cops," Jackie said. She gave Sarah a quick squeeze. Sarah gave her a grateful smile. Her body relaxed, and tears of relief welled up in her eyes.

Just then another police cruiser pulled up in front of the Cat Lady's home. The door opened and out stepped Chief Johnson.

"There's my dad," Scott said, shoving his hands in his pockets.

"Yep. I bet we're in a lot of trouble, aren't we?" Sarah asked.

"You could say that."

"Yeah, especially since our plan didn't work." Tears of frustration filled Sarah's eyes. She wiped them away, and Jackie gave her another squeeze. Grateful for her support, Sarah leaned on Jackie and sighed. "I think I figured out who Klonsky's sidekick is."

Jackie twisted toward Sarah, her eyes widening. "Who is he?"

Before Sarah could reply Chief Johnson spotted them from across the street.

"You kids get over here!"

Sarah gulped. "Here we go."

She reluctantly stepped out from behind the oak tree. The rest of the Super Spies followed her. They walked to the cruiser Chief Johnson had just exited.

"What do you kids think you're doing?"

"Dad, just listen to us."

Chief Johnson glared at each individual Super Spy. His blazing gaze rested on Sarah the longest. She squirmed and avoided eye contact.

"I certainly will. You kids are coming downtown and giving us statements." His frosty tone contrasted with the fire blazing in his eyes.

"Chief Johnson, Lon Klonsky murdered the Cat Lady," Sarah blurted out.

"Yeah, where's your proof? Do you have a confession?" His sarcastic tone cut Sarah to the quick.

Her shoulders slumped. "No."

"I didn't think so. You kids certainly made a mess of things. Now get in the car, you're going downtown."

Just then, Klonsky and D.W. were led to another cruiser. The criminals wore handcuffs, and their eyes were swollen shut. Neither one could see. They stumbled down the stairs and would have fallen if not for the support of the officers.

"Chief? Are you there?" Klonsky asked.

Sarah noticed he resembled a schoolyard bully, rather than a raging hulk that committed a brutal murder.

"I'm here, Lon."

"Chief, I'm innocent. I didn't do anything."

"That's what all the criminals say." Sarah spat the words at him, her body rigid with anger.

The chief turned toward the kids and gave Sarah a menacing look. "Get. In. The. Car."

"Chief, tell them to take the cuffs off."

Spinning back toward Klonsky, he said, "Can't do that, Lon. You're riding in the back. Consider this an education."

Sarah and the Super Spies climbed into the back of the cruiser, and for the third time that treacherous summer, they were on their way to the police station.

Chapter Twelve

Sarah groaned as the cruiser pulled up to the station. She stared out at the parking lot and saw the lone parking light high on its pole. It cast an eerie shadow on the area below. Watching the bugs flit around the bulb, she compared herself to the insects, contemplating them as they flew close to the heat, and then fluttered away when it grew too hot. *I feel like a moth attracted to a flame.* Going after Klonsky was a risk, she knew, but staying quiet would have been worse. Weighing the consequences in her mind, Sarah knew without a doubt she made the right choice. Taking a deep breath and squaring her shoulders, she focused on the officer in the front seat.

She watched as he shut off the engine, and opened his door. "Okay, kids, out of the car." He climbed out and opened the back door.

"Are you going to call our parents?" Jackie asked.

"Of course I am."

Sarah sighed. "We're in deep on this one."

Jackie nodded. "Yep."

"Come on kids, you know the routine," the policeman

said.

They followed him into the station and were once again escorted to separate interrogation rooms.

Sarah sat in the metal folding chair and let out a weary sigh. She remembered the frigid air from her first visit and welcomed the chill after the humid stuffiness of the Cat Lady's house. At least in here, she could breathe. Waiting for her uncle, she knew this time he wouldn't be so understanding.

The door opened, and Officer Wilson poked his head in. "Would you like something to drink before your parents get here?"

Sarah gave him a grateful smile and nodded. He left, and then returned a few seconds later with a soda.

Grabbing it, Sarah popped the top and guzzled. "Ahh, that hit the spot." Her voice echoed in the empty room, emphasizing her aloneness. She felt small in a big world.

Another fifteen minutes went by before the door opened and Sarah's uncle stormed in, his wispy hair standing on end. Chief Johnson and Officer Wilson followed him. *Uh-oh.* Sarah gulped as she realized she would be facing all three men at the same time.

"Uncle Walt," Sarah faked a smile.

"What in the world have you girls gotten yourselves into?" he demanded.

Sarah groaned. "It's a long story."

"I'm all ears." He pulled the chair out, and sat down crossing his arms over his chest.

There was no sympathy from him this time. The officers sat across from Sarah. She noticed they were waiting for her uncle to stop talking.

"I am not happy. It's three o'clock in the morning."

Sarah sighed and gazed down at the floor. "I know, I know."

Officer Wilson cleared his throat. "Okay, Sarah, why don't you tell us what happened tonight?"

"Spit it out," her uncle demanded.

Sarah told them the whole story. While she spilled her guts, Officer Wilson jotted furiously on his notepad. Uncle Walt, on the other hand, tugged on his hair so often she was positive he'd be bald by the time the story was finished. Chief Johnson hovered in the back of the room pacing and listening.

"That's how we ended up at the Cat Lady's," Sarah finished.

Officer Wilson leaned in. "Did you ever get a confession?"

Sarah shook her head. "When I tried, I was told it was none of my concern."

"Almost." Officer Wilson glanced at the Chief.

Sarah didn't dare look at her uncle; she could tell by his agitated tugging, he was still angry.

"You mean to tell me you crawled through your bedroom window in the middle of the night?" Uncle Walt asked.

Sarah's shoulders sagged. *Here we go.* "Yes."

"You even had the gall to drag your sister into this?"

"She wanted to come. She could've stayed home."

"So, that's how you see it?" Uncle Walt muttered.

Looking at him out of the corner of her eye, Sarah noticed his face was a frightening shade of red. He stood and paced. Her shoulders slumped, and she sighed again. She had escaped his rage for the moment.

Officer Wilson glanced at her uncle before continuing. "At any time did Officer Klonsky say anything to incriminate himself?"

"What do you mean incriminate himself?"

"Did he say anything that only the killer would know?"

"No, but doesn't he incriminate himself just by showing up at the creek?" Sarah held her hands up at her sides with her palms facing up. "He did ask us for the knife."

"Good question." Officer Wilson winked. "It's circumstantial evidence. We'll have to see how the district attorney feels about it."

The chief and her uncle finally sat down. Sarah felt outnumbered as she faced the men. She slumped even further in her chair, wishing she could melt into the floor and get away.

"I know who Klonsky's sidekick is," Sarah blurted out. She sat straighter in her chair, and suddenly she beamed. *Maybe, just maybe, I can get out of this mess.*

"What?" Chief Johnson asked.

"I know who Klonsky's sidekick is," Sarah repeated, sitting even straighter and leaning forward.

"Well, who is he?"

"He's David Fedewa," Sarah proclaimed.

The three men stared at her in stunned silence.

"For real," Sarah raised her eyebrows and nodded.

"What are you talking about?" Chief Johnson demanded.

"How do you know?" Officer Wilson asked.

"Because, when I asked Lon why he murdered Mrs. Fedewa, D.W. said she had the same last name as him."

The chief lunged out of his chair, sending it to the floor. "Oh my…Are you sure?" He stared at Sarah as he returned his chair to an upright position.

"Yes, I'm sure."

The chief strode to the door, pulled it open, and stormed down the hall. Sarah heard him holler at one of the detectives to hurry up with the prints.

Officer Wilson winked at Sarah. "When we get the prints back, we'll know for sure."

"It's him. That's why Klonsky killed the Cat Lady."

"I'm not following you." Officer Wilson frowned.

Sarah sighed, but stopped herself from rolling her eyes.

"Klonsky killed the Cat Lady to get David's inheritance."

"So, you think the Klonskys had David this whole time?" her uncle asked.

"Yeah, I think they kidnapped David and hid him."

"We have to prove it," Officer Wilson said.

"Why don't you ask David?"

Officer Wilson gave Sarah a rueful smile. "If it were only that simple."

"I see it on detective shows all the time," Sarah insisted. "They're always getting one of the partners to turn on the other."

"Yes, they are." Officer Wilson glanced at his notes briefly, and then rose from his chair. "I'm going to go talk with the chief. I'll be right back." He stepped out of the room, leaving Sarah alone with her uncle.

Sarah avoided eye contact with him, and the tension between the two of them grew thicker by the minute.

"You are grounded for the rest of your life." Uncle Walt bristled, both of his hands were tugging at his hair. Sarah cast a furtive glance down to the floor, looking for tufts of snow-white hair.

She expelled a weary sigh. "No time off for good behavior?"

"No!" he thundered. "Sneaking out of the house at night, and that's just the beginning. You broke the law!"

Sarah knew he was just warming up. "We didn't know we were breaking the law."

"Oh, come on, Sarah."

"For real, we didn't. Besides we didn't have a choice. Klonsky was trying to frame us for the Cat Lady's murder."

"Breaking the law is never an option." He pivoted toward Sarah and gave her a long look. "You trespassed on a crime scene and removed evidence. That's a felony! That's jail time!" He glared at her, his face red with anger.

The image of an overripe tomato danced through Sarah's mind. She remembered the tomatoes the Wykowski boys had hurled at the Cat Lady's house. Her uncle's face resembled one of those tomatoes just before it hit the old woman's siding. Sarah averted her gaze as a bubble of nervous laughter rose in her throat. *I always laugh at the worst times.*

She took a couple of deep breaths and faced her uncle again. "Yes we did, but we didn't have any other choice. Klonsky was going to send us to jail."

"Why didn't you come to me or go to someone in authority?"

"We did!" Sarah exclaimed. "The chief didn't believe us."

"You went to the chief with what you found?" Uncle Walt asked, leaning forward in his chair.

"Yeah, we found Klonsky's service pin. The chief said he probably lost it during the investigation."

"You could've come to me, Sarah; I would have helped you."

"I didn't think of that at the time." Sarah stared down at her hands and sighed. There was silence in the room as her uncle digested what she told him.

"So, the only way the police can prove their case is by getting David to talk."

Sarah noticed her uncle sounded calmer, and his hands were trying to tame his wild hair.

"Yeah, our 'get the confession plan' didn't work." Sarah sighed again, relieved she had diverted her uncle's focus for a little while.

She closed her eyes and laid her head on the table. Visions of the Cat Lady paraded through her mind. A deep sorrow coursed through her veins for the misunderstood woman and the tragedy she endured at the hands of the Klonsky family. The unfairness of it all hit Sarah like a punch in the stomach.

Officer Wilson walked back into the room, interrupting her thoughts. "We did get a hit on those prints, and it's a good probability he is David Fedewa."

"No kidding?" Uncle Walt asked.

Officer Wilson nodded. "No kidding. Now all we have to do is get him talking. We're going to start the interrogations right away."

"Did you have his prints on file, or something?" Sarah asked.

"Yes, when he was kidnapped the detectives lifted prints from his bedroom, for identification purposes."

"I want to hear David's interview," Sarah blurted out.

"You could probably sit in the observation area," Officer Wilson said. He glanced at her uncle.

Uncle Walt sighed. "We'll talk about it. You're still grounded, though."

"I know." Sarah clasped her hands again and laid her head down on them, turning away from her uncle. She concealed the smile bursting out on her face. Just by the way Uncle Walt answered the last question, she knew she was going to hear the police question David Fedewa. Sarah needed answers to the questions haunting her. She needed to know the whole story.

Chief Johnson walked back into the room. "All right, young lady, tomorrow morning I want you down here to discuss your punishment."

"Punishment?" Sarah asked, raising her head.

"She'll be here," her uncle answered, giving Sarah a stern look.

"Not only did you girls break the law, you put your lives in danger," the chief ranted.

Sarah sighed. "I know, I know."

"You meddled in a police investigation."

"We were trying to help." Sarah sat up straight in her chair and put her hands in her lap.

"Did I ask for your help?"

"No, but if we didn't help Klonsky would've gotten away with everything."

"You don't know that."

"Admit it, we helped put Klonsky away," Sarah pushed.

"It's not over yet, young lady. Don't go counting your chickens before they're hatched." The chief opened the door to leave the room. "Now, go home, and get some sleep."

"Chief, she wants to listen to the interviews," Officer Wilson said.

Chief Johnson looked up at the ceiling and sighed. "I guess it's all right. We're starting in a few minutes."

Sarah's heart leapt at the reprieve. *Good, I'm sick of these lectures.*

Uncle Walt stood, and Sarah followed his lead. Officer Wilson escorted them to the lobby.

Lacey and her aunt were waiting for them. Sarah saw the angry look on Aunt June's face, and she knew this wasn't over by a long shot. She squared her shoulders, steadying herself for another confrontation.

"You're in so much trouble," Aunt June fumed.

Sarah stifled a groan when she saw the frown line appear between her aunt's brows. "I know. I've already been chewed out."

"I can't believe you dragged your sister into this."

"She wanted to come." Sarah shot Lacey a look that said 'you can step in at any time.'

"That's not the story she told me," her aunt replied, still in a huff.

"What story did she tell you?" Sarah asked, staring at Lacey.

"June," Uncle Walt interrupted. "They're going to interrogate the criminals and Sarah wants to listen."

"What?" Aunt June stared at Sarah with an angry expression.

Sarah nodded and looked at the floor as she spoke. "Yeah, I want to find out the whole story."

"I don't think that's really app—."

"Let her, June. She's worked hard to bring these criminals to justice."

"Walt, I don't think it's appropriate."

Uncle Walt sighed. "She's worked hard."

"She broke the law."

"I know." Uncle Walt nodded and sighed again. "But, she didn't have a choice, Junie. I'll explain everything later."

Aunt June opened her mouth to argue, but no words came out. She clamped her lips together in a tight line. "All right, but you're still grounded." She pulled her hair away from her face. "I've got patients to see in the morning, so I'm going home."

"We can give the girls a ride home," Officer Wilson said.

Uncle Walt sighed. "All right." He looked at Sarah. "We'll talk more about this tomorrow."

Sarah nodded as her lips twitched. She could barely hold back the smile that was trying to burst out on her face.

Uncle Walt put his arm around Aunt June and guided her to the door. Suddenly, he stopped and spun toward the girls. "Lacey, you can come home if you want to."

Lacey shook her head. "No, I want to hear the story, too."

Uncle Walt nodded and proceeded out the door.

Just then, Jackie bustled down the hall, followed by her parents.

"Hey, Beanpole, we're going to hear them interrogate Klonsky. Do you want to listen?" Sarah asked as a huge grin spread across her face.

Jackie nodded, sending her curls into a frenzy. She spun around and eyed her parents. "They're going to interrogate Klonsky. I want to hear the whole story." She crossed her arms over her chest and stared at her parents.

"I don't think so," Jackie's mother responded.

"Oh come on!" Jackie pleaded.

"Let her go, Claire." Jackie's father winked at his daughter.

"I can give the girls a ride home afterward," Officer Wilson said.

Jackie's mother shook her head.

"Mom, I can't believe you're not going to let me!" Jackie spun away and trounced toward the door.

"Claire, let her finish this."

Jackie's mother glared at her father. "I've always got to be the bad guy."

"Not if you let her." Jackie's father winked at her mother.

"Oh, all right." Her mother threw her hands up in the air and stomped out into the night.

"Thanks Mom!"

Jackie's father pivoted toward Officer Wilson. "You'll give the girls a ride home?"

"Absolutely."

He nodded and followed Jackie's mother out to the car.

"Let's go kids." Officer Wilson motioned for the girls to follow him.

The Super Spies traveled behind the officer toward the interrogation rooms. As they walked, weariness washed over Sarah's body. Her head still throbbed slightly, and the pain in her leg flared into a fiery rage every time she put weight on it.

"I just can't believe David Fedewa murdered his mother." Lacey frowned. Her hands found the hem of her T-shirt and she twisted it in her fingers.

"I know." Sarah shook her head. "That part doesn't make any sense to me." She winced as she hobbled down the hall.

"We'll find out the whole story in a few minutes," Jackie said.

Sarah nodded. "You got that right."

The Super Spies rounded the corner and continued to the interrogation room. They came to the viewing area right in front of interrogation room one.

Sarah peeked through the window and found Klonksy sitting in a chair. His eyes were red and puffy, but some of the swelling had gone down. He seemed agitated as he fidgeted and he looked uncomfortable. *Good.* Anger suddenly swirled through Sarah's body as she stared at her captor. *Who does he think he is? What right did he have to destroy the Fedewa family?*

As Sarah stared into the room, she realized the big picture window in the middle of the wall was actually a two-way mirror. She could see Klonsky, but he couldn't see her. Breathing a sigh of relief, she realized her captor wouldn't even know she was there.

Sarah hobbled toward the interrogation room two. She found David Fedewa hunched in a chair, looking small and scared.

She pivoted toward Officer Wilson. "When are they going to start?"

"In a few minutes. Why don't you take a seat?" He pointed toward the folding chairs in front of the windows.

Sarah limped to a chair and sat down. Jackie and Lacey were close on her heels. All three girls waited for the questioning to begin.

Just then, Scott ambled over with Detective Swift. Traveling behind them was Scoop Davis.

"So I guess you heard that we found David Fedewa?" Sarah said.

"Yes, I heard. I just can't believe it." Detective Swift rubbed his eyes.

"I'm finding it hard to believe he was involved with his mother's murder." Sarah pursed her lips and shook her head.

"Don't jump to any conclusions," the detective warned. "We don't know what the Klonskys have been telling him all these years."

"Are you here for the interrogation, too?"

"Yes, I am. I've been searching for that boy for thirty years. I want to hear his story."

"How about you?" Sarah asked, cocking her head in Scoop's direction.

"Wouldn't miss it," Scoop answered, smoothing his hair with his hands. "I thought I told you kids not to do anything until you heard from me?" He gave Sarah a reproachful look.

"You did, but we couldn't wait," Sarah said with a shrug. *What difference does it make now?* She brushed her hair from her face. "Did you find out anything?"

Scoop nodded. "I sure did."

"Well...?"

Scoop pursed his lips again. "I found out there's no statute of limitations on an heir making a claim to an estate."

"Huh?"

"Yeah, speak English please," Jackie piped up.

"It means David could reappear at any time and claim the Fedewa estate."

Sarah slapped her forehead with her palm. "So that was Klonsky's plan."

Scoop nodded and crossed his arms over his chest. Detective Swift sighed and shook his head, an expression of deep sorrow on his face.

"I feel so sorry for Mrs. Fedewa," Sarah said as a lump rose in her throat.

"I do too," Lacey chimed in.

"I wish we could have done more for her."

Sarah choked back tears as she remembered the cruel rumors that had been circulated about Mrs. Fedewa. A deep sense of shame overwhelmed her when she thought about the circumstances surrounding the old woman's death and how her body had been found. The poor woman hadn't been a witch or crazy or anything like that. She had been overwhelmed by the loss of her son.

"I'm never going to make fun of a weird person again," Sarah vowed. Her voice sounded far away and high, as if her air supply were slowly being cut off.

"Me neither," Jackie said, putting her arm around Sarah and giving her a quick squeeze.

"You just don't know what they've gone through." Sarah glanced down at the floor and exhaled a ragged breath.

At that moment, Chief Johnson strode into the room. He was startled to see the Super Spies and he peered at Wilson with a disapproving frown. "What are these kids doing here?"

Officer Wilson stepped toward the chief. "You said they could listen, remember?"

The chief snorted in response, but didn't ask the Super Spies to leave. Instead he gestured and said, "Okay, Wilson, why don't you start with Klonsky first."

"Yes, sir." Officer Wilson walked into the first interrogation room where Lon Klonsky sat hunched in his chair.

Chapter Thirteen

The Super Spies walked a few steps to the right and sat in front of the first window. Sarah peered into the room and examined the man who had terrified her the night before.

The swelling around his eyes had diminished, but they still watered occasionally and the scar by his eye was an angry red gash. Klonsky's rage erupted as he spewed curses and rants.

"Wilson, what is going on?" he demanded.

"What do you mean?"

"I was put in a cell like a common criminal."

"That's where we put murderers."

"What are you talking about?" Klonsky made a fist and pounded the table.

"You've been arrested for the murder of Frieda Fedewa."

"That's what they said earlier." Klonsky shook his head. "I just can't believe it."

"It's true."

"Come on, Wilson…you know I didn't murder anybody."

"We've got eyewitness testimony and evidence."

"You don't have any evidence," Klonsky sneered.

"What makes you say that?"

"I was the lead investigator on the case. I know what you guys have. You got nothing."

"That's not true, Lon."

"You're bluffing."

"We've got David Fedewa, and he's talking."

Officer Wilson gave the dirty cop a withering look. A fearful expression danced across Klonsky's face, but he quickly recovered. He stared at the officer, daring him to push the envelope.

"It's not looking good for you." Officer Wilson tapped his pencil on his notepad and eyed Klonsky.

"I want a lawyer."

"Suit yourself."

Officer Wilson stood and turned toward the door, then stopped. "There's nothing worse than a dirty cop."

"Get out of here!" Klonsky screamed. He lunged across the table at Wilson.

Wilson opened the door, walked out, and closed it behind him.

"Doesn't look like he's going to talk, does it?" Chief Johnson asked.

"No, it doesn't." Wilson shook his head.

"Try your luck with David."

"All right." He walked up to the window and studied David for a few minutes. "I'm going to try a softer approach with him."

The chief pursed his lips and nodded. "All right. Give it a shot."

Officer Wilson opened the door to David's room. Sarah shifted her position and the rest of the Super Spies followed her.

"Hello, David."

Sarah watched— hoping David would answer. He didn't, he sat in his chair bouncing his legs.

She studied him as he cowered in his seat. His curly, dark hair was long and needed trimming. David's brown eyes flitted around the room, never fixing on one object at a time. He resembled a neglected child, wearing overalls and a dirty T-shirt.

"Hello, David."

This time, the officer's voice registered.

"Where's Lon?" David squeaked.

The sound of David's voice surprised Sarah. It sounded childlike and innocent.

"Don't worry about Lon right now. He's all right. I would like to talk with you."

"I need to talk to Lon."

"We'll let you talk with him in a little bit," Officer Wilson said. His voice sounded smooth as dark honey. "But right now we need to talk with you and hear your story."

"I want to talk to Lon right now," David said.

David's legs bounced faster. Sarah could tell his anxiety had turned up a notch.

"Okay, David. I'll go see if he's available. Would you like a soda while you wait?"

"Yeah."

"Could you answer one question for me before I talk to Lon?"

"No." David gazed down at the table, his legs still bouncing.

"Okay, I'll be right back." Officer Wilson walked out of the room, and glanced at the chief. "We need to call the forensic psychologist in."

Chief Johnson shifted his weight and nodded. "I agree." He turned toward another officer. "Michaels, get Dr. Stiles here, ASAP."

The officer left to follow his orders.

"He's got some mental issues, boss," Wilson said as he studied David.

"Yes." The chief rubbed his eyes and sighed. "Hopefully, Stiles will get his story out of him."

Sarah groaned. "I hope this doesn't take too long."

"I know what you mean," Jackie said as she gave Sarah's arm a squeeze.

"Detective Swift, why are they calling a forensic psychologist?" Sarah asked.

"They've got to evaluate him, to find out if he's mentally competent."

"Mentally competent?" Sarah pivoted in her seat and gazed at the detective.

"Yes, see if he can be questioned, if he knows right from wrong, if he can assist in his own defense, that kind of thing."

"Oh." Sarah stared at the floor, deep in thought. *Maybe David's mental state was the reason for his odd behavior.* She sighed and slumped in her chair; she hated waiting.

The Super Spies hung out in the viewing area waiting for the doctor to arrive. After what seemed like hours, he walked through the door with a confident stride.

"Chief, how are you?" Dr. Stiles asked.

He was a stocky man with a compassionate demeanor and a friendly, open face.

"You won't believe who we have in interrogation room two," Chief Johnson said.

"Who?"

"David Fedewa."

"Are you serious?" Dr. Stiles spun toward the interrogation room and studied David.

"As a heart attack."

"This is unbelievable." The doctor peered at David through the glass. "Isn't he the one who disappeared thirty years ago?"

"That's right."

"I don't believe it."

"We're all shocked. We need you to evaluate him and see if you can build a relationship with him. The only cop he wants to talk to is Lon."

"Why can't he talk to Lon?"

"Because Lon is a suspect in his mother's murder."

"Are you serious?" Dr. Stiles pivoted back and locked eyes with the chief.

"Absolutely. Can you give it a go?"

The psychologist nodded.

"Here" Officer Wilson handed him a soda. "He wanted this."

"All right, let's give it a shot." He walked toward the room and stepped through the door. Sarah's eyes were on the glass, anticipating the interaction about to take place.

"Hello, David. Here's your soda."

"Ah, thanks. Who are you?" David grabbed the soda and eyed the doctor.

"I'm a doctor. I help the police sometimes."

David took a long swig of the soda. "I ain't sick. I don't need a doc."

"Well, I'm a different kind of doctor. I'm more of a doctor for your mind."

"I ain't crazy, either." His legs started their nervous bounce again.

"Oh, I know that. I'm here to help you. Everything is going to be all right."

"Where's Lon?" David asked, sinking into his chair and staring at the Doctor.

"Lon's in the next room. He's pretty busy now. He told

me to tell you it was okay to talk with me."

"He did, huh?"

"Yes, we need to figure out this puzzle."

"Puzzle?"

"Yeah, you know, you've been gone for a long time. The police have been looking for you for thirty years," Dr. Stiles said with a reassuring smile. "We just want to know where you've been, and if you're all right."

"I've been with Lon and his dad." David's body relaxed and his legs stopped dancing.

Dr. Stiles pointed to the chair opposite David. "May I?"

David shrugged. "I guess."

The doctor sat down and gave David another paternal smile. "So you've been with Lon and his dad the whole time?"

"Yep." David nodded.

"Did you go to school?"

"No, we was homeschooled by Lon's dad."

"Home schooled, huh?"

"Yep."

He took another drink of his soda and burped. He glanced at the doctor and laughed just like a five-year-old would.

Doctor Stiles gave David another disarming smile. "David, do you know who the president is?"

David gave the doctor a hesitant grin. "The president?"

"Yeah, you know, the man who runs the country?"

"Nope. Lon told me I didn't need ta know that stuff."

"I see." Dr. Stiles frowned. "Do you know the capital of this state?"

"Dunno." David shook his head and pushed his soda can between his hands.

"Do you remember the day you went to live with Lon?"

"Where is Lon?"

"He's in another room. You're not in trouble here, David.

Everything is going to be all right. We just want to hear your story."

"What story?"

"The story about when you went to live with Lon."

"I'm not supposed to tell that story," David whispered.

Sarah saw a shadow of grief flit across his features.

"It's okay. Everything is going to be all right. Lon said it was okay to tell it now," the doctor leaned forward and whispered.

"Could I get another pop?"

"Sure, I'll be right back."

Doctor Stiles stood and walked through the door into the viewing area.

The chief rushed up to him. "What do you think?"

"It appears David has some developmental issues and is probably suffering from Stockholm's Syndrome." The doctor rubbed his forehead.

"Stockholm's Syndrome, huh?" Chief Johnson frowned. "How can you tell? You haven't asked him many questions."

"Because of his total dependence on Lon. Of course, I would need to do an extensive evaluation to be sure."

"Ah, I see." The chief tapped his chin with his fingertips, deep in thought.

Sarah tugged on Detective Swift's sleeve. "What's Stockholm's Syndrome?"

"It's where a kidnap victim identifies with his captors. He's dependent on them for his survival."

"Dependent?" Sarah cocked her head and studied him.

"Yes, he depended on the Klonskys' to take care of him."

"Is that why David didn't run away?"

"Yes, it is." He pointed at Dr. Stiles. "They're going to continue the interview."

Sarah focused her attention back on the doctor for a moment and then studied David. He seemed more at ease than he had earlier.

"He wants another soda." Dr. Stiles told the chief as he glanced at David.

"Yeah, I sent Michaels to get one for you."

"I'm going to find out about the day he was kidnapped. He's dropped his guard. I think he'll spill it."

"All right. I want you to wear an ear piece, so I can feed you questions." Chief Johnson motioned for Detective Wilson.

"Sure."

"Wilson, go get one of our ear pieces for the doctor."

"Sure, boss."

Wilson disappeared and reappeared within minutes. He handed the earpiece to the doctor. Sarah strained in her seat to see it. It resembled a hearing aid.

"It's not uncomfortable," Wilson said.

The doctor nodded. "Where's that soda?" He fumbled with the tiny instrument, trying to put it in his ear.

"Right here." Michaels trotted up.

"I'm back at it." Dr. Stiles walked back into the interrogation room and handed David his drink. "So, David, can you tell me about the day you went to live with Lon?" He sat back down in his chair.

"Are you sure Lon said it was okay to talk to you?"

Dr. Stiles smiled. "Yes, he said it was okay."

"All right. We was at the pool with my dad, then Lon says, 'hey, let's get some ice cream.' I says, 'okay.'"

"So you went to get ice cream?"

"Yeah."

"You didn't think to tell your dad?"

David shrugged. "We was gonna be back before he got out of the bathroom."

The doctor nodded and pursed his lips. "I see."

"So, then Lon's dad pulls up and says there's trouble at the mill. I need to go home with them."

"What happened next?" Dr. Stiles clasped his hands in front of him.

"I jumped in the car with Lon and his dad."

"Then what?"

"Then we got to Lon's house, and I asked when my dad was gonna come git me."

"What did Mr. Klonsky say?"

"He said there was still trouble at the mill. I had to stay with them for a week or two."

"What happened when the two weeks were up?" Dr. Stiles leaned forward in his seat and studied David.

"I asked Mr. Klonsky when my dad was gonna come git me, and he said my dad didn't want me anymore." David choked back tears.

"I see. And you believed Mr. Klonsky?"

"Not at first, but my dad never came." David couldn't hold back his tears any longer. They rolled down his cheeks like fat raindrops. "I would sit on their porch just waitin' for my dad to show up, and he never came." David put his face in the crook of his arm and wept.

A small cry escaped Sarah's lips as she listened to this story. Tears welled in her eyes and cascaded down her cheeks as she pictured a lonely boy sitting on a porch, watching as one car after another drove by.

"That poor kid," she whispered to Jackie.

"I know," Jackie said, never taking her gaze from David.

Sarah wiped her eyes and returned her focus to the interview. She didn't want to miss a thing.

"I bet that hurt," Dr. Stiles said. He gave David a compassionate pat on the arm.

David wiped his face on his sleeve. "Yeah, it did. I just couldn't believe my dad didn't want me. I was so grateful for Lon and his dad taking me in."

"So, you just stayed with Lon and his dad?"

"Yep."

"Why didn't you run away?"

"Where would I run to? My mom and dad didn't want me." David choked back a sob.

"Okay, David. We're going to take a little break. Do you want another soda?"

"No, but I gotta pee."

"All right, I'll have Officer Wilson take you to the bathroom."

Dr. Stiles stood and walked out of the room. He met the chief in the viewing area.

"I think we've got enough to pick up John Klonsky, don't you?"

"We sure do."

"Is he still alive?" Dr. Stiles asked, watching Wilson lead David down the hall.

"As far as I know. I'll send Michaels and his partner out with a warrant for his arrest."

"David is definitely suffering from Stockholm's Syndrome. It's a textbook case." Dr. Stiles sighed and shook his head.

"Doc, I need to find out what role he played in his mother's death and if he knew she was his mother. Do you think you can ask him about that night?"

"I'll give it a try."

The chief and the doctor huddled together and spoke in low voices. Sarah could no longer hear the conversation. After a few minutes, David returned to his seat and Dr. Stiles went back into the interrogation room.

Sarah focused her attention back on the interview. Tears welled in her eyes again as she thought about Mrs. Fedewa and her tragic life.

"David, I just have a few more questions for you," Dr. Stiles said.

"Okay."

David appeared relaxed. He put his elbows on the table and leaned on them, pushing the soda can between his hands.

"About a week ago a lady was murdered. Do you know anything about that?"

Sarah saw David grow rigid, and he didn't speak.

"David?"

David closed his eyes, and whispered, "She has the same last name as me."

"Yes, she does."

"Who was that lady?" David opened his eyes, and stared at the doctor.

"How do you know she has the same last name as you?"

"Cuz one of them kids said her name was Mrs. Fedewa...Who is she?"

Dr. Stiles glanced down at his hands. "David, before I answer, you need to tell me what happened to her."

David squeezed his eyes shut. His hands dropped to his sides, and he clenched them. "I was there the night she was kilt."

"What happened?"

David's eyes remained shut as he spoke. "Lon knocked on this lady's door. He jus kept knockin' and knockin'. It seemed like forever before a lady came to the door. I could see her lookin' out the window at us. She looked kinda scared, and then she looked at me and started to cry. The lady tried to unlock the door, but she was havin' trouble, like she was in a hurry or somethin'."

"What happened next?"

"I was wonderin' what she was cryin' about, then when she opened the door she said, 'David,' like she knowed me. She was so happy, and I was confused. How did this lady know me?" David paused and tears started to leak from his eyes.

"Then what happened?" Dr. Stiles leaned forward in his seat.

"It happened fast." David snuffled and wiped his face on his sleeve.

"What happened fast?"

"Lon pulled out this knife, and he stabbed the lady! She had this surprised look on her face, and there was blood! I just wanted to get out of there!"

"Did you know what Lon was going to do before you got there?"

"No, I hadn' a clue!" David said. His eyes flew open, and he gestured frantically with his hands.

"Then what happened?"

"I kinda went crazy. I couldn't believe what Lon had done."

"What happened next?"

"It took a while, but Lon calmed me down, then he had to change his shirt."

"Lon had to change his shirt?" Dr. Stiles asked.

"Yeah, he got blood on it, and he wanted to change," David said.

"Do you know why Lon wanted to kill her?" Dr. Stiles stared at David as he waited for his answer.

"He said she owed us money. That by killin' her, we would get our money." David slumped in his seat, looking spent. "Now, Doc, tell me who she was." His voice was low and insistent.

Dr. Stiles took a deep breath and let it out slowly. "She was your mother, David."

Sarah watched as Dr. Stiles studied David, waiting for his reaction. She sat rigid in her chair, repulsed by what the Klonskys had done to the Fedewa family. All of a sudden a wave of nausea overwhelmed her; she gulped, keeping it at bay.

"Noo00!" David moaned and squeezed his eyes closed.

"Yes, I'm afraid so, David. She never stopped looking for you."

"Looking for me? She knew I was with the Klonskys."

"No, she didn't. The Klonskys lied to her." The doctor reached across the table and touched David's arm.

David pulled away from the doctor's touch. "No, I don't believe that. They took me in and took care of me."

"The Klonskys lied to you, too."

David shook his head. "No way, Lon and his dad took care of me."

"I know this is a lot of information to digest. Why don't we take a little break? I'll be right back."

Poor David Fedewa, Sarah cried silently. She wanted to comfort him. He looked like a train had struck him. He slumped in his chair like he was in physical pain. His face turned white, accentuating the dark circles under his eyes.

As Sarah watched, David struggled with the information Dr. Stiles had given him. A lump rose in her throat, choking her. She let out a strangled sob and tears fell from her eyes; she couldn't stop them. It was like a dam bursting.

Sarah felt an arm pull her close; she realized it was Jackie when she smelled her flowery perfume. She knew Jackie meant to comfort her, but it just made her cry harder as she realized David had never had anyone comfort him. Sobbing, Sarah cried for the lonely little boy, who never knew his mother, and for the mother who never got over the loss of her son.

"Klonsky used him as bait," Sarah wept.

"I know, Sarah," Jackie said in a soothing tone. "But we got him."

Sarah nodded and wiped her eyes on the sleeve of her T-shirt. "Yes, we did. We stopped him."

"You stopped him, Sarah. Lacey and I just went along for the ride."

"You guys helped, Jackie."

"Yes, but it was your guts that kept us going. Lacey and I wouldn't have done anything if it hadn't been for your stubbornness."

"That is so true," Lacey said.

"I'm glad you guys are here." Sarah sniffled. "I keep thinking about that poor little boy sitting on the porch waiting for his dad."

New tears filled Sarah's eyes, and she swung away trying to compose herself. She took several deep breaths. She felt spent, like she'd cried herself empty. Sighing, she spun around and faced the interrogation room.

She found Dr. Stiles and the chief speaking in hushed tones right outside the interview room. Sarah watched as they came to a decision. The doctor quickly walked back into the room. Concern was written on his face, and she leaned forward to hear the rest of the interview.

"I don't unnerstand," David said.

"I know, I don't quite understand it myself, but what you need to focus on is the fact your mother loved you very much."

Sarah watched the doctor as he walked around the table and sat in a chair next to David. He put his arm around the man-child, attempting to console him.

"Lon was my friend." David's face contorted with the pain of betrayal.

"David, he wasn't your friend. I know it's hard to believe, but he lied to you and your family."

"I just can't believe the Klonskys lied."

"It was very cruel, but let's focus on moving forward. I'm going to have an officer escort you back to your ce—uh, your room, and I want you to lie down for a while."

David suddenly broke out in a sweat. "I'm going to be sick."

Dr. Stiles jumped up and grabbed a wastebasket. He quickly placed it in front of David.

He vomited and then wiped his mouth with his sleeve. "Can I have a piece of gum?"

"Certainly." Dr. Stiles handed him a piece of gum.

"Is it bubble gum?" David asked.

Sarah noticed his voice became child-like, and he seemed to act like a five-year-old.

"I'm afraid not."

David sighed and grudgingly took the gum.

The doctor pursed his lips. "Do you feel better?"

"Better."

"Okay, David, I think it's time for you to lie down."

"Okay."

Dr. Stiles walked out of the room. "We need to put David on suicide watch."

"I agree." Chief Johnson motioned for Officer Wilson. "Wilson, take him back to his cell. Stay with him. We want him watched."

"Yes sir."

Sarah's heart lurched in her chest. *Suicide watch! Poor David Fedewa; he never had a real life to begin with, and now everyone's afraid he'll try to end it.* She glanced at Jackie and saw the compassion in her friend's eyes. Tears filled Sarah's eyes once again. Shaking her head, she twisted away, hoping to get her emotions under control.

Her tears dried up as soon as she thought about Klonsky. *What a worm! A total loser!* Anger coursed through her body and she clenched her hands. Once again, she felt Jackie's arm around her. She took some deep breaths to calm down and then swung back to face the others.

The chief sighed. "I think it's time to get something to eat. Stiles, why don't we head over to Hinkle's?" He dipped his head toward the retired detective and the reporter. "Do you two want to come along?"

Sarah saw the weariness in the chief's face and realized the emotional interview had drained him.

"Sounds good to me," Detective Swift said.

Scoop shook his head. "I've got another appointment."

"Dad, can we come?" Scott asked.

"I suppose," his father sighed.

Sarah watched as Officer Wilson led David away. He sagged against the cop as if he had no strength left in his body. David looked like he had just been beaten.

"I don't unnerstand," he mumbled over and over.

Officer Wilson whispered encouraging words to him to keep him moving forward.

Jackie nudged Sarah. "Is this enough to put Klonsky away?"

"I think so; we'll ask at Hinkle's." Sarah wiped her eyes and took another deep breath.

"Let's get going," Jackie said.

"Yeah, let's get over there and grab some tables."

"I want to see if Lon's lawyer has been contacted. I'll meet you there, Swift," Chief Johnson said.

"All right."

Detective Swift stood and put his arm around Sarah. He led her down the hall and motioned for the rest of the Super Spies to follow him. "Come on kids, let's go." Together, they left the station.

Sarah blinked rapidly for several seconds when she walked out into the blazing sun. The bright sunlight surprised her. She expected the darkness of night. What time was it? Shading her eyes with her hand, she peered down the street and noticed the people of Harrisburg were simply strolling down the sidewalk. They were oblivious to the tragedy that had been exposed in the police station. It amazed her they could be so unaware. She walked to the restaurant with a heavy heart.

Hinkle's was alive with the noon rush. Sarah glanced at the patrons as she waited to be seated. They appeared animated, living under the fragile illusion nothing evil would puncture their little bubble. Sarah knew better; she was changed by this whole experience, somehow less fragile, less innocent. Suddenly, a wave of loneliness swept over her; she felt separated from these people who were untouched by tragedy.

The hostess appeared and motioned for Sarah and her group to follow her. She led them to a large table. Sarah sat down and opened her menu, grateful for the opportunity to think of something besides the Fedewa tragedy. They had just finished placing their orders when Chief Johnson sat down.

"It looks like we closed two cases today," he said as he got comfortable in his seat.

"I hope you have enough to put Klonsky away," Sarah said, shaking her head. "He's a total worm."

"Yeah," Jackie agreed and gave Sarah a quick squeeze.

"Yes, I believe we do. We've got David's testimony. I don't know if he'll be able to testify at the trial, but the district attorney has other ways to present his testimony."

"Is David going to go to jail?"

"I highly doubt it. He'll probably go to a psychiatric hospital for a while."

Sarah nodded and glanced down at the table. "I see." Relief flooded through her body and tears threatened to spill down her cheeks again. She clenched her hands, trying to keep her swirling emotions under control.

"I just can't get the image of David sitting on the Klonsky's porch out of my mind," Lacey whimpered.

Sarah grimaced. "I know what you mean. I hate the Klonskys for what they did to the Fedewa family."

"Well, if it's any consolation, you kids helped catch Klonsky," the chief admitted.

"I'm glad to hear that," Sarah said and gave the chief a tentative smile. "So, that means we're in the clear about the crime scene issue?"

Chief Johnson chuckled. "I didn't say that."

"What do you mean?"

"You're still going to be punished. You kids are lucky I don't arrest you."

"I don't get it." Sarah frowned. "We helped you catch him."

"That's true, but you also broke the law. You trespassed on my crime scene, removed evidence, and put your lives in danger. You kids need to be taught a lesson."

"You did ignore the evidence we gave you. You're partially at fault here," Sarah declared, her rebellious streak rearing its ugly head.

The chief burst out laughing. "You're kidding me, right?"

Sarah grimaced. She couldn't think of one retort to hurl back at the chief. She sat fuming.

"Dad, they didn't know it was against the law," Scott reasoned.

"Ignorance of the law is no excuse."

"Oh, come on, Dad."

"Did you know tampering with evidence is a felony? That could mean prison time." His voice sounded stern, and the smile in his eyes disappeared. He was an officer of the law now. The girls were no longer Scott's friends but criminals in his eyes.

Sarah's throat constricted. Visions of the Super Spies behind bars filled her mind, each one rotting in their own cell. She heard Jackie complaining about the orange jumpsuits.

"I wonder if we'll get tattoos?" Sarah mused out loud.

She gazed at Jackie and Lacey and saw their wide, frightened eyes.

"Tattoos?" Chief Johnson asked.

"Yeah, it sounds like a prison thing to do."

"You know prison time stays with you forever," Detective Swift added.

"It'll be hard to get into college with that kind of mark on your record," Chief Johnson winked at Detective Swift.

He caught the wink and twisted his head away from the Super Spies. Sarah saw his shoulders shaking as he tried to hide his laughter.

She relaxed. "It can't be that bad if you're laughing, Detective Swift."

"You're busted," Scott laughed.

"Yes, I'm afraid I am."

Sarah giggled in relief, and Jackie squeezed her hand under the table. Sarah squeezed back and winked at her friend.

"Your punishment will be community service, with the understanding you won't do this again." Chief Johnson gave the girls a wide grin.

"I'm so glad. I so hate those orange jumpsuits," Jackie laughed.

The waitress came and took the chief's order. She scurried away but returned a few minutes later and placed a huge piece of strawberry pie in front of Sarah.

Sarah cracked a wide smile. "I love strawberry pie."

"You're not getting lunch?" Detective Swift asked.

"This is my lunch. I'm celebrating solving our first mystery."

"I want to change my order," Jackie declared.

"Me too," Lacey piped up.

"I'm having what she's having." Jackie pointed at Sarah's pie.

"Me too."

The waitress hurried away to change the order.

Sarah took a huge bite of her strawberry pie, relishing the sweetness. She wondered if David ever got to eat pie like this.

"Can I buy David Fedewa a piece of pie?" she asked.

Chief Johnson seemed taken aback by the suggestion, but he recovered and nodded. "Sure, why not? I'll take it back with me after lunch."

The waitress returned with two plates of pie, and Sarah ordered a piece to go. She knew it didn't make up for all David had lost, but she felt it was a start. Sarah didn't want him to spend the rest of his life thinking the world was a horrible place.

After lunch, Sarah, Jackie, and Lacey declined Chief Johnson's offer of a ride and made their way toward the creek. The sun baked Sarah's shoulders, and she welcomed the heat. It felt like a warm blanket after the frigid air conditioning inside Hinkle's.

Reaching the cul-de-sac, Sarah walked along the sandy trail toward their willow tree. She heard the crackle of dry weeds as Lacey and Jackie followed her.

Walking beneath the branches of the willow tree, Sarah sighed and collapsed on the ground. She was bone-tired and her leg ached, a reminder of the horror of the previous night.

Jackie sat down next to her. "I can't believe it. We solved the Cat Lady murder."

"The Super Spies are number one!" Sarah raised her arm and chanted in a weary voice.

"No doubt, girlfriend."

"I feel so bad for David right now," Sarah said. Tears welled in her eyes.

"Me too," Lacey responded.

Jackie frowned. "I do too. I think he got blown away today."

"You can say that again." Sarah brushed the hair out of her face. "How do you get over something like that?"

"I don't know." Jackie shook her head and picked at her shoe.

"It's been a very interesting summer," Sarah said.

Jackie snorted. "That is a major understatement."

"I'm glad I met you, Jackie Jenkins." Sarah couldn't look at her because if she did, she knew she'd start crying again.

"I'm glad I met you, too." Jackie reached over and squeezed her hand.

"Me too," Lacey piped in.

"I'm so glad we're not going to jail," Sarah laughed.

"Me too," Jackie giggled and pushed her wild curls out of her face. "I mean orange jumpsuits? Come on. They couldn't have picked a more fashionable color?"

Sarah gazed at the other girls and laughed, then grew quiet. They sat that way for quite some time, and Sarah realized each one was lost in her own thoughts.

"We caught the Cat Lady killer; that makes me happy. I'm so-o glad that creep Klonsky didn't get away with it," she said.

"Yeah," Lacey replied.

"Hopefully, David will have a chance at a normal life. I think Mrs. Fedewa would've wanted that, don't you?"

"Mrs. Fedewa?" Lacey asked.

"Yeah, calling her the Cat Lady sounds—I don't know, disrespectful or something. Don't you think?"

"Yeah, I do," Jackie sighed.

"I bet Mrs. Fedewa is happy with the way things turned out," Sarah said. Her voice caught as she spoke. She wondered if she would ever be able to talk about the Fedewas without crying.

"We did good, Sarah." Jackie reached over and gave Sarah's arm a squeeze.

The girls grew quiet again and Sarah's eyelids drooped. She heard Jackie get more comfortable under the tree. Soon all three girls were lying on the ground. Sarah sighed, enjoying the shade and the cool breeze. Growing sleepy, she closed her eyes.

"It's strange we're back here under the willow tree," she said. Her voice sounded far away and snoozy.

"Why's that?" Jackie asked.

"Well, this is kind of where it all started." Sarah pulled some grass from the ground and chewed on a blade. "We were playing Truth or Dare, remember?"

"I remember."

"Maybe we'll get to come back next summer," Sarah said with a lazy smile. Her body was heavy with weariness, and she knew if she didn't keep talking, she would fall asleep.

Jackie beamed. "Wouldn't that be awesome?"

A smile spread across Sarah's face. Jackie's voice had that sleepy sound too. "Maybe there'll be another mystery to solve."

"Wouldn't that be a blast?"

"Umm-hmmm."

Lacy giggled. "Jackie, truth or dare?"

The Super Spies cracked up laughing. They laughed so hard they curled up and hugged their bellies. These were full belly laughs, and it felt good to Sarah. All the tension of the last few weeks disappeared. Sarah loved the sound of that laughter and realized the three girls shared a strong bond. She felt grateful for that bond and couldn't wait for the next mystery the Super Spies would solve together.

About the Author

Lisa Orchard grew up loving books. Her debut novel "The Super Spies and the Cat Lady Killer," is a suspenseful thriller about three young girls thrust into a situation and the choices they make. The setting is Harrisburg, a small town in Michigan, much like the town where Lisa grew up. Many of her characters' adventures stem from her exploits as a young teen. After graduating from Central Michigan University with a Marketing Degree she spent many years in the insurance industry, pining to express her creative side. Deciding to stay home with her children gave her the opportunity to follow her dream and become a writer. She currently resides in Rockford Michigan with her husband, Steve, and two wonderful boys, Kyle and Ethan. Currently, she's working on the second novel that stars the same quirky teens, and she hopes to turn the Super Spies into a series. When she's not writing she enjoys spending time with her family, running, hiking, and reading.

Made in the USA
Charleston, SC
16 January 2016